GODS, MEMES AND MONSTERS

A 21st Century Bestiary

Edited by Heather J. Wood

Published by Stone Skin Press 2015.

Stone Skin Press is an imprint of Pelgrane Press Ltd. Spectrum House, 9 Bromell's Road, Clapham Common, London, SW4 0BN.

ISBN 978-1-908983-11-4

A CIP catalogue record for this book is available from the British Library.

1 2 3 4 5 6 7 8 9 10

Printed in the USA.

This book can be ordered direct from the publisher at www.stoneskinpress.com

Contents

Meet the New Beasts

An Introduction by Heather J. Wood

Welcome to our nightmares, welcome to our dreams, welcome to our fears and secret desires, welcome to *Gods, Memes and Monsters*. You're invited to enter and spend some quality time in our mythological house of monsters, creatures and beasts. Lexicons of creatures go back to ancient and medieval times, but this is categorically not a bestiary in the style of Pliny the Elder or Anne Walshe. This bestiary is a different animal — cheap pun most definitely intended.

From the agave spirit to the zmeu, from the banaroc to the yelyelsee, this bestiary sheds light on the mythological creatures of old coping — and sometimes thriving — in the contemporary world. It introduces you to beasts previously undiscovered or newly born. You'll get reacquainted with some familiar names that have evolved since the times of Aristotle and Pliny the Elder. Echidna is still giving birth to monsters. The gorgon now has a job and a boyfriend. The griffin has found a home in a modern casino. Emily Care Boss' sphinx happily resides in Manhattan. Steve Berman resurrects the medieval bonnacon and finally enlightens us about the cause of the Great Chicago Fire of 1871.

Contemporary police reports potentially reveal the existence of Kyla Lee Ward's leucrotta and Richard Dansky's Bigfoot variation — the Trashsquatch.

You'll also meet lesser-known beasts such as Kathryn Kuitenbrouwer's battlefield banaroc, Kate Harrad's urbantelope, Julia Bond Ellingboe's skinwalker and Ekaterina Sedia's urban mimic. There is Patrick O'Duffy's catoblepas, whose unfortunate invisibility has made noticing it almost impossible. In a similar vein, Nick Mamatas' parasitic yelyelsee is also invisible to the human eye. Researchers have been required to comb through some messy evidence to confirm its existence. Speaking of research, cranky scholars and scientists are peppered throughout the anthology. Whether they are pursuing doppelgängers, tedious finches, black thylacines or half-cats, they persist in their quests for mythological beasts, unfazed by the disbelief of others or even a myriad of mysterious deaths. You won't always be able to trust the accounts of these intrepid researchers, and the entries by law enforcement officers may be equally suspect.

The anthology illuminates that the United States of the 1980s was a fertile time and place for the emergence of new creatures. Greg Stafford's American singing swan was reportedly sighted in the first year of that decade. A year later, Dennis Detwiller's chronovore made its appearance and potentially accounts for why New York City's subway trains never get you to your destination on time. 1984 was the year of Orwell, but it also brought us that party-hearty college campus favourite and all round righteous dude, Chad Fifer's weredad. Coincidentally or not, 1984 was also the year that Jonathan Blum's meme mosquitoes were responsible for a disturbing outbreak of the "Where's the Beef" plague.

Fittingly, our modern cyber age is the source of both new creatures and the revitalization of older ones. The wendigo, the genie, the succubus and the furies are growing more powerful on the Internet. Ed Greenwood knows there is a dragon living in your computer systems — one that even St. George would be hard-pressed to slay. James Wallis' memetic parasites and James Ashton's The Eaters could not even exist without cyberspace. Considering that careers can be both made and destroyed by the World Wide Web, it's no surprise that for many contemporary bestiary authors the Internet itself is the most horrifying monster of all.

As a compendium of mythological beings, this book offers you a smorgasbord of entries. By bringing together pieces from writers from different genres and countries, you can metaphorically feast on a vast cross section of international legends. (Note to omnivores: you can't literally dine on any of the critters herein, but a few of them may very well wish to eat *you*.) There are particulars on beasts from locations around the globe, including the vagabond gingko, Australia's bunyip and whippen, Romania's zmeu, Mexico's ahuizotl and the North American lake monster, Memphre-Magog. Many of these creatures are immortal, while others such as the daylings only live for a single day. The bestiary does contain pet-like animals, yet you really wouldn't want to keep jackalopes in your home. Cat creatures rule the Internet these days, and they figure prominently in the anthology, but Rupert Booth's StiffMogs are far from the ubiquitous adorable felines on your Facebook feed.

Some entries will frighten you; some will challenge you; a few will even shock or offend you. Other beasts will serve as warnings. For example, the next time you are in Central America, we caution you to shield yourself from John Scott Tynes' marsupial monster, the black thylacine. Please also be careful to stay far away from black dogs in underground train systems. Should you see one in your house, try not to squish Robin D. Laws' seer beetle, as it lives vicariously through your memories.

Some of the creatures will make you laugh, others shudder in horror or afraid to go out alone at night. Others might put you in the mood for candlelight and romantic company, although perhaps not quite the kind of company you would normally bring home to Mother.

Peter Birch (Aishling Morgan) presents some delicious — and we assume 100% factual — details about his career as an erotic writer and the many goblins and human-animal hybrid beings he has been inspired to create over the years. Helen Marshall's

"Minotaur" starts out as a racy tale of a rich social climber with a proclivity for bulls but ends up as a charming love story of two bovine-human hybrids. The satyr is now a sexy yoga teacher. In J.M. Frey's subversive retelling of an old "ogre kidnapping the maiden" story, the zmeu becomes a hilarious account of an unorthodox first date.

Some entries are satires and parodies or quick *amuse-bouches*, while vampire writer Nancy Kilpatrick's article offers you a fascinating historical examination of the undead from the past to the present day. Peter Dubé's gargoyle entry poses the question: are gargoyles mere architectural decorations or are they living monstrous beings?

Further beast pieces are engrossing tall tales. Jonathan L. Howard's skriker is a scary campfire story set near the village where the writer grew up. Marie Davis and Margaret Hultz's brain monster wreaks havoc on a landlocked pirate ship. Bill Zaget's samsa offers a compelling re-working of the human cockroach saga from Kafka's *The Metamorphosis*.

So, as you make yourself at home in this bestiary, maybe slip into something comfortable yet sexy. Turn down the lights. Or better yet, shine a brighter one. Pop some popcorn before reading about the adventures of Godisaurus — a giant lizard monster, who may still be gracing a silver screen near you. When necessary, don't forget to grab the appropriate apotropaic to ward off the more sinister beings: garlic for the vampire, wolfsbane for the doppelgänger. If you can get your hands on a bottle of absinthe, pour yourself a glass before tackling Molly Tanzer's fée verte or decant the best wine in your cellar. Kenneth Hite's manticore might best be savoured with a twelve-year-old Scotch. I'm convinced you'll come up with some clever libations for the other creatures depicted, including beings, line waifs, pipers, subterrs, and unicorns. The greater spotted capital requires a bottle of expensive champagne should you wish to share in its opulent tastes. Fortunately for your bank account, a cheap bag of crisps or chips should suffice as accompaniments for the magpie, sojourner, taximan rat, and tentagoon entries. Whatever you choose to sip or snack on, make certain there are no leftovers when you tackle the long-tongued mulgara.

Many of the beasts in this lexicon are elusive and hard to track down. You may not be able to see them, but you'll want to avoid being infected by some of the invasive and parasitic species detailed in this volume. Some of the beasts trick us, a few want to kill us or make love to us. Some, including Gareth Ryder-Hanrahan's gods, small and terrible, live with us. Others are lonely and want to befriend us. Some watch us; others just want to be us. All of the creatures teach us about ourselves, about who were are, what we long for and where we are heading — holding a mirror up to our twenty-first-century lives. Remember, our bestiary door is open now. Come on in and be amused, scared, horrified and delighted. Turn the page; the gods and beasts are waiting.

Agave

Arinn Dembo

She comes down just once a year from the dry hills of *Los Altos*, when the midwinter streams trickle through the canyons at their lowest ebb, and the thorn forests burn. Accompanied by long-nosed bats rising into the deep purple sky, She emerges at dusk from the rocks at the edge of town, and moves toward the plaza and its lights and music.

With the smoke of burning sage and *copal* blowing through Her long, loose hair, She comes hunting for a man who has been drinking Her blood.

Some families have been here since before the Spanish came. The elders of those families forbid young men to drink in winter, and will not let the boys go to the *pulquerias* or *cantinas* even if they promise only to sit and smoke and play cards. But it has always been the nature of some young men to ignore their elders, since the first people came here thousands of years ago. There have always been young men who drank forbidden liquor and cast fearless eyes on strange, beautiful women. And every year for thousands of years, in one of the villages of Jalisco, a boy of this description has died.

When the boys disappear, they have always been seen recently with a beautiful woman. Yet when witnesses are questioned, no description of this mysterious woman matches any other: Her beauty is shaped by the one who beholds Her, and its details are fluid. Regardless of Her outward appearance, however, She always moves like a jaguar, with the stride of a hunter. And survivors say that Her skin is cool to the touch, as smooth and fine as river clay. Her lips are always lush, Her teeth white and sharp, Her voice low and sweet. When She smiles, and speaks their names, men come to Her bidding.

Sometimes She stands in the shadows just outside the *pulqueria*, waiting for a man to emerge alone. When She sees one who pleases Her, She calls to him, drawing him away from his friends and the lively thrum of the *pulqueria*, where only men can drink. Before he quite understands what has happened he is walking beside Her, reaching for a slim hand which She always seems to keep just out of his reach.

When at last She does touch him, Her hand will rest on his chest, Her fingertips close to his heart. He will hardly notice the piercing pain, the thick needle sinking into his flesh so quickly and so quickly gone that in his drunken haze he barely feels it. She may disappear soon after, or stay with him for the rest of the evening, studying him with solemn eyes. But by morning She has always disappeared.

The Aztecs once worshipped Her as *Mayahuel*, the Goddess of the Maguey. In ancient times as now, the *agave* was a generous gift, a manifold blessing to Her people. The thick flat succulent leaves of the *agave* surround its high stalk crowned with flowers like a nest of swords, and they can be used in a hundred ways: roasted and eaten, pounded into paper like papyrus, dried and used to thatch a roof, stripped of fiber to make cloth and rope, even stripped of Her sharp thorns at each tip to make pins, pens, needles, and nails. Her tall stalk may be cut and roasted and eaten like sugar cane, or even used to make a musical instrument. Her flowers may be boiled and eaten, Her root baked and consumed as well. But by far the richest gift is at the heart of the plant, where the sap collects.

Aguamiel is the true treasure of the *agave*, a thin syrup of varying depth and color, milky and full of sugar. Freshly harvested it can be used to sweeten food, or mixed with salt and used as a poultice for wounds, for it kills pus-causing bacteria. But when fermented, the sweet nectar of the Goddess becomes *pulque*, the sacred liquor of the ancient Aztecs, thick and slick and milky-white, tasting faintly of the juices of love. Among the Aztecs the white beer was drunk only by priests and the victims of sacrifice, by victors in war or by pregnant women and the elderly — for it roused fervor and soothed suffering in equal measure, just as one might expect from the blood of a Goddess.

When the Spanish came the *pulque* was no longer reserved for the sacred elite, for killers and the dying. Common people could drink it, and even build cantinas to serve it, *pulquerias* where one could sit and drink the divine blood without censure. But however potent and widely available it might be, the viscous white brew was still unstable, and could not be exported far from the place where the *aguamiel* was harvested. *Pulque* would continue to ferment over time after it was harvested, and always became undrinkable.

It was the Spanish who began to distill the *pulque* into *mescal*, a stable hard liquor made from *agave* mash. And you yourself have likely tasted the blood of the Goddess, if you have drunk tequila — for tequila is only a mescal made from the blue *agave*, which grows in the cold mountains of Jalisco.

The ancient myth of *Mayahuel* is a bloody one, the gruesome story of a woman torn apart by star demons, her magickal body raining in chunks to the earth. And the sufferings of the *agave* plant as it dies are also acute. A single *agave* can produce hundreds of liters of sweet sap during its death throes, as the farmers come daily to collect the pool of its seeping blood for many months.

The sufferings of *Mayahuel* are repaid by the boy who encounters the Lady of Thorns. The morning after this first meeting, the flesh surrounding the pierced hole in his chest has turned mottled and thunderous with deep violet bruises. The wound and the surrounding meat of his chest burn and hurt, as if he has been bitten by a poisonous spider. Within two days the pain and distress will fade, his alarm and any sense of urgent fear melting away. In its place a strange and even blissful calm will come over him, as well as a desire to go walking in the hills.

This state of intoxication and desire to walk in the high desert will only increase as days pass, until the state of delirium and the urge to leave the village and walk up into the rugged mountains alone is completely overpowering. If restrained, the maddened boy will fight savagely to escape, fight like a man trying to reach his true love and die in Her arms, his burning love for Her consummated at last.

There are some who have tried to restrain a thorn-struck boy over the years, locking him in a windowless room or even a cell of the local jail. The results are inevitably tragic, as his slowly fermenting blood goes rancid, like *pulque*, and rots in his very veins. No medicine, spiritual or scientific, can treat the condition, and the pain he experiences, both emotional and physical, is heartrending to behold. What is left at the end is a pulpy sack of skin and swimming bones, dark rot leaking from every orifice, which weeps inconsolably until at last it expires. What remains is unfit for a funeral or even a Christian burial: it can only be shoveled into a hole somewhere and forgotten.

Meanwhile, somewhere in the mountains a tall maguey stalk is rising, crowned with flowers, and among the blade-like leaves at its base, one might find a scattering of human bones.

Ahuizotl

Silvia Moreno-Garcia

There, in the alley, a starving dog, all bones and matted black fur.

Look more carefully. You'll notice its tail ends in a gnarled hand, like that of a monkey. Look carefully and you'll discover its eyes glow softly, like certain fish and mushrooms. A soft, blue-green glow. Not a dog, then.

The ahuizotl.

♦

Tenochtitlan, the mighty city upon a lake, its twin pyramids shadowing the main plaza. The ahuizotl lives in the canals crisscrossing the water and nestles next to the axolotls. It listens to the murmur of the water, the bustle of the market, the conversations of slaves and of merchants, the secrets of courtesans and the songs of the priests. It listens. It waits.

♦

The ahuizotl drags people into the depths of Lake Texcoco with its long tail; warriors and peasants and noblemen drown in the creature's loving embrace. Alas, the lake disappears, drained by the Spanish conquistadors. The ahuizotl mourns it with its thin, piercing wail. And though the lake vanishes, the ahuizotl remains.

◆

Mexico City sinks slowly every year upon its silty bed and there are no barges floating through canals, no noblemen with bright feathers upon their brow or soldiers holding the shield of the jaguar. Cars, buses, taxis, rumble over the city's ancient foundations. The subway snakes beneath crumbling palaces. People with cellphones yell their conversations and others with music players drown the voices out with headphones. The ahuizotl listens. It waits.

The ahuizotl devours the eyes, nails, teeth, of its victims, leaving the rest. This has not changed. The rest has, for it is an adaptable creature. Nowadays, it can be found in the sewers or the subway station, in the garbage-littered streets when the rains come and the avenues flood. That splashing sound that you sometimes hear behind you as you walk home at night? That's the ahuizotl.

The ahuizotl hunts alone and employs tricks to lure its prey. It often imitates the sound of baby's wail to draw humans towards it. And it need not have a lake to inhabit: it can hide in the shallow puddles that form after the rain. It can come in through the moist walls where mold grows. It can slink through tiny holes in the ceiling, where the water drip drip drips. It can even slide through old pipes and spill upon the tiles, ink that takes the shape of a dog.

Tonight there will be rain and that is why I say: watch out for the ahuizotl when you walk home.

The ahuizotl listens. The ahuizotl waits.

Watch out for dogs that are not dogs and do not heed the cry of a screaming child. Watch out and walk faster, avoiding the puddles. Watch out, my dear, for there are eyeless corpses that float through the sewers of our city, float dreamily towards the palace of Tlaloc where the drowned swim.

The American Singing Swan

Greg Stafford

There has appeared in America a peculiar and beautiful creature. Sightings reportedly began on November 5, 1980, although these can be questioned for lack of public verification, a photo, or any recording of its song. Such verification has proved elusive, yet the large and increasing number of encounters with it, or more often its song, has gained it veracity as great as Bigfoot. As such, it must be considered in a manual of modern creatures.

Its appearance is contested. Some observers claim it is blue, white, and red;[1] others that it is red, blue, and white;[2] and yet others say it is red, white and blue.[3] Fewer of the witnesses have claimed it is blue, red, and white; or white, blue, and red. This might indicate that there is more than one type, that it has gender differentiation, differences between age groups, or any combination of all these. These uncertainties have brought scholars of a prominent New England University to speculate

---

1 Francis, *Swan in the Union Hall?* Columbia University, 2012

2 Stafford, *Cacophonous Noise — Plebeians Whine Some More*, Beloit College, 1990

3 Gregory, *The Cry of the Upper Class Swan*, Humboldt State University, 2014

that it is actually a spectral creature, or perhaps a shape shifter.[4] These disagreements inevitably lead to name-calling and mockery when supporters of each type meet in public or on media. These public quarrels lead us to one of the most mysterious aspects of the creature, and the origin of its name: its song.

The actual song of this creature is said to be a kind of "plaintive moan,"[5] a "cacophony of squawks, mumbles and cries,"[6] and "not unlike the roar of opposed political marchers meeting on a street corner."[7] The approximately common nature of these descriptions doubles back on itself when witnesses claim that their verbal arguments, via media or in person, inevitably sound like its song. This statement is universal among claimants and ought to offer some hint of a solution, although the author cannot think of any such resolution. One thing seems certain: that this swan song will continue to erupt and mystify participants until several of the participants can resolve their differences and find a solution together.

4 Petersen, *The Mystical Nature of the American Singing Swan*, Miskatonic University Press, 2013

5 Gregory, *ibid.*

6 Francis, *ibid.*

7 Stafford, *ibid.*

Banaroc

(Of the Banaroc)

Kathryn Kuitenbrouwer

The battle creature, or banaroc, is an unsteady and quickly dematerializing homunculus known only to emerge out of the viscera of fallen soldiers. Initially sighted during the First Battle of Bull Run at Manassas in 1861 and last seen dissipating into the late day fog at the Battle of Palmito Ranch, 1865, the banaroc lives in every warrior's lower bowel and causes a great stench to be emitted when it is released upon the violent death of its host. The banaroc is said to be birthed by the coupling of fear and bravado, which copulate in the stomach chambers of duped young men. In appearance it is identical to its singular host, except in two ways: in size, for it is miniature in every way, and also in materiality, for it is wet and blurred and fleeting. The banaroc feeds on the flesh and bone of the man who housed it, and so does a hygienic service to the battlefield, even as it repulses us. The banaroc is associated with Job: *And Satan answered the Lord, and said, Skin for skin, yea, all that a man hath will he give for his life.* (Job 2:4). Conjecturally, some instances were witnessed of the banaroc emerging before the last soldierly expiration, and especially in the chaos of death throes. The banaroc's teeth are tiny, monstrous, and many — like filed ivory. There is a nearly lost, possibly apocryphal "Song of the Banaroc," which, it is said, doomed soldiers sang in rounds:

♦

The Banaroc, the Banaroc,
We fear his teeth, we fear his claw,
He cleans my bones, he scours the field,
Good-bye!!
Hello!!

♦

There is one ancient photograph of a banaroc hovering in starved anticipation over the corpse of its soldier. The image is damaged and hidden away in the American Civil War section in a musty university library, the location of which is lost to angst and memory. It is said that one Private Russell Boyt was the last to know of the photograph's whereabouts; we have an unsigned letter, in what a forensics team declare is Boyt's handwriting, and that is all we have. The letter reads: "Ah, mother, the Banaroc of lore came all at once from the tangled stomachs of the dead and dying. The creatures hover and scream their ghastly scream across the battlefield. They are like tiny, misted men, all sloe-eyed and bewildered, which then feed with ravenous intensity before dissipating into the ether. I never saw the like before and recounting it to you here is my worst transgression. I am yours, R.S.B."

Beings

Rupert Booth

We've all met one. Almost every individual on this planet has encountered several and yet has never known it. Other than a vague sense of wrongness, there is very little to give a Being away from a humanoid, yet they are so ancient and far removed from us as a species that to turn the mind to the concept is to invite a potentially terminal boggle. Yet the human reaction to a Being is and will always be the same, a profound and dominating fury, which surges up from deep in the hindbrain and rapidly removes any veneer of civilisation. This phenomenon can be partially explained by the Beings' origin, they are not indigenous to Earth, to our Galaxy or even to the Hubble Telescope's most distantly imaged Star-bobbles.

For the Beings are leftovers from the very first Universe of all. The Protoverse: the quietly ignored initial prototype from which all subsequent Universes were developed. A place with worlds of provocative flatness lit by light bulbs the size of which would have given Edison a scientific hard on, and each world seeded with its own identity, or Reality. This distinctly strange yet utterly familiar Omni-System came to an end in 1999, burning under the weight of its own conflicting time streams and fundamental daftness, a design flaw mostly, but one not completely eliminated for the second attempt, our own Universe. I mean look at string theory. String theory??? How can string have a whole theory?

The origin of the Beings is mysterious, what with the whole problem of porting data storage formats from one universe to another, a task which makes the VHS/Betamax war look like a battle between a dead ant and an uninterested fragment of leaf. However, it's known that there was a time in the Protoverse before the rise of the Being Empire, when great damage was done to the moil in between the Realities by the earliest inhabitants, the BigClevers, leaving filigree conduits of energy lancing dangerously between the flat worlds. It is postulated that the Beings may have evolved to counteract this discord in the Protoversial harmonies.

There were, as might be assumed, millions upon thousands of species populating the Protoverse, from Gods to Monstrances, to massive Gas Hands, but by far the dominant shape was the two arms, two legs and hopefully a head, humanoid form which has since proven so successful in our own Universe. As far as we know from *Star Trek* anyway. It is therefore likely the Beings evolved from perfectly ordinary people but alas, those people took the pursuit of ordinariness too far, so much so that even their original species name was lost and they became simply "Beings". Feared, hated and generally avoided by everyone with any sense in the Protoverse which was about a third of the total population.

The Being Empire was a widespread organisation in every sense of the latter word and this is the core of the Being existence; to regulate, to bring order, where before there was only freedom. The early Beings made two crucial discoveries which gave them almost unassailable power in the Protoverse, the first being a pure flowing Red Tape Spring, the basic power source for their monolithic dominance. Every new Being, whether a convert to the cause or of natural (well, as far as natural could be in triplicate) birth was exposed to the spring and grew a Red Tapeworm in their brain, a symbiotic piece of Bureaucratic ribbon twined with the central nervous system and allowing all Beings a hive mind of sorts.

That hive mind gave the Beings the raw thinking power to actually hold a cogent argument with the Protoverse itself, the result of which was immortalised on the very first form. This edict, written in shades of opalescent grey, black ink having been discarded as being too decisive, decreed that the Protoverse should damn well shut up: do as it was told and plug all potentially destructive energy conduits, damaging the fabric of Protoversial Time/Space into the back of a shed. Thus, they were harnessed into a transportation network which could deliver cohorts of Beings instantly to almost any point in their cosmos. The Beings had hit upon one of the few immutable laws of the Protoverse, which was that an idea, once written down, signed and witnessed by enough conscious things, became fact. With the Being hive mind (now more of a filing cabinet for the soul) able to witness any one document thousands of times, the resultant influence over events and ability to shape reality gave them extraordinary power.

The Being Empire was eventually brought down in a legendary yet quickly forgotten event. Such was the logic of the Protoverse. Lost to the mystery of history is the moment when a man, wrongfully persecuted by the Beings themselves for inadvertently causing a misfile, simply picked up a rock and blocked up the Red Tape spring, instantly causing every Being linked to it to go into irreversible Spewis (*noun, polite Being term for complete Brainfuck*).

Allegedly after this event, the man in question turned into an empty picture frame for 13 years, possibly as a spectacular overreaction to the guilt. The destruction of the one controlling force left in the Protoverse speeded its irreversible decline and eventual demise as it spiralled out of control, leaving many of those who had reviled the Beings to stand on country fences, sucking on pipes and claiming things were much better in the old days.

This is all very well, but what relevance do dead hyper-bureaucrats from an equally dead universe have to everyday life in the 21st century? It turns out, more than one might have expected. The Beings were for a long time aware of the existence of our Universe and were concerned that travel between the two was in fact readily accessible to those who knew the secret. They therefore determined that it would be advisable under Section 4771/P of the Inter Universal Wrangling Act (fifteenth revision), Sub Clause 8a (awaiting acceptance and underwriting of ninth draft), paragraph googolplex (beginning "We the undersigned") to establish branches in "Reality" as they called it, confusingly, to ensure that any unauthorised travel was stamped out, controlled and thoroughly made difficult. Despite their basically highly OCD intentions, this did spare our universe from all manner of ridiculous invaders and indeed, as the gateway was frequently used by Uber Criminals fleeing from justice, can actually be seen as one of the few genuinely useful services the Being Empire provided.

Protected from the catastrophic disintegration of their empire, the Beings left in this Universe faced an uncertain future and therefore set about the task of bringing certainty to it. Over the centuries, each nest of Beings established its individuals as members of society, all in positions of extreme boredom yet each with a certain small influence which cumulatively allow them to further their goal unnoticed. That goal? To achieve a state of perfect inertia, where there is no change, no development and, as a by product, very little joy, unless correctly applied for.

Which brings us back to the initial assertion that we have all met a Being. They can be distinguished from normal human Bureaucrats by their single-minded determination to hinder, in the face of logic, reason or desperate need. Even if a Being's arcane procedure has been followed to the letter, they will find a way to enforce the only power they have left to them, the lifeless power of "no". A fully functioning Being is the kind of preventative that Durex can only dream of, to them, without the presence of correct documentation to back up your existence, you simply don't. To a Being, "expedite" is a swear word and even the most carefully worded letter of protest will be discarded if its capitals are not blocky enough. To reason with a Being is to invite either gibbering madness or complete body function failure and their wielding of stress is perhaps their greatest weapon in this world.

However, Protoverse researchers, of which there are three, note if an applicant can successfully turn that very stress back upon the Being itself, there is a chance of at least breaking that one link in the chain, though very rarely of actually achieving one's objective. To do so, one must maintain one's own calm demeanour, give the Being no sign of weakness and feed it with such a conflicting stream of information that it is pushed so vastly far outside its comfort zone, where no precedent exists to cover the eventuality you have presented to it. At this point, the average Being is likely to turn a radiant shade of puce and be forced into "Failsafe Mode". This final sanction was, in the Protoverse, a method of instantly transporting the Being in question to a null zone of total relaxation, a large, comfortingly grey room filled with a soothing amount of nothing bar one ballpoint pen and a form full of simple yes/no answers. Since the demise of the Protoverse, however, this inbuilt biological teleport simply dissipates the Being when activated or, in more spectacular instances, misfires, reducing the Being to a small pile of ash in a violent yet completely controlled conflagration.

For the skilled Being watcher there are a few giveaway signs, bar the absolute banning of a sense of humour. Beings have completely odourless ears, unnaturally boring though not toneless voices and one slightly flaccid eyelid from squinting at small print from their "Necessary Developmental Small-time" (the Being phrase for "Childhood"). Though hugely disempowered by existing in the wrong Universe (a fact which makes them seethe within stated anger limits), Beings nevertheless wield a considerable influence over the lives of us all and must be treated with great trepidation and if possible avoided.

If you think you have a Being in your midst, tread carefully: think before you speak, sniff their ears and make sure you have your badge of official identity on you at all times. Otherwise, they will infiltrate every aspect of your life and dominate every waking thought, eventually bringing down your existence to an irreversible spiral of negative hell.

In triplicate.

The Black Dog
(We Apologize for the Delay)

Sam Agro

If not for David Spurling, and an elderly Asian man at the west end of the platform, the subway would have been completely deserted. This was no surprise to David, considering the time. It was nearly one in the morning.

With his artist's eye, David regarded the Asian man, taking note for future reference. The man looked to be in his late fifties, and appeared to be completely bald. His coat was long, and too heavy for the weather. It hung loosely on the man's body, as though it had once fit, but the man had recently shriveled. Several plastic shopping bags lay scattered on the floor next to the old gentleman's feet. He stood, placidly, blinking occasionally, completely unconcerned with David, who was leaning against the wall at the other end of the station.

David turned away from his fellow subway denizen, tilted his head back, and looked at the ceiling. He took a moment to log the cracks, blisters, and water stains that marred the plaster surface. His eyes itched. He closed them, but this did little to alleviate the dry, scratchy feeling. The long hours he'd been putting in at the studio had left them in a nearly permanent state of dehydration. It had been worth the time, though. His first one-man show would debut at Gallery Pretext in less than three weeks. David was still a few canvasses short of a complete show, but he'd come a long way, and he was confident he'd be ready in time.

David rubbed his eyes, yawned, and glanced back at the old man. The old fellow rummaged through one of his plastic bags and came up with a baggie of almonds. He plucked one out, popped it in his mouth, and munched away. He seemed very serene.

A sudden blast of cold air gusted out of the tunnel, and David shivered. Maybe the old guy had a good idea after all, with that heavy coat of his. David stood, walked to the edge of the platform and looked down into the tunnel. He expected to see the lights of an oncoming train pushing a column of wind ahead of it, but he didn't.

No train.

No anything, in fact.

Usually, a few dim lights could be seen down the tube, but tonight the tunnel was pitch black. David peered intently into the abyssal darkness and heard a soft, animal *huff*. The hackles on the back of David's neck prickled, and he shivered again. He sensed a living presence in the shadow. He rubbed his eyes once more and looked back into the tunnel. His tired eyes struggled to separate black from more black.

At that moment, the blackness seemed to ripple, as though it were a muscle flexing itself.

Then came the howl.

It was a canine wail of such agonized tone and malicious intent that David took an involuntary step backward.

"What the fuck?" David whispered to himself.

He looked over at the Asian man, seeking independent confirmation of what he'd heard, but the man offered no such reaction. He seemed not to have heard the howl. The man stood there, peacefully munching away on his almonds, oblivious to all. David wondered if he was hearing things.

He shook his head and gave himself a little slap on the cheek. Obviously, he was in desperate need of some sleep.

♦

It had been an intense ten days, but David had finished three more canvasses. They'd all turned out beautifully, even if he did say so himself. It was another late night, but he had just enough time to catch the last subway train of the day. He dropped his token in the cup, exchanged a friendly nod with the collector, and plodded down the steps to the tunnel.

It was totally deserted. Not a soul in sight.

He ambled over to the end of the platform and stopped near the opening. He was tired, but also wired, excited about his show, about the big leap forward his career was about to take. His mind entertained small fantasies of sold out shows, fawning critics, and throngs of admiring women dressed in chic Bohemian fashions. The thought of finally having a little money and respect brought a soft grin to his lips.

Then he heard a noise.

It was a wheezy *huff*, followed by a low snort.

He looked into the tunnel, black as night, and once again the jet-black darkness seemed to spasm. This time a figure emerged from the gloom. A dog.

An enormous black hound, easily four feet tall at the shoulder, wide and muscular, built like a cross between a bulldog and a Great Dane.

The huge creature stood in the middle of the tracks, just inside the opening of the tunnel. It observed him intently with its immense, yellow eyes. The beast did not seem crazed or rabid, but he sensed some threatening implication in its bearing. David looked back at the platform, but there was no one there. No one to confirm or deny what his sore eyes told him. He ached for the company of the elderly Asian man who'd shared the station with him last week.

David steeled himself, and looked back at the hound. The beast fixed him with its jaundiced glare and howled. If the howl he'd heard ten days before had been chilling, this one was downright bloodcurdling. It seemed to rattle his bones and echo endlessly in the empty caverns of the tunnel. David stood, rooted to the spot, unable to move. He could feel frigid droplets of sweat oozing from every pore.

The hound coughed out a half-bark, lifted its forepaws and turned tail. In an instant the creature disappeared into the impenetrable murk of the tube.

♦

David paced across the cold floor of his one-room apartment, his sock feet shuffling quietly on the cheap laminate flooring. Part of him believed that he'd been witness to an unlikely, but feasible occurrence. That somehow a dog had gotten into the subway system and learned to survive in there. Another part of him believed he'd imagined the entire frightening incident.

But there was another part, the part of him that remembered his Aunt Hannah. She was his great aunt, in fact, his grandfather's sister. She'd said something to him once, when he was five or six, about a black dog. *Black Shuck*, she'd called it, or *Old Shuck*, maybe. Some tall tale from Suffolk, where his family had originated.

"If *Old Shuck* comes to visit you three times, Davey," she'd said, "you're not long for this world."

He remembered something else, too, a phone call about four years later. He recalled his mother whispering with Aunt Hannah. Curious, he'd quietly lifted the receiver and listened in on the extension.

"It's just an old wives' tale, Auntie, there's no such thing as —"

"No, my darlin', it's the God's honest truth. I've seen him once in the garden, and once again in old Emmerson's corn field. He howled his death call, and I know he'll come again."

"Don't be ridiculous. It's just some stray."

"No, it's the way of the Spurling family. Three visits from the black hound and it's all over. I just called to let you know that I love all of you."

"It's a crock of shit, Hannah, I'll see you in Kitchener at Christmas."

But they hadn't seen her at Christmas, David remembered. They'd gone to her funeral less than a week later. He'd been fourteen, and it had been his first time as a pallbearer. Even though the experience was a bit weird, it had made him feel grown up, somehow.

And now Black Shuck was after him. One more visit, and he'd be dead.

"How can I be about to die?" he thought. "I'm only thirty-two."

His first show was coming up, and he had an agent now. His paintings were starting to sell. His life was just beginning.

"Well, to hell with that noise, *Old Shuck*!" he thought, "I'm not the one who's going to die."

David raced to the closet and pulled down a beat-up old banker's box from the shelf. He yanked off the lid and rummaged through all his high school art awards, old photos, and other jumbled keepsakes, and came out with a small oak case. He opened the case and gingerly removed his granddad's old service pistol, a Browning .40 caliber semi-automatic.

It would need to be cleaned and oiled, but Granddad had taught him how to use it. If Old Shuck wanted a fight, David would give him one.

♦

The paintings were all boxed up and on their way to Gallery Pretext. For a few nights David had taken a taxi to and from the studio, but he couldn't keep up the cash outlay until some of the canvasses were sold.

The first night he'd relented and taken the subway had been rough. He'd been sweating like a pig, and kept reaching into the pocket of his coat to feel the hard, cold, reassuring shape of the pistol he carried there. But, nothing had happened that night, or the six that came after. He was beginning to feel the entire thing was some sort of fever dream, brought on by too much work and his overactive imagination.

There was no one else on the platform except a young couple, looking a bit tipsy, necking on a bench. He walked past them, taking a moment to ogle the girl's cleavage along the way.

He found the end of the platform and leaned back against the wall.

He felt good.

Elaine, his agent, was predicting a sellout for the show. That could mean a lot of money for him, along with a better apartment, and not having to bullshit his studio space landlord when he was late with the rent.

A rush of cold air blew out of the tunnel and David looked up, expecting to see the train.

There was nothing there.

Nothing.

The darkness pulsed like a black bubble and the hound emerged.

It was bigger than ever, easily taller than a man. Even standing on the tracks below him, the beast's eyes were nearly even with his own. Its eyes were enormous now, as big as platters, and its massive mouth lolled open, revealing its dripping fangs. The beast howled, and it felt like an earthquake. David thought the sound alone might kill him, but it finally stopped, and the echoes faded.

He felt as if his blood had turned to dust and his heart was pumping dry.

Then he remembered the gun.

He reached into his pocket and fumbled out the pistol. He pointed the weapon, shouted, "Screw you, Old Shuck!" and fired at the beast.

His shot went wide and ricocheted off a pillar. The girl behind him screamed and the man yelled, "Jesus Christ!"

The dog *huffed* and ran back into the tunnel.

David leapt down onto the tracks and followed the creature. He fired another two shots, but this seemed to have no effect on the monster. It loped easily ahead of him, titanic in size now, nearly filling the entire tube. He fired again and again until the clip was empty and the hammer clacked impotently against the cylinder.

The brute turned and faced him. Its eyes glowed, no longer yellow, but fiery white, and its hot breath blew against him like a gale. It howled, and the sound rose in pitch to become a terrible whine.

Then, the great beast burst suddenly into mist, and was scattered away by the squealing rush of the oncoming train.

Bonnacon

Steve Berman

Beef created Chicago. No other city in the world has slaughtered so many cattle.

Ambrose Bierce referred to that metropolis as the "abattoir of anything with a hoof." He was just shy of thirty when the Great Chicago Fire of 1871 happened, and, as a journalist, investigated the cause of the terrible blaze. The below entry appeared in the original manuscript of his book *The Devil's Dictionary*, but the banker to the publisher, Doubleday, Page and Company, was married to a member of the wealthy Armour family and thus had this entry excised before publication. Supposedly furious at such censorship, Bierce left America for England, a land that appreciated cuts of lamb over beef. The truth may be more sinister, as Bierce was purported to state he feared for his life while on American soil.

BONNACON, n. A species of cow that uses its fiery dung as a weapon. Discovered by Nero. Bull-headed, like any elected official, with horns that are useless, much like the deeds of any elected official. The most famous bonnacon was owned by Kate O'Leary of Chicago. Second most famous was the martial Philip Henry Sheridan, who set his bonnacon to scorch the earth ahead of his hungry troops.

Legend has it that one of Kate O'Leary's cows kicked over a lantern and started the blaze that would consume much of Chicago. How did a poor Irish immigrant come to own four cows? How could, as the newspapers claim, one blackened calf survive? Daniel "Peg Leg" Sullivan, a witness to the barn accident, testified that he was the man who sold O'Leary that surviving cow but would not state where or how he came into ownership of the livestock. A former Union soldier maimed at the Battle of Corrick's Ford, Sullivan was a known vagrant, who often slept near an abandoned armory by the rail stations. Sullivan later disappeared. A pariah, O'Leary was forced to sell the surviving calf. Some say that the mayor purchased the cow; some claim a wealthy former soldier resembling Sheridan took possession of the animal.

Ambrose Bierce traveled to Mexico in 1913 during the tumult of the Mexican Revolution. In 1914, Bierce was last seen alive at the port of Veracruz when a German merchant ship, the *Ypiranga*, arrived. Dock workers complained of the stink rising off the *Ypiranga*, a stench so foul, so redolent of manure, that none would agree to unload the vessel. Soldiers of the Federal Army unloaded the many great crates aboard. Locals said these crates were singed and swayed — they held beasts that snorted and bellowed like bulls.

In the papers of one H. Finn,[1] formerly of St. Petersburg, Missouri, who was an abolitionist and claimed to spy for the Union, are personal correspondence from Bierce dated late October of 1871 that mention Sheridan, a former Union general, who presided over martial law in the days after the Great Chicago Fire. Sheridan's manor was unscathed by the blaze, yet, during an inquiry as to the cause of the fire, it was revealed that all his personal papers and military attaché documents had burned to ashes. Further correspondence with Bierce reveals the man suspected the bonnacon to be some sort of weapon, perhaps

1 The Finn papers are housed in The State Historical Society of Missouri. However, many historians question the veracity of these documents, namely because the man was a known thespian who would only perform female roles while cross-dressed under the stage name of Rebecca Finn, and likely a sodomite. Whether he ever appeared as Marguerite in Faust is unknown.

artillery, commissioned to decimate the Confederate States Army. Bierce goes on to suggest that the bonnacon was given to Sheridan by Simon Cameron, who later became secretary of war in President Lincoln's cabinet, and that Cameron had discovered a secret, referred to as the *vilde kow*, among a particularly degenerate clan of German immigrants in the coal region of Pennsylvania. Even more mysterious among the Finn documents is a tattered telegram to Finn from an A. B. dated April 13, 1914, which offers a strange message taken straight from Gounod's *Faust: Le veau d'or est toujours debout*.

Brain Monster
(Dynamite-Packing, Slightly Cannibalistic)

Marie Davis and Margaret Hultz

This year fall came too gently, causing Bunny to have a loving memory of Sara. That was it — Bunny was highly allergic to good thoughts. Bunny, as she was so frightfully named, was roughly three and a half feet tall. Her orange hair stood up on top of her head clumped together in eight-inch spears. Countless people had looked at the spikes and thought all they really needed was an olive stuck on the end of each one. Then Bunny could swizzle her head around in a giant gin martini, which just might loosen the scowl she constantly wore as an empathetic gesture towards humankind. Mistakenly so, oh so many mistakes ago, Bunny had loved Sara. But mutinous Sara had never *ever* loved Bunny.

Unconsciously bending down to haplessly pick up the first scrap of litter, Bunny was clueless that she had — once again — been kidnapped by her brain. This time, her brain maneuvered Bunny all the way across town, and she was exhausted after days of mindlessly collecting trash without any sleep. Huddled up next to a post office box, in an alley between a coffee shop and the grocery store, Bunny desperately needed rest, but Bunny's brain had an entirely different idea.

Was it a dream, or had a pirate's life saved me? Bunny glanced down at the weight on her hip. A *cutlass? Maybe it's true? Why else do I gotta sword on my belt? But where's the ship — my mates? What 'bout those big-ass cannons? And dammit, if a pirate's life really saved me, why'd it give up on me now?*

"A life of piratedom..." she muttered as her voice drifted off. Sleep finally arrived and a snore rumbled in her throat and growled out her nose.

This was not the first time the pirate crew had gone looking for Master Gunner Bunny. Bunny's brain had absconded with her in the past, and the pirates knew that she would not be easy to find. Her brain, Bunny's nemesis, was always attempting to steer her off course. It whispered in her ear a sort of running commentary, never kind, always treacherous. In her entire life Bunny had reserved the only kind word she'd ever said for the first time her daughter told her that she would become a grandmother. "Fine!" Bunny grunted, perilously close to smiling. That spot of joy was eighteen grandchildren ago.

Cap'n Lizzy had a soft place in her heart for Bunny's meanness and the whole ship and crew were now well accustomed to the short, bitter woman's foul disposition. Even with one eye covered by a patch, a hook for a right hand, and one peg leg, Cap'n Lizzy was a handsome woman — tall with broad shoulders, an olive complexion, short dark hair and one big, bright blue eye. In speech, appearance and personality, Lizzy was a classic. She fancied herself a kind of traditional pirate, someone who took women with bravado, pillaging their virtues, and leaving a wreck in her wake. But Lizzy's crew? They were a motley assortment of misfits, thankfully minus failed mutineer Sara, forced to walk the plank into the catfish pond despite Bunny's pleas. The remaining crew made up of motherly, dynamite-packing Esmeralda, stuttering, slightly cannibalistic Rosie and *unsunny* Bunny were more like family. No matter how strange they might be, you just couldn't let any one of them go roaming around nabbed by a malcontent brain. You just don't do that. After all, this was an odd posse of four landlocked lesbian pirates on this side of the 21st century.

Captain Lizzy commanded, "Stick nigh, me hearties. Follow my lead."

Tiptoeing close behind, Esmeralda wrung her hands. "Captain? What if we can't fix Bunny this time, what if her brain's got her for good? What if she won't ever come back?"

"It's n-n-n-not like you to be gl-gloom and doom, Esme," Rosie stammered.

"Things are *not* promising," Esmeralda fretted.

"What are promises anyway — just a-a-a crap shoot," Rosie mumbled.

Creeping quietly around the side of the coffee shop, the Captain whispered, "Promises-shromishes! The honor between pirates is much more certain!" Lizzy drew her sword, "Halt. Thar be monsters ahead."

Slumped on her side by the mailbox, poor Bunny had built a flimsy fortress surrounding herself with shopping bags stuffed full of garbage, a pitiful attempt to keep safe. But Bunny's brain had finally escaped its cranial incarceration. The pint-sized organ, encephalitic and enraged, hopped about agitatedly while patrolling the bags' perimeter.

Captain Lizzy murmured. "Aye maties, I think I spies our rotten Bunny — guarded by some ugly grey beast."

Startled, Rosie exclaimed, "Ohhhh… L-L-L-ookie there! It's s-s-so… little! It don't looks *beasty* at all?"

"What'llwedo? Lordyhowstrange? That's a brain! Aww… it's so little. I swear I've heard of this condition, but never seen it with my own eyeballs. Let's get out there — see if we can catch the teeny darlin'."

"I 'spec that ain't no li'l darlin', Esmeralda. That there be Bunny's brain I reckon, and there ain't nothing darlin' coming outta Bunny. Outta her head and outta its mind with a mission all its own — wreakin' havoc on the world. Damn scary if'n you ask me."

"Well hell's bells, how are we gonna get that shriveled up li'l noggin-filler back where it belongs, Cap'n?"

"Don't fret, me Boatswain, somehow we'll finagle that bitty beast back inna her head. Now hush, me hearties, don't be letting its small size hornswoggle ye," warned the Captain.

"Shoulda one of us go out there and try to talk to it? Maybe it would be a little more reasonable *outside* of that woman's infernal cranium?" Esmeralda suggested.

The Captain put her finger to her lips, "Shhh... that blasted brain might hear ye, and besides, ye can't reason with crazy. The brain — and Bunny's brain in 'ticular — it be the meanest kind of monster thar be. It's more liable to snatch you up and stuff the likes of ye into one of those bags of trash — or worse yet — knowing our vicious Bunny."

"Well, i-i-f-f it's that dangerous, Captain, l-let's leave that crazy woman be and g-get the hell out of here — this is serious — and I'm g-getting scared..." Rosie's voice broke as she began frantically gnawing on her fingernails.

"I'll never leave any of me shipmates behind, Rosie, not never!"

Bunny's brain perked up at the sound of tiny whispers, spotting the women in its peripheral vision. Turning to confront them, a fifteen-foot roaring furnace of fire came spewing out of its extraordinarily cavernous mouth.

"ACK!" The pirates screamed and ran, crouched down behind a pickup truck. Knees knocking, they clustered together.

Wild-eyed, Rosie stuttered, "Holy Sh-Shit! It's a f-f-fire breathing brain!" A snippet of flame caught Rosie on the ass, burning through her breeches. Slapping the fire out with her hand, Rosie repeatedly rubbed the charred flesh and then smelled her fingers, mumbling, "Mmm, home cooking."

"Rosie, get yer hand off yer ass and pay attention!" The Captain rolled her eyes.

roar Roar ROAR! Again the brain spewed flames toward the women!

Esmeralda wiped her forehead with her forearm. "Sheesh! No wonder Bunny's so hateful. Do you think this calls for dynamite,

Captain? I got a stick or two in my hosiery, you know I'm always packing." The Boatswain grinned hopefully.

"CRR*RAP*!" Lizzy grumbled under her breath, "No dynamite this time, Esme, and blimey, me sword's not gonna help much either."

Just then Bunny's bitty brain careened around the corner, breathing fire to the left and then to the right. Pedestrians scattered in all directions, tufts of clothing fell like fiery rain while the reek of scorched hair and flesh filled the scene.

Lizzy whispered to her crew, "Avast, Bunny — err — her brain I suppose, has gotten worser than I imagined."

Knees knocking, Esmeralda asked, "What do you think set her off this time?"

"M-m-may-maybe something good happened? You *know* how good thoughts upset her."

Roar! ROAR!! Brain-flames licked the sides of buildings.

When Bunny loudly moaned the brain darted back to her side — stalked cautiously by the pirates. Smoldering, the brain hopped up onto her chest and looked with care at Bunny — softy nuzzling up to the woman's cheek. Without warning it spewed a shot of orange-white flames at point-blank range. Bunny's face reddened — skin boiling and blistering — her red-haired spikes charred while fire steadily burned at their tips.

On hands and knees the pirates crawled behind the next car to get a better view as the brain jumped on top of the post office box. Peering down and closely examining Bunny's seared face, her brain began to cry. Dripping tears doused flickering flames. Sooty, burning flesh smells and Bunny's moans oozed through the air.

Esmeralda watched the scene in awe. "Wow… look at that. That monster of a brain is crying for her. Maybe Bunny ain't so rotten after all?"

"Naw…" Lizzy said, "anger ain't nuttin' but fear turned upside down."

Rosie spouted, "That ol' f-f-fight or flight idea."

Esmeralda nodded her head, "Yeah, except Bunny ain't got no flight in her."

"BUNNY! Over here, can you hear me?" Captain Lizzy popped out hollering and waving her arms.

The brain jerked around spitting fireballs toward the Captain.

"*Shit!*" Lizzy ducked. "That's it, crew, there ain't nothing to do but appeal to that brain's inner pirate."

Esmeralda nodded, "Sure… there's gotta be a pirate down in there somewheres."

"Wh-wh-what does it want?" Rosie shouted out, then clasped her mouth with two hands shaking her head.

Hearing Rosie, the brain turned to disgorge more fire.

"ACK!" The pirates bolted and dived behind a nearby delivery truck.

"That pirate brain of Bunny's is gonna m-m-murderize us… that's what it wants," Rosie uttered, as she ravenously gnawed on her fingers.

"Hmmm… no, but she'd be wantin' her cannons now wouldn't she?" Lizzy thought hard on the predicament and summoning up her courage she screamed to her crew, "ATTACK!"

Without a second's pause the pirates obeyed their Captain and ran toward Bunny. Captain Lizzy ordered, "Grab a bag o' garbage and run! Hurry up, grab a bag o' garbage and run!"

Each woman nabbed a bag and took off fast in the direction of their ship. *Poof!* The brain disappeared and Bunny's eyelids flew open — her rage-filled consciousness fully returned.

"Quick, fling the trash as ye run!" Lizzy ordered as the crew raced away in the direction of their ship.

Bunny sprang to her feet and set chase, spewing vengeful words at the bolting pirates, "You ain't pirates, not even close! Give me back my treasures! Pirates don't run away, y'all are nothin' but scairt little girls playing dress up. Lizzy, your damn boat won't even float, just wait, you'll see. Thieves! Stupid little scairt thieves is all — stealin' my treasures and treatin' 'em like trash — I never cared fer a one of ya…"

Bunny's words burnt like flames, but Cap'n Lizzy just laughed all her way back to her ship.

Bunyip

Laura Lush

Smooth yet tusked — claws so sharp that he dare not groom his own darkened fur. Hind legs thick and squat, but the fore legs long, lean. Anomaly of a beast. Never has he met another like himself, never has he gotten close to another creature long enough. He is burdened by his own strange body, by his flavour for both water and land, by the stories that have grown from his monster-like appearance. And for this, he remains — alone, singular.

For days, he has been watching an animal graze on the swamp's edge. The animal is soft and slow, spotted with black and white dots. And to the bunyip's amazement, when he looks at the animal, the animal does not look away. He does not run or howl or jump. He just settles his eyes — big, brown, and moist — on the bunyip, then lowers his head to eat the grasses.

"Ah," the bunyip says aloud. "Finally — one who is not afraid." The bunyip imagines the animal and him as fast friends. He imagines them spending their days along the swamp's edge munching on grasses. Or maybe even casually basking by the swamp's edge. But the animal does not approach, does not seem afraid or un-afraid.

Then one day, the bunyip gathers his courage, decides to visit the animal. But the animal is no longer at the swamp's edge. The bunyip raises his clawed hand to his face and looks. He looks beyond the swamp, around the swamp, and finally his eyes search the surface of the swamp. That's when he sees him — the animal in the water-hole, his whole body unmoving, stuck. He will rescue him and then he will not only be a hero, but he will be a friend. A friend and a hero! The bunyip lowers himself into the swamp and begins his slow and careful crossing. He alerts with each slow glide forward. *Swash—swash-swash* — his horse-like tail slapping the swamp's surface as he slowly swims toward the lone animal bogged in the water-hole. *Swash—swash-swash*, he signals. But the animal does not look up. For the first time, the bunyip cannot see the animal's large moist eyes looking at him.

In a far-off place, a mother sits down to read her son a bedtime story. The mother always chooses the same book — the one with the oddly shaped creature who watches rather than acts, who halts rather than advances, the creature who is neither animal nor fish, neither completely fin nor fur.

The boy turns his head away.

But the mother loves this creature. This bunyip, this strange mixture of fur and anguish.

How he skips the heat and the sun. How he avoids, eludes — how he hides in the water, feared and rivalled, but never fully seen by any. And for this, he remains fascinating — an enigma.

"Where does he live?" the boy asks his mother.

"Somewhere," she says.

"Here?"

"Not here," she says.

The boy allows himself a sigh of relief.

"Is he big?"

"Not so big," she says, smiling.

"How big?" he presses.

"The size of a dog, maybe."

The boy grabs the book, flips to the page to the bunyip. "That's not true. A bunyip is *much much* bigger than a dog!" The boy shouts: "He's bigger than you! He's bigger than you and me together!" Then the boy pulls the covers over his head.

"It's okay," the mother says.

"Does he eat people?"

"No."

"How about cats — foxes?"

"No." She rubs his head. "That's just a story."

The boy starts to cry.

"Don't be afraid."

"Why do you always have to read the same book?"

"Because," the mother says. "Because, he's interesting."

The boy tosses off his cover and glares at his mother.

"He's not interesting! He's horrible!"

She turns the page, then closes the book.

"He's interesting," she continues, "because he's a bit of everything."

The boy thinks a bit. "Okay," he agrees. "A bit of everything." But the boy does not understand.

"And because he's a bit of everything," his mother says as she tucks her son into bed, "he has to hide."

♦

The bunyip keeps swimming toward the animal. Tail serrated, he cuts through the thick murk of swamp-water. When he reaches the animal, he lifts him from the grip of the water-hole, then hugs him close to his body. But the animal is already dead, body stiff and rigid.

The bunyip releases the animal, then throws back his head, and yowls — a sound so pained that small fish surround him, warming him with their fins.

Then, on shore, he curves his water-body to earth-body until he stands ten — twelve — thirteen feet. Then he walks slowly and beautifully. He walks slowly with his head erect.

The Catoblepas

Patrick O'Duffy

Eye contact is an integral part of human communication. When we speak to each other we look to the eyes for meaning, for stop and go signals, for signs that what we're saying is sinking in. For the constant feedback loop that tells you that yes, you're speaking to someone right now, not just to dead air. Take that feedback away and your conversation partner might as well be invisible.

Such is the quandary of the catoblepas, the creature that is visible but isn't.

Descriptions of the catoblepas have varied over the centuries, and the few sightings that any have recorded (or remembered) are inconsistent. Its body resembles that of a buffalo or a bison, but its legs are probably short and stumpy. Its back is covered with scales, or maybe a mane of thick and greasy hair, or perhaps warts and scabs. It definitely smells terrible — all accounts agree on that. And while versions differ over whether its head (which is like a camel's, or warthog's, or gnu's) just points down due to its weight or whether its long, snaky neck is too weak to hold it up, it's certain that it constantly looks down at the ground, never meeting the eye of those around it.

This may be a blessing for its neighbours; its gaze can kill. But it's a terrible burden to the sad, lonely catoblepas, since it can't make eye contact with other people. And so they never really see it. They're aware of it, more or less, if only because of its appalling odour, but that's not the same thing as seeing it, as acknowledging it, as saying 'Hello, how are you, would you like fries with that?'

No one ever asks the catoblepas if it would like fries. They just wrinkle their noses, look askance at each other and overlook the muddy-footed quadruped awkwardly shuffling before them, hoping to buy a Happy Meal just this once. 'What is that godawful stink?' they say, and no amount of throat-clearing or hopeful staring at their shoes will drag their attention to the unfortunate monster before them.

Privacy is all well and good should you ask for it; not so much when it is forced upon you. The catoblepas is a social creature, or it would be if given the option; it would very much like to be noticed, to be asked its opinion, to be brought into the circle of conversation. Hell, even to be pointed and screamed at every now and then, if only for variety. If only for a moment. But no, without a pupil and iris to latch upon, everyone around the catoblepas is too polite and oblivious to give it even this amount of heed, and so it is left alone. So alone.

And as for its love life... well. Eye contact is even more important when it comes to romance, be that casual flirting or exchanging vows. Take away the option of gazing lovingly into someone's eyes, or even their kneecaps, and romance is replaced by scratching one's back on broken tree trunks every Friday night and trying to hide the tears that no-one is looking for anyway.

There is a sensitive soul behind the indescribable face and kill-vision, you know.

The Internet was supposed to fix this; it was meant to connect people via text, tweet and avatar, letting them make friends and enter relationships without ever needing to see each other. And for many people that's the case, but the catoblepas faces a significant number of challenges in online interaction, chief of which is the difficulty of getting a computer. It has no money, no credit rating, no electricity in the soggy swamps it calls home, and while it can wander into Apple stores or Internet cafés, it's rare to find a monitor lying face-up on the ground with a keyboard nearby, put aside just for the use of the eyeline-challenged. Left to its own devices, the catoblepas has been unable to pass the hurdle that might see it post Photoshopped selfies on OKCupid or grumble about being friendzoned — worse, nonexistentzoned — on Facebook.

But in truth, the catoblepas isn't too keen on this whole Internet thing. It prefers print to digital; it has a respect for tradition, not to mention that it's easier to find newspapers lying on the ground than iPads. It writes letters to the editor — in longhand, pen clamped in its rhino/elephant/frog-like paws, handwriting remarkably neat — and places classified ads. And, of course, plants news stories about catoblepas sightings.

After all, while the catoblepas is reluctantly forced into the role of recluse, it is not a totally unknown quantity; there are records of sightings, encounters, unfortunate deaths. And yes, most of these are engineered by the catoblepas itself — who else is going to do it? They're usually ignored, but every now and then an amateur cryptozoologist or community access TV show will come looking for evidence of the Sobbing Swamp Monster, and even if they go away disappointed (which they always do), at least it gives the catoblepas a couple of column inches and the momentary hope of discovery and perhaps a really nice chat about the weather.

(Sometimes these stories whip up fear and attract men with guns, which is a bit unkind. It's true that the catoblepas eats people. But in fairness, most of them were like that when it found them. It's a carrion eater, and one too hamstrung by strong emotion and a weak neck to go turning its death-ray glare upon anyone save those already on the ground who look up into its face, such as snakes, frogs and drunkards. Anyway, its hide is impervious to bullets and its environs unwelcoming, so those folks usually give up and go back to planning airstrikes on Loch Ness.)

These fleeting moments of almost-recognition are all right for what they are, but in truth they aren't much, and the catoblepas is just about sick of it. Lately it's been thinking about leaving its swamp home and moving to another place — no, another country, one where eye contact isn't as strong a part of social interaction. It's heard tell that in many Asian and African countries, people avoid eye contact as a mark of respect, a way of showing deference to the wealthy and influential. It likes the sound of that, and the notion of being called 'Catoblepas Effendi' or something similar. But booking a plane flight is pretty much out of the question, and learning a new language difficult, so the catoblepas is stuck in its familiar rut for the moment.

Sometimes it's easier to be sad than to change your habits; sometimes it's simpler to be lonely than to go in a totally new direction. Perhaps one day misery can push past inertia and the catoblepas can transform itself completely, break through the barriers it's put in its own path.

One day. Not today. Not now.

For now… stop reading. Step out into your yard or onto your balcony, close your eyes and listen. Can you hear it? The resigned weeping of a soul forever alone? The slow rasp of a warty back scratching invisibly along a concrete abutment? The sloppy crunch of something eating a day-old bird carcass that was hidden in the long grass?

Have a heart. Say 'Hello, catoblepas. Come sit and talk for a while.' Give it a little of your time. Reach out.

But for God's sake, keep your eyes closed or the paramedics will be collecting you in bags come the morning. Don't give the poor creature one more thing to feel bad about.

Chronovore

Dennis Detwiller

There again.

The man sat, head down, on the D, morning rush hour, New York City, 1981. Tony watched him. It was becoming their routine.

The man was fat. Morbidly so, squeezed into a double seat, arms hung at his sides, wheezing. His face had all the openness of a pig face, tiny eyes buried in the mound of pink, a nose somewhere down there, small, yellow teeth occasionally clicking in time with the train. He never looked at anything. He just sat, slightly moving in a rocking, repetitive movement. A calming action an animal might take, like Pepe used to do before sitting down, circling her dog bed, before curling up. Instinctual.

Tony was late again. The train seemed to take forever. It moved, but somehow defied arrival. Mr. Sanucci would, as usual, be in an apoplectic seizure of displeasure. Tony would walk into the school — he was already doing it in his mind — and walk past. They would not fight. He would not tell the old man to go fuck himself. He needed to stay in school.

Which is why he left so early.

The fat man looked up, startled, as the car *finally* came to a halt.

Tony stood, but the fat man did not move. Instead, his jowled face looked confused, interrupted, and then was lost in the spray of people leaving the train, each mumbling their personal hatred for the force that had made them so terribly late.

Tony took the steps two at a time, but was still twenty minutes late.

♦

He fought with Mr. Sanucci. Just a little.

What?

♦

His school hours just missed rush hour, so he'd find a seat on the train home and sprawl. A young guy with curly black hair, jeans and a KISS T-Shirt, eyes lidded in an empty car.

The man who threw the door open between cars smelled like hell. Cigarettes and B.O. and dried shit. A vet maybe? Old army jacket, duct taped shoes that were throwing off chunks of leather, newspapers poking from the edges of his pants. It wasn't winter, so Tony guessed they'd be from *last year*.

The bum's face was stained black from uncleaned years of city sputum. He sat directly across from Tony. Bums always found him.

The bum tried to make eye contact, but Tony flicked his gaze away, watching the dark reflective windows, where an angled version of himself hovered in the air, looking back, unimpressed.

"You know why you always late, man?" the bum announced to the otherwise empty car.

"Because I ride the New York Subway?" Tony replied, half-smiling, not looking.

"Nah man, you ain't seen —"

The train arrived at his stop, *finally* and he hopped up, crossing through a solid cloud of stench.

"Sorry, man," Tony said, and left.

"I BEEN UP THERE!" The bum shouted after him, but the train was already leaving.

♦

At home he watched Roger Grimsby on Eyewitness News, eating Fruity Pebbles on the chipped formica folding table. His dad wouldn't be back until 9, and his mom was working a double at the hospital, so he wouldn't see her tonight.

Upstairs, a giant in tap shoes danced a jig while bowling, or that's what the noise sounded like. That's what New York was. There were two settings for neighbors, *somebody lives there*? Or *call the cops*.

The fight with Sanucci was unfair. Tony had been late after all. He shouldn't have mouthed off. What irked him was the preparation, the pride in being early he truly felt. If Sanucci could see his father — and the military precision of everything in his life to this point, he would have been ashamed to call him a slob.

For the last five mornings, he had been late, and after the first two, he adjusted his schedule. The D was a short jaunt uptown, ten minutes tops, but time seemed to stretch out down there. It didn't *feel* like more than ten minutes, but it was. Sometimes a lot longer.

The last time, the amount of time from stop to stop was about the amount of time it would have taken to walk.

Tomorrow, he'd leave an *hour* early.

♦

Fat man again. Filled train. Time spun out like taffy. Movement continued, the train bucked and rocked. Outside, occasional tiles, pipes and doors flashed by the windows. There was no idea of slowing down, no concept of a hold up, yet they never arrived. No one seemed to notice.

Tony eyed the fat man, who was lost in his trance, head down. His clothes were… odd.

Clean, but form fitting and somehow… neat? Suede or mohair, tan with a fine fuzz on it. His skin was pale pink, and plunged into the shadows under his non-neck into the gap of the suit. No shirt was visible beneath his jacket. His face was a marshmallow puff with holes popped in it, as expressive as a parking meter.

His one visible boot was strange as well. Thin and tall, rising to disappear into pants made of the same odd suede as the jacket, just slightly darker.

Finally, interminably, the car came to a halt.

Nine minutes late after leaving forty-five minutes early.

Motherfucker.

♦

"He eats up your time, man," the bum said to him, teeth close enough to his ear that the breath blew Tony's hair back. The stench was unreal. Tony leaned away. The same bum.

"Fuck off!"

"Huh, fuck off? Fuck you. I'm trying to help you, little brother," the bum said, eyes fixed in the glare of a correcting teacher. "The porker who sits here, ever wonder why you don't see him when you get off?"

Something in Tony clicked.

"What?"

"You wonder where he gone?"

Tony didn't know what the fuck was going on, anymore. He gazed around the empty car for the fat man, but he already knew they were alone.

"He ain't here, man, 'cause he done feeding for the day, and gone to ground."

The train stopped.

"Want to trip? Get one of those digital jobbies and time yourself," the bum smiled. He pulled back a jacket arm and revealed a graveyard of watches, each more ruined than the last, floating on black, scabbed skin.

Tony stood, and looked back at him.

"Think about that, young brother," the bum said through his rotted teeth.

◆

Sanucci sat him down in his guidance counselor's office: four walls and a door made of cardboard with a brass handle half hanging out of it. Someone had hit that door once, hard, and the interior — nothing more than paper, had folded and cracked. Now it wouldn't shut.

"Listen, kid, I know we go at it sometimes, but you're alright."

"Thanks, Mr. Sanucci."

"I like you. You a good kid."

"I like the school too, Mr. Sanucci."

"So, we ain't going to have no more problems, okay?"

"No more problems."

"Good, cause I'd dearly hate to throw out your Puerto Rican ass."

The day drifted by in a haze, and the threat hardly registered. Tony was thinking about other things.

◆

"So, the animals feed on one another in an organization called the…"

Mrs. Carcaterra was pointing at him. She waited while recognition and then fear set in on Tony's face. She cut him off before he could speak.

"The food chain," she said.

"Can anyone tell me something that is neither a predator, or prey species?"

Michael Dunphy raised his hands.

"A parasite?"

"You're a fuckin' parasite," someone mumbled in the back.

Everyone laughed.

Tony watched the fat man the next morning, carefully. He put his TIMEX watch on the edge of the seat in front of him, so the watch face *and* the fat man were visible at the same time. The fat man was lost in his rocking, repetitive motions.

On the watch, every ticking second defied the train to arrive. He kept pace with the seconds count, and found his internal count failing to make time with the seconds on the watch face. The watch seemed to slow, imperceptibly at first, like it was slowly spinning out of sequence. Still, his disbelief fought this conclusion. He kept restarting his count, certain he was mistaken.

Tony observed it, eyes growing wider, as he counted off the time and the watch failed to keep up. For one, glorious minute of internal counting, the watch hung, improbably, at :33.

The moment it resumed, the fat man's head came up, and the doors opened.

Tony fled the train, giving the fat man a wide berth.

School was a blur. Sanucci lobbed a few at him in bombing runs up the hallways between classes, but Tony failed to engage. His mind was elsewhere.

He found himself counting along as the watch evenly spun out hours, minutes, seconds, days…

The plan formed in his head, glacial pieces, most under water, slowly slamming one into another until his mission was clear. He dressed in a Mets jacket and cap, and left long after his early morning time.

It took him several tries to find the fat man, but when he did, he sat across from him and watched his movements.

Same pattern. Same slowness.

The first new thing he saw was the liquid. It seemed the fat man had pissed himself. A wave of clear, sweet-smelling liquid drifted in a thin puddle from his seat area down the train, to the muffled curses of the travelers. Like dog pee only with a stronger smell.

At each station, the fat man stopped a moment before the train did, looking up, blinking.

This seemed to go on forever. Hours. Though his watch failed to register much of it.

♦

Tony woke suddenly on an empty train, just as the fat man's back exited the door at… 196th street, the… Bronx? No man's land.

Tony leapt and caught the door just as it began to close, blocking it with his shoulder. He fell onto the wrecked platform with a grunt, as the doors slammed shut behind him and the train left.

He looked up to find the fat man, hung forward on thin, black booted legs in an odd gait, looking back at him with tiny eyes.

There was no recognition there.

Tony stood, and wiped himself off as the fat man scurried away.

Dusk. Ruined streets of tri-levels with abandoned yards, boarded storefronts, and empty intersections. Doors hung like rotting teeth. Empty windows. Smashed cars. No one but Tony and the fat man.

"Hey!" Tony shouted, and it echoed.

The fat man shambled away at high speed, hunched forward, feet clacking on the ground.

Tony followed.

The factory had a clown, worn away with time, painted on its side, and the fence which once surrounded it looked like it had fallen to enemy invaders, collapsed under the weight of bodies.

The building was huge, cut with ruined fire escapes and pipes, and had long since fallen to disuse.

Tony cut the corner just in time to see the fat man's tan blot enter a building at the end of the street.

Tony covered the distance in a few seconds, just as the fat man's door slammed shut. He found his knees, wheezing. It had been a long time since he had run that fast.

There was a grunt from above which made him jump.

Improbably, thirty feet up from the roof, the fat man's pig face looked down at Tony, backlit by purple and grey sky. Somehow, the enormous man had climbed three stories in a second or two.

"Fuck this," Tony said and ran.

School called twice, and then not again. He knew it was them, because the only other person who called him was his grandma, on Sundays.

Tony didn't need to talk to Sanucci to know he was expelled. He wished he still cared, but he couldn't stop thinking about the pig man.

Tony packed his aluminum baseball bat and emergency flashlight in an Adidas bag and left early in the morning.

The clown factory was silent, and smelled of sick-sweet urine. He left the bag at the door, held the bat in his good hand, and the big flashlight in the other.

The beam crossed the factory's ruined innards, cutting a circle of light to reveal an overturned, rusted tricycle, wood pallets rotted into a green mush, completely eroded metal cogs sunk into the cement.

The second floor was rickety, many of its wood planks rotted or fallen away.

A noise from further in the structure made him realize how terrified he actually was. His breath was coming in great gasps, his heart clopping along.

Something moved.

Tony slowly placed the lamp down, and it cast his shadows in bizarre exaggeration on the far wall. An old tarp stretched across discarded equipment came into sharp focus. The tarp had blue and white paint flecks, as it had once been painted with the face of the clown.

"Hello!" Tony shouted.

Rustling.

"Come out, fucker!" He yelled, trying to sound menacing.

Then, he wasn't alone.

The pig man slammed into him from behind, knocking him backwards, screeching. Like a bird. Spittle flying from yellow teeth, eyes glowing pink in the dark.

Tony collided into a pillar, found his footing and swung the bat. It connected perfectly. Finding the pig man's head with all the practice Tony had put into making it find a ball.

There was an enormous CLANG and the pig man fell back, crashing onto the ground. Then, he was gone with a crack and a BOOM as the floor beneath him gave way.

Tony found the pig man on the cement thirty feet below, sprawled and unmoving.

He dropped the lamp, kicking up crazy circular shadows on the beam in front of him.

Tony leaned in to see if the pig man was breathing, but he wasn't.

Tony reached to feel for a heartbeat, and when his hand touched the jacket, he recoiled.

It was warm, soft and yielding.

Lips pulled back in disgust, Tony grabbed the jacket lapel, found that it was skin, like the flap of an ear, folded in on itself to *look* like a suit.

Then he heard the mewling.

Tiny pig men were crawling from the corpse of the big one. Their legs were curled tusks of white, unlike the grown pig man's black boot-like things, but otherwise they were tiny, fat, scrabbling versions of their parent.

They struggled and squealed on the ground, tiny not-people, moving away from the corpse.

Tony ran, leaving everything behind.

♦

He fell to the ground, outside, and didn't even feel the bloody cuts on his knees. His chest kept hitching, like he couldn't catch his breath.

When he finally wiped his face and looked up, his breath stopped in his chest and his eyes were wide.

At the fence, a hundred pig men, all identical, waited silently, staring at him. A thousand parasites feeding on the city's time, returned to nest.

Daylings

Jerry Schaefer

Daylings come from small, hard eggs produced by chickens of ill repute. (The less said about that the better.) These eggs are laid in shame — far from the disapproving eyes of others — after which they gestate for seven hundred years.

Upon hatching, daylings resemble clumsy bats. The head is like that of a human infant, but feathered and much smaller, with large eyes and tall, peaked ears. The skin is soft and translucent; a thin membrane connects all four limbs to the torso.

Daylings are not capable of powered flight, but can glide like flying squirrels. Without the stabilizing influence of a tail, however, their movement is less like that of a beautiful bird than a psychotic butterfly with a fear of heights.

Having emerged from their embryonic state, these tiny creatures flit about, observing humans unseen. If you ever thought you saw something moving in the corner of your eye, or had the feeling that you were being watched, then you have been in the presence of a newly hatched dayling.

At this point, they are visible only to lunatics and Irish monks. This is why images of daylings sometimes appear in the borders of illuminated manuscripts. The depictions are not flattering or accurate. Here and there, hiding within the Celtic lacework, you may see a wretched figure with wings, wide googly eyes, and horns instead of ears. They are often shown tormenting the souls of people they've never met, or fleeing a saint with a pageboy haircut.

Why such animosity toward such a small creature?

Well, daylings are ugly, quite common, and so frustrating they sometimes drive the best of us mad.

Yet, they are perhaps the most neglected of creatures. Daylings are easily dismissed by mythographers, who often cite the dearth of reliable source materials. For the eighth edition of *The White Goddess*, Robert Graves prepared an appendix on daylings, which made an argument for their actual existence.

His editor rejected the addendum, saying, "Oh Bob, don't be a twat."

Nor will you see any mention of daylings in the *Physiologus*, or any other bestiary, and this is just as well. These largely undocumented creatures are possessed of a "deformed comeliness," about which they are strangely vain. Thus, daylings would rather not be seen in manuscripts featuring such a-zoological improbabilities as fire-breathing "porcupigs." And who could blame them? Imagine being immortalized on a page beside a two-headed bird that sings duets with itself while pooping chocolate-covered cherries into the sweaty palms of vestal virgins.

The "dayling" is so named because it only lives for twenty-four hours. By midday, however, it has grown out of its little, bat-like body to assume the form of a fully grown human. Unfortunately, its brain is still quite small, but after incubating for so many years, the dayling is eager to begin living and rushes out into the world.

Sometimes into the path of a bus. Most do not, though, and spend their one and only day alive annoying people. Chances are, you've met one.

Some daylings find their voices right away, but can only ask questions, possibly the same questions over and over.

"Why *can't* I order pancakes? Is there a *law* around here against eating pancakes? What do you mean you don't serve breakfast?

What kind of restaurant *is* this, anyway? A *steak* house? Okay, so… can I have a steak? With a pancake on it? *Why not?*"

Other daylings amble about like cattle, taking pictures and pointing at things they've never seen before. They may accost you with strange words and broad gestures while shoving a map in your face. Presumably, they want to see the aquarium, or some other attraction that none of the locals ever visit. If this happens to you, nod vigorously while smiling and point in any direction until they go away.

You might find yourself stuck behind a dayling who has no idea how to use a bank machine, or maybe this ignorant creature is trying to buy an entire shopping cart full of tinned meat in the "8 Items or Less" lane of a grocery store.

One may run into you on the street because it isn't smart enough to walk and play *Candy Crush* at the same time. Another may drive slowly in front of you for miles while signalling a left turn. Caution: daylings are prone to slamming on their brakes for no apparent reason, causing you to have an accident.

Because their time is so short, many daylings try to leave behind some evidence of their existence, something that says, "Look at me! I'm special!" For this reason, they are drawn to train wrecks and tenement fires, where they stand behind TV reporters, grinning and waving their arms overhead.

All of this is very irritating, but as I mentioned earlier, daylings are short-lived. Before their day is done, many are crushed under vending machines. The rest die a natural death brought on by an excess of sentimentality. This usually happens in a pub where you may see them tearing up over "the good old days" that never were, or hugging strangers and saying things like "Come 'ere, come 'ere, *lissen* to me — I love you, man. Seriously. *And* I'm rilly sorry about pukin' on your girlfriend, eh?"

If you happen to live or work with people who behave like this, I'm afraid they aren't daylings; they're just stupid.

Doppelgänger

Chris Lackey

Dear President Obama,

Please allow me to introduce myself. I'm Dr. Carl Peaslee, a bioengineer formally with the University of Chicago. I'm writing you in regard to a possible threat to national security and, perhaps, all of human civilization. I'm sure you receive letters like this on a daily basis from all types of mentally unstable people, but I assure you that I am quite sane. I've been looking into the possible existence of intelligent creatures, living among us, that can assume the shape, and appearance, of any human.

I hesitate to use the word 'doppelgänger' to define this creature as it doesn't quite fit the folklore. Common legend has the doppelgänger as more of a duplicate of a person that is a harbinger of bad luck, doom or even death, while this modern equivalent seems to be something much more sinister.

I assure you I did not set out to find a mythological creature. My years of study and research all stem from an incident that happened in 2010 while I was working on my Ph.D. in Bioengineering at UCLA. A close friend was having a Halloween party and I thought it would be fun to bring a bouquet of wolfsbane (minus the roots), as a bit of a joke. My friend placed the flowers in the foyer of her home. Later that evening, a horrific sound from the front of the house halted all conversation. So disturbing was this noise that some people actually ran out of the back of the house. Despite this sound (what I can only describe as a hacking scream), I ran to see what was happening.

A woman (or possibly man) was on the floor of the foyer. The sex was hard to determine as what I thought was a Halloween costume obscured the gender. The person was dressed in tattered, black clothing, that was in stark contrast to, what I believed to be, an elaborate makeup job. It was bald with two large black orbs for eyes. This 'person' had stopped making that horrific sound, but was coughing and gagging. A few of us just stood there. One woman timidly asked it if it was okay. It quickly stood up and ran off into the night. The creature's sound and appearance was so shocking, that I am still haunted by this experience.

The following day I spoke to some friends who were also at the party. We were all disturbed by what we heard and saw, but one friend (who will remain nameless) saw more than the rest of us. According to his account, he was walking to the house behind an attractive woman dressed as a witch. He joked that he was looking forward to talking to her at the party, but when she entered the house she violently dropped to the ground and started making that pained sound. He shamefully admitted that he ran away as fast as he could, before he saw anything.

I knew that what we all saw was no Halloween prank. I was compelled by my scientific curiosity to investigate further… to understand this perplexing incident. I began looking for accounts of creatures that fit the events of that evening. I searched on and off for days having little luck, until I found an account from the early 20th century.

In 1928 a Chicago police officer named Danny Staniec related, in a letter to his cousin, the story of a fellow officer, Mike Connor. One night, Officer Connor returned from a raid of a local speak-easy visibly shaken. When Staniec asked Connor what had happened, he explained that the raid went badly, causing many injuries and one death. Staniec commented that he knew Connor well, and thought that Connor didn't seem disturbed or remorseful, but frightened. Staniec pressed him on the issue, but Connor wouldn't say anything further. It wasn't until a week later, that Connor came to Staniec's home in the middle of the night, terrified.

Connor was afraid he was being followed, by someone or something. He related that on the night of the raid, Connor followed a man trying to sneak out of the building. Alone, Connor pursued the suspect through a tunnel under the club. The suspect drew a pistol, but Connor, having his already drawn, shot the suspect before he could fire. When Connor checked on the fallen suspect, he said it was not human. It was bald with pinkish grey skin, but the creature's most notable feature was its large, completely black eyes. Even stranger still was the fact it was wearing an expensive three-piece suit. Connor left to get help, but on returning found the creature gone. Ever since that night, Connor claimed he felt like he was being watched.

The day after the raid, the police chief called Connor into his office and questioned him about seeing anything odd during the raid. Connor had told no one about what he had seen, for fear of being labeled insane. The fact that the chief was asking pointed questions seemed very unusual to Connor, and suspicious. Not trusting the chief, Connor told him he saw nothing unusual.

At this point in Connor's telling of the story, Staniec thought Connor had lost his mind and called Connor's wife to bring him home. The next day, Connor failed to show up for work. Staniec assumed he took the day off, but that evening got a call from Connor's wife, that he hadn't returned home from work. Connor was found the next morning in the Chicago River. The incident was ruled a suicide and there was no further investigation.

The next doppelgänger account is almost 40 years later from the Soviet Union. A former KGB agent, Pyotr Kozlov, in his book *Strange Russia* (1992), wrote that in 1967 his commanding officer, Lev Vershvovski, had killed an oborot (one who transforms). As

Kozlov relates it, Vershvovski had shot a man he believed to be an American spy in East Berlin. After the man died, his skin turned an 'ashy pink,' his hair receded into his skin and his eyes grew large and black. According to Kozlov, Vershvovski had ordered an extensive examination of the creature, including blood analysis and anatomical photos. Kozlov claims to have even seen the body, personally, on one occasion.

Vershvovski took his findings to his superiors, in the hopes of gaining more support to look into a possible conspiracy. When Vershvovski returned the following day, he called his team (including Kozlov) to a meeting. Kozlov believed that their findings might change the face of the Cold War, but Veshvovski stood solemnly and told everyone that the creature was a hoax. Veshvovski ignored all questions from his staff and threatened anyone who ever spoke of it again. He had the body burned along with all documents and photographs. Kozlov said that Veshvovski behaved strangely for the rest of the day acting withdrawn and cold. After that day, Veshvovski was never seen again.

The third doppelgänger event I discovered was in 1995, involving the assassination attempt made on Georgian President Eduard Shevardnadze. His motorcade was attacked with anti-tank rockets and small firearms in Tbilisi. One of the assailants, captured and questioned, had some strange ideas. According to one of the investigating officers, the man claimed that Shevardnadze was not human, but a creature that could take the form of any person. The attacker insisted that this creature did not work alone but was part of a large conspiracy of creatures who secretly controlled the world. He begged the interrogators to get aconitum (wolfsbane) anywhere near the President and they would see him change into a "dead thing… with large black eyes of shadow." Reports state that this man hung himself in his cell that night, but no medical reports, autopsies, or even a name, of this man exist.

I know most of these stories only provide secondary sources, but the consistency of the description is very concerning and gives me cause to continue investigating. I have never been one for conspiracy theories, but if creatures who can take the form of any person exist, there would be nowhere they couldn't go. No information that they could not gain. For all I know, this letter may never get to you. And even if it does, there is no way to know if you are human. Even with my fears, I must reach out and inform any who will listen, especially those in power.

My questioning seems to have gotten the notice of police, who I assume are at least somewhat compromised. I fear for my own safety and have gone into hiding. I move as often as I can and even use assumed names. I'm not sure how long I can remain hidden.

I realize this letter sounds like the ravings of a madman, but I assure you my sources can be verified. I believe if you spend even a small amount of time considering my letter, you might come to the same conclusions.

At the very least, I recommend keeping a large vase of wolfsbane in your office.

Sincerely,
Dr. Carl Peaslee

The Dragon

Ed Greenwood

"It's frozen *again*," Tarvo snarled.

Chen looked up from his own work, only mildly interested. "So try another browser."

"On my third one already. Hung, just like the others. At the second screen in, this time. No Spinning Beachball of Death, no — no *nothing*!"

"The Dragon is hungry tonight," Walter von Bredemeyer said quietly, not turning his head from the columns of figures scrolling down his own computer screen.

Something in his voice made the younger programmers turn to look at him. They were in time to see him touch the head of a little plastic gold dragon figurine perched atop the far corner of his monitor.

"What?" Tarvo asked irritably, trying to shove the power button right through his computer, and force a hard reboot. He had to hold the damned thing in for so *long*…

Chen craned his head. "Plastic dragon. Off a swizzle stick from Wong's Ho Lee Chow Golden Dragon House, if I'm not mistaken."

"You're not," the old man assured him, doing something to his compiler that made his screen flash, dialog boxes appear all over, in a brief blizzard, and then vanish again just as quickly, and a chime sound that resembled an organ chord.

Chen and Tarvo waited, but von Bredemeyer said no more.

Silence stretched until Tarvo's computer complained loudly at the end of its reboot.

"Walter!" Chen said reproachfully. "Don't leave us hanging! What is this hungry dragon you speak of?"

"And what's with the little gold dragon?" Tarvo joined in. "Joined some crazy cult, have you?"

The old German turned and regarded them both solemnly over his half-moon spectacles. "Not crazy, and not a cult. If you mock the Dragon, don't be surprised if your work is lost, your compiling goes awry, your data corrupts. *I* know. I learned the hard way."

"You're joking," Tarvo said scornfully, as a loud sizzling sound arose from his computer. Its screen flashed blindingly and then went dark. A tiny wisp of smoke curled up out of the CPU.

"He's not joking," Chen concluded, voice getting a little smaller. Then he looked at Tarvo's dying machine.

Walter touched the little dragon figurine again. Gently, almost reverently.

"Laugh," he told them flatly, "and computers will die under your fingers from now on, as that one did."

Tarvo looked very far from laughing, and Chen took off his thick glasses and said almost earnestly, "We're not laughing, Walter. We won't laugh."

Walter leaned forward, and said in a low voice, "I am not a madman. Things went verrückt on me two years ago, and… I learned why. The Dragon spoke to me." He waved a hand. "On that screen."

"And who's the Dragon? Some really good hacker? Or a gang? A tong?"

"Nein, nein, do you not hear me? A *dragon*. Long tail, bat wings, size of a castle, long snout and fangs, breathes fire."

Chen and Tarvo stared at Walter.

He stared right back. "They are not all dead, you see. They are old and wise and much, much smarter than us. So those who are left, they went into hiding. Where smartness is always with them."

"Inside *computers*?"

"On the Internet. They lurk in the clouds of cloud computing, and amid the dataflows of the Web, where it is always warm, and power flows through them endlessly."

"You're… you're not joking."

"I do not joke about such things. The dragons are with us always. They watch and listen. They curl up in our e-mails, and they feed at will, devouring energies and lore whenever apps are used, whenever packet flows are fastest and heaviest. They take especial interest in those who know of them. Me, one Dragon always watches."

Tarvo reared back, shaking his head. "You're *nuts*!"

At that moment Chen's computer spat sudden flames out of its vents, shrieked like a man dying messily between sharp moving edges of metal, and shuddered to a halt.

Walter sadly observed both Chen and Tarvo over his glasses.

"Am I?"

The Eaters

James Ashton

Francis Manjee's sole ambition was to create the greatest Internet horror meme ever. It began as a hobby. Night after night he would return home from his customer service job at the TD Bank, where he tried to convince people to get more credit than they needed, and work away at his meme all night. He lived alone, with his three goldfish, Mia, Zia and Pia, and his cat, Edgar Allan Poe. These four were his only friends. His apartment was on Palmerston Street, in a hulking Victorian that had been subdivided into eight units. He barely spoke to his neighbors.

A huge bowl of Cheetos and a 2 litre bottle of Diet Coke at his side, he would research other memes, trying to figure out what worked, and what didn't. Francis posted the results on creepypasta and other sites devoted to horror memes. He called his monsters *The Eaters*, established a website and invented creepy short stories around them. He photoshopped images of the monsters into existing pictures: the little figures hanging around the periphery of funerals, at the edge of playgrounds. The Eaters looked like very small, shrunken people, with huge heads, bulging eyes and enormous rows of teeth. They traveled in swarms, attaching themselves to living things and sucking the life from them, quickly or slowly. They were demons who hunted through the Internet for their prey.

The tagline Francis created, and which he was particularly proud of, was: *Once they see something they want, they never give up*. He used that in many stories, hoping it would catch on.

But it didn't.

Something was missing.

At work, Francis would occasionally slip a mention of The Eaters into a conversation, but none of his web savvy coworkers had heard of them. He once had an extremely uncomfortable conversation with Sandi, a girl who sat four dividers down from him. He tried to interest her in The Eaters, but she merely feigned politeness, hoping he would go away.

When two teenage girls tried to murder a friend as an offering to the infamous tall, thin man meme, Francis became despondent, almost suicidal. He was consumed with envy. This was exactly the sort of devotion he was trying to generate with The Eaters. He had thought his idea was foolproof: The Eaters would piggyback on the zombie craze. Everyone loved *The Walking Dead*, so what could be more frightening than creatures that hunted humans through the Internet — the very medium that seemed to offer people freedom and anonymity. Why weren't The Eaters going viral?

The answer came, one day, while he was riding the subway home. He had been mulling over the question of The Eaters, as usual, when the solution came to him. What was missing was *involvement*. He needed to generate an event, something with *frisson*. He needed to break the third wall.

He decided to become an actor in his own meme. Like *The Blair Witch Project*.

After a dinner that consisted of a bucket of fried chicken and potato salad from KFC, which Francis consumed alone at his kitchen table, he practically ran to his computer.

He opened a copy of his desktop wallpaper in Photoshop, a misty forest scene. Over several hours Francis added some Eater figures into the background, very far away and very small, peeking out from behind tree trunks. He activated the new wallpaper onto his desktop and opened a small window on his computer to show one of his earlier scenes of Eaters menacing a group of people. Then he merged that image with the wallpaper scene.

Francis wrote a blog entry called *THEY'VE FOUND ME!!!* recounting how he had become casually interested in The Eaters and studied their website over a few weeks, and now, all of a sudden, he had found Eater images on his computer's desktop. He posted the article on reddit.com/r/nosleep and creepypasta and a few other fear sites.

The next night he published another article. This one was called: *THEY'RE GETTING CLOSER!!!!!* He photoshopped more of his wallpaper, adding additional Eaters, who were peeking out from behind tree trunks that were much closer to the front of the screen. He spent a lot of time making the images look both real and frightening. In the article he talked about waking up in the morning and turning on his computer to find that The Eaters had gotten closer during the night. He begged people for help.

Something began happening out there in memeland, some faint stirrings of interest.

The readership of his blog articles started to uptick. Suddenly, there were more hits to The Eaters website. Something was happening. That night he couldn't wait to get home after work. He found a new wallpaper image, this one of a bunch of multi-coloured stones in a riverbed. He produced multiple versions of this new desktop. When he published his next article late that night, he called it *I'VE CHANGED MY DESKTOP!!!! AND THEY'RE STILL COMING!!!! HELP!!!!*

The article described how Francis changed his desktop to get rid of the approaching figures, and how the new desktop seemed fine when he went to sleep. Screen captures were posted as evidence. The entry then explained how he had woken at four in the morning and checked the screen, and found, in the far bottom left, a tiny figure that appeared to be digging its way out of the riverbed. By the time he woke up in the morning the stones were crawling with Eaters figures, all staring at him. They encircled the edge of his computer screen, as though clawing at the glass to get through.

After he posted the help article, the floodgates opened. His hits exploded into the hundreds of thousands, and the meme went viral, showing up on other unrelated sites. People were forwarding the story. The next day he heard The Eaters being discussed at work. A small group of coworkers, Sandi among them, was discussing the phenomenon. They usually had nothing to do with Francis, who spent his breaks surfing the web alone. Sandi called him over to ask his opinion, since she remembered him mentioning The Eaters. He expressed no knowledge and let them explain how the story was evolving. Inside, he was euphoric. *Sandi had remembered something he had said!*

On the subway ride home that night he felt a sudden wave of panic. What if it was just a fluke? How could he keep it going?

He had to escalate. He had to increase the jeopardy.

At home he fished Mia, Zia and Pia out of their tank and put them in a jar of water on the kitchen counter. Then he took photos of the empty tank. He called this article *THEY'RE IN MY APARTMENT!!!!! MY FISH ARE GONE!!!!!!* Francis detailed coming home to find his fish tank empty. He posted pictures he had taken of his fish with earlier time stamps, and shots of the empty tank.

And he described hearing furtive rustling sounds coming from a closet.

In the morning he checked the metrics. The Eaters site had had *two million* visitors overnight!!!

As he got ready for work, humming to himself, he noticed that the bowl of water on the counter was empty. Stupidly, he had not returned the fish to their tank. Edgar Allan Poe must have gotten them. Where was he anyway? He wanted to scold the cat, but he could not find him anywhere.

That day, at work, was the sweetest day of his life.

Everyone was talking about The Eaters. The subway ride home was like Ulysses returning home from the sacking of Troy. His audience was insatiable. They would need more, more, more.

The cat eating the fish gave him an idea. He took photos of Edgar Allen Poe's favourite spots in the apartment, the litter box, the climbing tower, the window — all cat free. Edgar Allan Poe had gone to ground somewhere, which was odd but not unprecedented. A year ago, when Francis had accidentally stepped on his tail, Poe had gone into hiding for three days. This article Francis titled: *MY CAT IS MISSING NOW!!!!!*

Two hours after posting the article, it reached full meme status, popping up everywhere. The Eaters were now a true Internet phenomenon, one that would live on after him. He spent nine hours in front of the computer, eating a huge bowl of Honey Nut Cheerios, and chasing it down with many litres of Diet Coke. He read every article, followed every reference. When he went to sleep, at four in the morning, amid whispers and rustlings, he felt he had finally gotten his fill.

♦

Three weeks later, after a rent cheque bounced, the Francis's landlord finally came to check on his reclusive tenant. When the man opened the apartment he was hit with a heavy rotting smell. The rot seemed to be coming from the bedroom, where a large shape lay concealed completely beneath a mound of blankets. Morbidly curious, the man pulled back the sheets, to stare at Francis Manjee's bloated, rotting face, upon which was pasted a satisfied smile.

Several days passed before it was discovered that all the other units in the apartment building were empty. The occupants were missing.

Echidna
(Typhon & Echidna: A Love Story)

Sandra Kasturi

1 *Out of Tartarus*

You are taller than the sky.
Your hands are dragons, your face a typhoon.
It's no wonder I love you.

We are both sprung from the abyss,
spawned from the earth, scaly and wondrous.
Our delight comes not from love
but from recognition.

You, my second self, my sinuous
beautiful monster.

We would eat each other if we could.
And we do.

2 The Mother of Monsters

I am daughter of the pit
and wife to the maw.

And now motherhood beckons
like some winged fury
beating at my future.

One, two, ten, a thousand?
Who can keep track
after so many children:
dogs, snakes, eagles, cows
in any jigsaw combination
imagined and unimaginable.

All of them biting
and furious, sent forth
to be some hero's trial
before I can even finish
suckling the little horrors.

3 Under the Mountain

They tell me you've been conquered.
Lightning-struck and thrown
under Etna, where your rages
spew lava to the heavens.

Love comes quickly
to the monstrous,
to the ugly.

We want to grasp it, hold
it tight in our mutant hands
or it'll leap right into the jaws
of bright-shielded heroes.

Love goes quickly, too –
running sped-up through
some trickster god's hourglass.

4 Mythology and Its End

And I am alone again.

Half woman, half snake,
all-devouring –
who would have me but you,
my sweet carnage, my viper?

Now we are nothing but story,
tales told to squalling brats,
fresh-limbed and full
of the promise of death.

Your rages are quieting.
Our children are long-slaughtered,
their deeds hung in the stars –
an infinite array of bright lies.

I wait in the pit for that final
silence, the one foretold
by the sibyl hung up in her bottle.

There — a new weighty footstep
on the threshold. I can hear
the blinking of his hundred eyelids.

Look, you, godservant of Olympus:
I shall be as if asleep, vulnerable.
Unmake me; make the myth.
And it is done.

Erotic Goblins & Hybrids

(Sex and the Anthropomorphised Being: A Personal Take)

Peter Birch (Aishling Morgan)

The idea of beings with both human and animal characteristics goes back a long way, perhaps to the dawn of human consciousness. Pick an ancient culture and there it is, from the Stone Age cave paintings, through the gods of the Egyptians to the mythical monsters of the Greeks. Imagination and the blending of human and animal characteristics go hand in hand. Sex of course is even older, a prime ingredient in the drive for evolution. That the two have often become intertwined I see as inevitable, and this has exercised my imagination for years, leading me to ponder on the erotic possibilities of everything from the sensuality of winged Babylonian demonesses to the grotesque virility of the minotaur.

Fortunately I'm not the only one, and with the decline of repressive monotheism and the freedom of expression provided by the Internet, these concepts have taken wing as never before. It would be impossible to enumerate the creatures blended of human and animal characteristics that have been created over the last couple of decades, but a substantial proportion of them have an erotic dimension. Some don't, and I have no issue with those who prefer an asexual approach, but that falls outside this article's scope. My own creations are strongly sexual, which is hardly a surprise when I make my living by writing erotica. I think I've come up with some quite good ones too, and while I claim no greater imagination, I come to the subject from an unusual angle.

I trained as a scientist, taking two degrees in Zoology, which is why I'm not content to let such creatures exist in my imagination without asking the question: how did they come to be? A being must have an origin, and while I accept the existence of one-off creations spawned from the vats of a crazed scientist or some malignant magician, that usually means conventional sexual reproduction, and preferably within the bounds of the animal kingdom as we know it. Thus, if you have a jabberwock (as depicted by Tenniel and clearly reptilian — although the six limbs offend my sense of physiological probability) then somewhere you have a jabberwock nest, complete with eggs, unless the jabberwock is viviparous, and there must be young. Likewise, if you have furry tiger girls, goblins, lust-crazed teddy bears, as I do, then there must be a way more furry tiger girls, goblins and lust-crazed teddy bears are produced.

This may seem to be a bizarre blending of logic and the absurd, but the science of nonsense has long had a place in human culture, perhaps more in England than elsewhere. Look at Heath Robinson with his crazy but apparently functional contraptions, or Norman Hunter's Professor Branestawm. Add to this my other great love, erotica, and you have the basis for much of what I have written, which now stretches to over one hundred paperbacks and numerous hardbacks, magazine articles and ebooks, made up of some 10,000,000 words, and that doesn't include what I've written purely for fun.

My creations have kept me going quite comfortably for twenty years now, no doubt to the utter disgust of any serious but failed authors who've come across my work, and hopefully to the sniffy disapproval of any serious and successful ones. I make no excuses. I like rude and ridiculous situations. I like exploring the dark and often absurd underbelly of humanity. I like smut. Fortunately for me, so do other people, or at least enough to keep me in roast beef, Yorkshire pudding and the occasional bottle of decent claret.

I have been lucky, though. My writing career has benefitted from several strokes of good fortune, such as a certain big name of her era throwing a tantrum at a magazine editor. She got sacked and I was rushed in to take her place, allowing me to ride the mainstream publication gravy train long enough to put the money aside to support myself. More useful still was the appointment of James Marriott as editor at Nexus Books. James was unusual in that he was more concerned with publishing worthwhile stories than with his bosses' profits. Rather than steering me towards what the market wanted, or was supposed to want, he encouraged me to fully indulge my imagination. He was also intrigued by anthropomorphism, and particularly by furries, which led to the novels *Tiger, Tiger* and *Pleasure Toy*, in which the half-human products of genetic manipulation vie for supremacy in the far post-apocalyptic city of Susa.

The plots centre on political machination and sexual manipulation, but it's the nature of the factions involved that make the novels distinctive. The population of Susa is divided between three distinct forms: true humans, tigranthropes and suanthropes, these last two being part of the historic culture of human/mammal hybrids that has blossomed into fantastic complexity through the medium of the Internet. The books' main female protagonist, the Tigranthrope Tian-Sha, is a classic example of sexualised anthropomorphism. She is tall, powerful, elegant and beautiful, with her sleek, red and black furred body a temptation to all, a creature who made erotic scenes just slip from fingers to keyboard to screen. Oh, and she has six breasts, in two parallel rows running down her front, which is a characteristic typical of her genetic background.

If Tian-Sha expresses classic sexual themes, then the Suanthropes cater to another favourite human obsession, the love of the grotesque. The females are rather cute; plump, curvaceous creatures with well-rounded bottoms and a full twelve breasts (again accurate to their genetic origins), but the males are huge, tusk-faced, bristle-haired, rutting creatures of notably dirty habit, designed to horrify as much as to intrigue, depending on personal taste. Otomos, the dominant Suanthrope, I still regard as one of my finest expressions of erotic grotesquerie.

Looking back over *Tiger, Tiger* and *Pleasure Toy*, the sex is exotic, and that's one of the joys of anthropomorphic creatures. Variety in body shape makes for extra pleasure, be it the feel of fur on a lover's skin, the thrill of having a tail or half-a-dozen breasts to play with, or the sensations related to a corkscrew penis, piggy style. The potential for variety is enormous too, as a quick Internet search will demonstrate, but it's not for the unimaginative, and often not for the faint of heart.

My own feelings are that writing in general and erotica in particular shouldn't be for the faint of heart anyway. I despair of the current trend for bonking billionaires and politically correct heroes and heroines and far prefer to people my worlds with the outlandish and perverse, the obsessive and downright dangerous. After all, it's fiction, and while my characters might haunt the fantasies and dreams of my readers, Otomos will not actually come to get you in the night.

Nor will the goblins of the Maiden Saga, a four book series I started as a pastiche for the amusement of friends and which has gone on to become one of the pillars of my career. I'd always wanted to play with the conventions of adventure fantasy, and so created a world in order to explore the comic and erotic possibilities of old favourites such as goblins and trolls, Nordic warriors and sultry slave-girls, sadistic tyrants and wicked witches. It was never intended to be serious, and while I've occasionally felt obliged to swing my chair around and bang my head on the wall in response to reviewers who don't realise it's all parody, it has sold remarkably well. My proudest moment came when an online bookstore filed the Maiden Saga books under both erotica and horror, perhaps due to the goblins.

My goblins are squat, green-skinned creatures that live in holes in the ground and seek to lure human females below the earth by means of an overpowering pheromonal musk. Not surprisingly this makes them less than popular with the local human population, and allows for a whole spectrum of erotic possibilities. The goblins are exclusively male and can only reproduce by impregnating human females, a device at once awful and grotesque but also scientifically pleasing, at least within the deliberately absurd internal logic of the Maiden Saga world.

So, we have two styles of erotic monster, one the product of science, the second of nature. The third technique I've employed is to make the creature virtual, and in the case of the implausibly over-endowed teddy bears from *Slave to the Machine*, a product of the heroine's own imagination. I was rather pleased with this plot device, whereby everything exists within a virtual world created by the imagination of the cryogenically suspended pop princess Melody J. Whatever happens, it is born of her own imagination and so inherently consensual, which allowed her encounters with Teddy, her frequent spankings, the description of her being hunted through the woods by crazed rednecks and the incident with the four anthropomorphised cartoon bears to be written in the full, uninhibited detail they deserved.

There were others along the way: werewolves and vampires (almost inevitably), satyrs and succubae, creatures half-woman, half-seal, even an octopus god, but while you may think me perverse, even certifiable, and you're probably right, there is nothing I have created that does not draw from the great, dark well of the human psyche. These creatures are there, lurking in the corners of our minds, ready to terrify or to delight, perhaps even both at the same time. I recommend my creations to you in the sure knowledge that in the quiet of the night, when you let them out to roam, their behaviour will ultimately be dictated by your own, deeply human, imagination.

But why? I am no psychologist, but I know enough about the subject to be aware of its limitations, and the short answer is that we do not know. I also feel that it's only fair to point out that these are minority tastes. For every woman, or man for that matter, who likes to fantasise about being gang-banged by goblins or tortured by teddy bears, there are many more who don't. Many of my less ebullient reviews contain variations on the sentence "It was all right until…" followed by mention of some especially perverse incident. Often that incident involves anthropomorphism. So what I write isn't for everybody, but agree or disagree, I hope you will find some interest in my musings and perhaps an echo of your personal feelings.

Let's start then, with the beauty of fur, which is in itself a curiosity. Beauty is a purely human concept, meaningless beyond the confines of our psyche, and yet at least reasonably consistent between individuals. We find beauty in water, as water is essential to life, but we can also find beauty in a desert, which is not so easily explained. Nor is the beauty we find in fur, something we've largely lost and which is generally associated with animals that in the natural environment would be competitors, predators or prey. Nevertheless, most people consider fur beautiful, and as beauty often equates with sexual arousal, it is no great leap to imagine one's partner covered in fur. On the other hand, we don't usually consider our close, furry relatives to be especially beautiful — presumably an evolutionary response to prevent wasted attempts at crossbreeding. What we do consider beautiful are sleek, elegant predators, which represents yet another bizarre twist in the human psyche, as they like to eat us, and cute, vulnerable baby animals. Put all that together and the desire to dress up as a tiger with abnormally large, bay-blue eyes starts to make sense, as does the fantasy of becoming that creature in a perfected, highly eroticised form.

The flip side of the same coin is many people find a combination of the erotic and the grotesque arousing, especially as an element of masculine sexuality. Huge, powerful, gnarled beings stalk through the dark places of human sexual fantasy, and at the risk of sounding unfashionably Freudian, I suspect this derives from the mingled fear and desire aroused by engorged male genitalia. After all, few people would regard a towering, heavily veined penis and a great, fat set of balls as a pretty sight, and yet there is no doubt a deep fascination. This is not just a straight male reaction either; witness the frequent protests of women when presented with pictures of erect cocks online. So, given that there's something inherently grotesque in the sight of male genitalia, but also arousing, it's easy to extend that to the entire body. Thus an over-endowed goblin, a great, shambling troll or even some monstrosity composed largely of penis tipped tentacles can become an object of desire or a component of an erotic fantasy, even if you don't fancy being the one on the receiving end.

Next there's fetishism, which can relate to the above but also casts its own, separate influence. A sexual fetish is when an ordinarily asexual thing becomes charged with erotic significance, and can vary from a mild preference to an all-consuming need. In the case of anthropomorphic erotica the most obvious example is fur, but fetishes can spawn many such fantasies: blood for vampires, scales for mermaids, hooves for satyrs. Having got the fetish, it's perfectly normal to want a partner, real or fantasy, who best expresses that fetish, which often means taking on animal characteristics.

Related to this are power play, dominance and submission. Erotic fantasy often involves wanting to be stronger or weaker than in reality and thus able to dominate a situation or be powerless to resist. This is evident simply in the terms we apply to particular erotic types; a bull for an exceptionally virile male, a pansy for an exceptionally fragile, yielding one, a cougar for a predatory, older female, a bunny girl when the emphasis is on sexualisation and vulnerability. Give the bull horns or the bunny girl a fluffy white tail, and you have taken the first step to erotic anthropomorphism.

Another influence comes from the bonds we form with domesticated animals, particularly those whose characteristics we admire. Back in the nineties, when my wife and I were most active on the London fetish scene, I ran a club that specialised in anthropomorphic eroticism, especially pony-girl play. We had a good many members over the years, split evenly between male and female, but the mainstay of our club and what we did together deep in the Hertfordshire woods always related to women who loved and wanted to take on the roles they so admired. We also had plenty of puppy-girls and pussycat-girls, plus wilder variants such as zebra-girls, along with their male counterparts. Please note that to the best of my knowledge none of these people had any inclination towards real bestiality, also this was purely consensual fun, without money changing hands. The idea that exotic sexual practises happen only when perverted men pay reluctant or even desperate women is, I hope, well and truly debunked.

We shouldn't neglect the purely physical either. Just what could an octopus with human desires do with all those tentacles; or a snake do with its powerful, tubular body and long, forked tongue? How sensuous could a woman be if she were born of fire, or water or air? How would it feel to be humped by a ten foot man-ape or spanked by some strange tree being with paddles for hands? After all, there's only so much that a human body can do, but if you borrow characteristics from animals, let alone from your imagination, the possibilities are endless.

Lastly, we return to the products of human imagination and superstition — gods and demons displaying animal qualities but moved by the erotic appetites of men and women. All you need to get started is a combination of desire and plenty of imagination to populate the darkness with lustful and even dangerous creatures. The only real surprise is that not everybody goes in for it, although it might simply be that people prefer not to admit to what goes on in their hearts in the quiet, dark hours when there's nobody around to disapprove.

La Fée Verte

(Faierium thujonia)

Molly Tanzer

While references date back to the *Papyrus Insinger* of the ancient Egyptians and Aristotle's *Inquiries on Animals*, the modern *Faierium thujonia*, more commonly known as "la fée verte" or "green fairy" was discovered and named in Couvet, Switzerland, in 1792. According to the diary of Dr. Pierre Ordinaire, an eccentric French botanist, Dr. Ordinaire first encountered the unusual member of the genus *Faierium* while taking samples of the perennial *Artemisia absinthium*. Instantly entranced by the beauty of the delicate creature and its "bewitching" flying habits (Ordinaire 189), he captured several specimens with the intent to study them.

One of these captured fées was a fertilized, egg-laying female, and Ordinaire soon found himself caring for a host of the creatures. The wild species adapted to life in captivity with uncanny ease, and soon his small villa in the hills of the canton of Neuchâtel was, in a word, infested with them. A telling excerpt from Dr. Ordinaire's diary demonstrates his mixed feelings about this opportunity to observe the fées verte in close proximity:

Their flying patterns are seductive — sensual beyond any Parisian cabaret act or the gyrations of an Oriental harem-dweller taught since childhood to dance with the seven veils. I am frankly ashamed by how many afternoons I have lost sitting in my parlor watching them twisting and turning through the air, listening to the soft buzzing of their wings, bewitched by the undulations of their unclothed bodies. More than once I have wished myself one of their number, in order to cavort with the females, who are to my mind more perfect in figure than any human woman. The males seem of a similar mind, for they breed frequently and enthusiastically, and at all hours of the day or night.

Five days after fertilization the females lay a clutch of small eggs in nests made of scraps of cloth, shed hair, and slender branches. They have a maddening habit of nesting in the most improbable locations; I have uncovered fairy-nests atop bookshelves, under tables in the joints, in the specimen-boxes I use for displaying dried plants, underneath banisters and eaves, and among my personal effects in my closet. The cottage is become one large swarm of them, but while their presence plagues and distracts me, I cannot bring myself to destroy or cast out even a single one. But I shall have to find a way of arresting their reproduction if I am to persist in my studies. (Ordinaire, 235)

Unfortunately for Dr. Ordinaire he did no such thing, resulting in his demise. Not long after writing the above entry, his desiccated body was discovered by friends of his, the Henriod sisters. Concerned after he missed an engagement, they came to call and reported finding his dwelling "thick" with the creatures, "adorning every surface as if it were an emerald-mine rather than a villa" (Cherin 67). Too enthralled by his discovery to drink or eat, he had died amongst his subjects.

The beguiling influence of the odd creatures was not lost on the sisters, but, cautioned by Ordinaire's extraordinary demise, they sought to control and make use of it. Neither having married, the sisters had for some time been contemplating finding a trade to supplement their incomes, and seized this opportunity to do so. Couvet, situated on the banks of the Areuse, was at that time a popular tourist destination. The sisters therefore released most of Ordinaire's brood back into the wild, but retained the choicest specimens. Separating the males from the females and housing them in wicker cages, the sisters opened a shop where those passing through could buy an "authentic green fairy of Couvet" as a keepsake. The shop was a fantastic success (Cherin 115), though the Henriod sisters never guessed that their little moneymaking endeavor would have long-standing and international repercussions.

In 1797, a French major by the name of Dubied happened to be traveling through Couvet. Captivated by the Henriod sisters' fées verte and hoping to duplicate the shop's success, he purchased and exported ten females and five males. Along with his son-in-law Henry-Louis Pernod, Dubied spent several years selectively breeding the fairies in Pontarlier, France. Their aim was to cross the most elegant and beautiful of specimens with those who demonstrated less "licentiousness" (Cherin 308) in order to reduce their astonishing propensity to breed.

Once Dubied and Pernod were satisfied with the results of their efforts, they repaired to Paris and opened a shop similar to that of the Henriod sisters. It proved so wildly popular with locals and tourists that several imitators quickly sprang up, though not all were as concerned about monitoring the fairies' reproduction. Before long, fairy-shops could be found in cities in Spain, Great Britain, the United States, and the Kingdom of Bohemia, inevitably resulting in escaped fairies breeding in the wild in those countries.

Interestingly, the international phenomenon was fueled in part by artists, who for some reason were particularly taken with *Faierium thujonia*. Writers such as Charles Baudelaire and painters like Henri de Toulouse-Lautrec often referenced green fairies in their works; Ernest Hemingway became obsessed with fées verte, as well, and conducted his own breeding experiments with them, producing a distinctive breed known for possessing six or sometimes seven toes on their dainty little feet.

Eventually, however, the near-worldwide love of green fairies resulted in near-worldwide crackdowns on their breeding and sale. Those who did not heed the advice of fairy-sellers when it came to containment often released unwanted fées, resulting in the species being classified as an invasive one by most European nations by 1915. Possession or sale of green fairies was subsequently banned after reports of swarms causing the death of hikers in Germany and Spain gained international attention. New Orleans was especially plagued by fées imported from Europe; *Faierium thujonia* was found to be uniquely adapted to life in the swamps of Louisiana, becoming a major public nuisance around the turn of the century.

One fairy, kept in a cage, might bewitch an observer for a pleasant hour; a "mesmer" of fairies, as groups came to be known, can captivate a grown man in a matter of moments, causing disorientation and eventually complete disconnection with the necessaries of life. Tourists and locals alike were found dead of exposure after encountering flocks of wild green fairies outside of New Orleans, the result being not only a local but a federal ban on sale or breeding of green fairies in the United States.

In spite of the dangers, *Faierium thujonia* enthusiasts were not to be stopped. Private breeding and sale continued unchecked, even after the bans. For years, fées verte could be obtained via the black market, resulting in several sensational crackdowns and arrests that made international news (Wainwright 476).

In spite of green fairy breeding causing so many problems in New Orleans in particular, it was a Louisiana breeder who hit upon the solution to arresting their unchecked reproduction in the mid-1990s. After years of selective breeding of *Faierium thujonia* for personal pleasure and private sale, Lovell Edwards, a former biologist and green fairy enthusiast, noted that certain pairs of green fairies failed to reproduce even after extended (but sexually successful) exposure to one another. Curious, he began a series of experiments, resulting in the discovery that *Faierium thujonia* is unique in that the species possesses two sets of males — "sperm-producing" and "powder-producing." Females must breed with both types, first mingling their wing-powder with that of powder-producing males, a process which induces estrus, before mating with the sperm-producing type. As both types of males are visually indistinguishable and enjoy frequent and enthusiastic vaginal intercourse with females, this difference had never before been noticed. By identifying the microscopic external gland at the wing-base responsible for producing the estrus-inducing powder, Edwards inadvertently devised an effective method of population control among domestic green fairies.

Following the adoption of the modern classification system and the introduction of modified law, longstanding barriers to the breeding and sale of *Faierium thujonia* have disappeared. As of the publication of this bestiary, green fairies are being successfully, responsibly bred and kept as pets in over a dozen countries.

Sources:

1 Cherin, Samantha. (2011). *A delicate madness: The strange history of breeding the world's most hypnotic species*. London: Bloomsbury.

2 Ordinaire, Pierre. (1975). *The diary of Dr. Ordinaire*. W. M. Pagan (Ed.). New York: Anchor.

3 Tryon, J. (1998). Five Stories of Fairy Trafficking in Europe. *The Legal Review*, 94 (2), 45–99.

Furies
(Three of a Kind)

Monica Valentinelli

aWduaXRl
(Base 64)
"Ignite"

"...shots fired at yet another elementary school in Virginia just days after..."

"...though he's a veteran political commentator, his surprising set of remarks have forced women's organizations to withdraw funding from..."

"...when asked how should we get young people to care about major issues, she answered: Do what I did. Cast a little-known actress into the role of an iconic super heroine..."

I am one of three furies, sisters of spirit and flesh. When you first meet me, you won't recognize me when you do, for I will be invisible. Yet, I am everywhere. Nowhere.

I am online on a website, in the comments, on forums, and in chat rooms. I am lurking on your phone when you talk to your friends. I am spying on you when you send your lover naked pics, bitch about your mom, or tell your whiny best friend to chill. Can you see me now? My form becomes more solid each time you get angry; each time you get pissed off, each time you vent about something someone else said online.

The stronger I get, the more I surround you to fuck your shit up, toy with your emotions, get you so pissed off you accidentally say the wrong thing to a total stranger.

I don't care about gun rights or abortion or gay marriage or boo-fucking-hoo how you don't feel included in a book or a game or a movie. It's not my job to be passionate about corporations being ethical, educational reform, or climate change. It's not my responsibility to *be* responsible. I am not the rosy picture of youth, nor am I a portrait of your grandfather who fought for your country.

We furies are older than the invention of the printing press. References to me and my sisters — demons, succubi, trolls, gods, narcissists, vampires, goddesses, sociopaths and psychopaths — can be found in every culture, around the world. Our forms are ten million times ten thousand fold, and I'm just one of many. I am a drunk orisha named Ogoun who carries a machete, lords over politics, and is worshipped by artists. I am a long-dead patron of war — the flayed one — named Xipe Totec. I am as alive and well as the Morrigan in reconstructionist beliefs, inciting soldiers to battle on a field of words, with no outcome other than to destroy through the spread of rage. I am a demon according to one person. I'm a *YouTube* commenter to another.

"*...no such thing as geek culture...*"

"*...Beebs 4vr...*"

"*...wtf? Fatty's such a cocksucker...*"

I am fucking famous, but I don't care about fame or notoriety or becoming an Internet celebrity. What I do care about? Your anger. It makes me strong, feeds my insatiable hunger, ensures my body remains solid. Powerful. Validated. I reach through the screen, and suck the happiness from your fingertips, goading you on.

When was the last time you had a *good* day? You don't remember what that's like, do you? Let me guess. Self-loathing has started to set in, and now you're mad about being mad at yourself, too.

Anger follows impotence, helplessness. It's what you feel after you read about how a corporate fat cat embezzled thousands of dollars, paid no taxes, and spent no time in prison. Your rage begins with a hot spark sizzling after you hear that a seventy-five-year-old man raped a twelve-year-old girl — someone's daughter, sister, cousin, granddaughter — and she "asked for it" because she dared to wear a short skirt in front of him. She should've known better, after all. That director you admire said some pretty shitty things, too, about how you're not really a geek. You're a pathetic admirer of shit someone else said… did… created… had the balls to make — and you just pay for the privilege of being close to what someone else has done.

Your opinion doesn't matter.

"It feels like nobody's listening to me."

"Why wouldn't they ask a real expert like me? What the hell does a priest know about science?"

"Another day, another fake celebrity obituary. You'd think my mom would use Snopes.com for once."

Are you pissed off now? Have you burst into flames?

Thank you.

I am starving, and because of your angst? I can see my fingers, wrap my arms around you, heat you up — I am whole and staring right at you and you're too preoccupied to notice.

Let's make this a three course meal.
Did I forget to mention that I am not alone?
Aren't you glad? I bet you are.
Now *burn*.

6275726e
(Hexadecimal)
"Burn"

We are valkyries, succubi, poltergeists, imps, harpies, serpents and sinners who live on in bytes and pixels, feeding off your melting-cheese-on-the-asphalt rage, your hours wasted worrying about stupid bullshit, and your regret for diving into yet another flame war.

You've already met my sister, Ignite.

Thanks to the demon on your shoulder, the fires of your personal hell have been raging on in your mind.

I attack after Ignite, hit you hard every time you lash out and type a pissy comment, forcing you to stick around and wait for a response.

I can smell your fury burning through forum after blog after website. Burn, baby, burn.

This is what gets you p0wn3d, destroys friendships, pisses off family members and anybody else who reads the shit you post on the Internet.

Someone said something stupid on the Internet, so you posted that the commenter is too fucking dumb to live and should kill themselves now.

Someone said something stupid on the Internet and didn't bother apologizing, so you feel it's your duty to blog, raise the alarm, get everybody riled up to force that person to make amends.

Someone said something stupid on the Internet and believes what they said is true — so you decide to educate them and wind up getting into a flame war. How dare they ignore you? Marginalize you? Make you feel invisible?

Someone said something stupid on the Internet about you, that you said something stupid when you didn't, so you go on the attack — bitch, dick, cunt, ass.

Without even knowing it, you prove there's no such thing as justice, because you're conducting a trial-by-Internet, baby, and you've decided that a perfect stranger, that I-met-you-once-in-a-bar patron, that barely friends-of-friends' friend is guilty, guilty, *guilty*.

You don't second guess yourself. Your self-righteousness is warranted, for there's always more shit posted on the Internet to hate, another cause to champion, someone else to shit on. It's awareness, right?

'Course, it's not all bad. You post the occasional cat picture and watch pr0n.

What? Some bastard a thousand miles away dared to shoot a defenseless [Insert race here.] because the victim, a [Insert age and gender here.] dared to believe in [Insert deity of choice here.] which violated the [Insert appropriate U.S. Constitutional amendment here.]? Forget about verifying your sources, you'd better sound the alarm. Never mind getting proof. Can't be a hoax, can it?

Motherfucker, you can't let anyone else get away with this bullshit online, even if it is 2 a.m. No one else is as good and just and heroic as you.

Somebody somewhere is still awake — maybe even in [Insert that country you hate.], those [Insert a slur for people you've never met]. Fuck them. It's all *their* fault.

Fuck working, too. Write that twelve-thousand-word rant, and then scatter it across the following websites:

Facebook
Instagram
Twitter
Reddit
Tumblr
Google+
Blogger

WordPress
Flickr
Goodreads
LiveJournal

Oh, you're such a lame ass windbag, but your wasted breath reeks like greasy French fries.

You're my junk food, my bottom-of-the-barrel fast food paste that the rats won't even eat. Keep this up, and I'll lose my girlish figure.

Wait! Don't stop commenting yet.

I've got all the time in the world — to feed.

Want me to try a compliment? You're a shining example of humanity wrapped up in a frothy, mouth-breathing, rotten meat sack.

Tired talking about how Hollywood is pissing on your childhood? The wars in the Middle East? That next presidential election? Feminazis? Climate change? How China is taking over the world?

Try another topic, and let's see how long you'll dig in, make your point, piss people off with your stunning display of 133tsp3@k and rational thinking because you know *everything*.

Vaccines cause autism.

The new edition is a vast improvement over the original.

The Holocaust never happened.

Yes, by all means: *remake*.

No boobs.

Boobs.

Moobs.

Moobies.

Libtards.

Repugnicans.

Tea Party loons.

Go ahead, I *dare* you to make another comment, call another name, post when you're pissed, and make everybody else mad, too.

You are not the only one who's keeping me and my sisters alive.

011000010111001101101000
(Binary)
"Ash"

Regret.

(I feed off of your guilt.)

When you were with my sister, Burn, your eyes were bloodshot, flames were shooting out of your nostrils, and your fingers flew across your keyboard. You posted hundreds of comments that'll get lost in a matter of hours…

(And still completely searchable to anyone who cares.)

… which is the equivalent of *thousands* of Calories.

(How many pissy comments did you make before you turned off your computer?)

You won't delete what you said, because you've earned the right to say something. To be heard. To be acknowledged as a fucking human being. To be a voice — a unique individual — in a sea of millions. Over 7 *billion*.

(You're a stubborn one all right. So much remorse… yet you're *still* online for hours and hours and hours. Sucker.)

Holy shit! Don't get pissy with me for telling you the truth. I'm surprised you haven't shot anybody — not *yet*, anyway. Stop dealing with your problems face-to-face. This is the only way to get anything done, to assert how right *you* are. Isn't it so much fucking easier?

(Deep down you know that's not true. Guess you let yourself down, but you're not gonna cry about it. Internet rage does affect you in real life after all, and you'll never admit that little fact.)

You kicked your cat, yelled at your roommate, told a grieving widow to "get over it," and your dog is cowering in the corner. You've wasted days sitting in front of your computer, proving your point to people who don't give a damn about you.

(Why'd you do that? Don't you feel the least bit guilty about the time you wasted?)

You had to show that one Internet troll how smart you were. Now everybody just thinks you're an asshole, and they're avoiding you live and in the flesh, too.

(Pyrrhic victory. Bravo!)

This is all your fault, you know. This latest dust up, kerfuffle, flame war, and the exposure of every skeleton in every motherfucking stranger's closet was your idea. You should feel like shit, because there is another person on the other side of your monitor — but you've convinced yourself that handle can't possibly represent a real person. They post you hurt their feelings; you haven't even begun to bully them.

(Have no friends? Maybe that's because you're too busy being a royal asshat nobody wants to spend time with you.)

Please, stop trying to rationalize this bullshit. You got angry because you're beginning to realize you've been duped by us furies, by your invisible cheerleading squad egging you on to be mean, to waste your time, to post every bit of you that's wrong and bad and awful on a worldwide network for all to see. You — of all people — never thought you'd be suckered into our trap. You believed you were too intelligent, too *justified* to fall for our ruse, and you were wrong.

(I'm just here to feed off the aftermath. Gods, I just want to sink my teeth into your gut and suck you dry. Instead, I'll sit here and soak in your guilt when you read the responses to your douchebaggery.)

No, you can't kill me, because you won't ever *see* me.

(You'll never see my sisters, either.)

Oh, we're not invisible because we want to be.

(We're transparent because we have to be.)

You wouldn't believe that we existed otherwise.

(Vampires and trolls and fairies and harpies and demons and gods and shape shifters and ghosts can't be real — can they?)

The truth is right in your fucking face — we are a virus, a plague, a disease that exists on a microscopic level and can spread anywhere and infect anyone. We *want* you to feel like shit as much as possible — and you've become addicted to that feeling, because you think you can control it even when you can't. The only cure is to use that goddamn power button, and you know you can't/won't/shouldn't.

(It's better this way. Think of it like gambling. You put a comment in the Internet slot, out pops your angst — and 100 Calories for me. Play those slots!)

Sure, you might occasionally reach someone who agrees with you when you rant.

(Odds are 1 in 10.)

Oh, I'm sorry… are you an Internet celebrity? Then of *course*, everyone will agree with you.

(Too bad there isn't a sarcasm filter.)

Go right on feeling sorry for yourself, you little prick.

(It's not your fault. How could it be? It's always someone else's responsibility. It's obviously someone *else's* job to be the better human being.)

You should feel like shit about the time you've wasted posting nasty comments to total strangers. I hear you might get fired for being a dick to your boss, too.

(Moi? I feel spectacular. I am reborn from the ashes of your all-too-human emotions that you are so eager to feel. Flip flop. I'm on top. Screw peace.)

I smolder into spirit form, won't stop feeding until I am sated, and travel through the pipes looking for my next meal.

(I am *never* satisfied.)

Now, let's do this all over again. My sisters and I will be more subtle next time.

(If you believe that, then I'm the Queen of Sealand.)

Together, the three of us will work harder to make sure you have a pleasant experience online, free from people telling you what they really think.

(That's the nicest goddamn lie I'll tell you today.)

Cross my fingers.

(Cross your fingers.)

Can't fool you…

(… but we will.)

And it will be *delicious*.

(So tasty!)

Asshole.

Gargoyles

(Or, Grotesques: Being Pages from the Newly Discovered Notebooks of V.M., PhD)

Peter Dubé

Hybrid, impure, monstrous: three words that say one cannot determine the nature of a thing with any certainty, but these are the words that arise unbidden when my mind turns to the problem of gargoyles. This happens more than one might think; my professional life is dominated by the study of art and architecture, a field in which the creatures become a matter of debate from time to time, and in which — another instance of uncertainty — even their nomenclature is unfixed: they are called gargoyles, or grotesques, or chimeras. Or, what again? Among my colleagues there are many who insist their existence is entirely artificial; they are merely a functional ornament for buildings — and excessive even as that. This lack of clarity brings me back to the indeterminacy with which I began, because it is the questions implicit in my troublingly ambiguous words that are most tied to the monsters in my memory. Well, those words and the face of a young monk, *Brother Severino*, to whom I never got to speak; he died before the doors of his abbey church not quite a hundred years before I visited it. His twisted features were preserved for posterity in a series of yellowing images depicting him sprawled across the steps. His eyes and his mouth frozen open: pale, tense and empty. His tongue was missing and his eyes fixed on a curious new shape that clung to the abbey's spire with scarlet claws. I had gone to the church, in fact, to study the presiding legion of gargoyles that grew up around that form, each one added in defiance, commemoration, or — sometimes — subversion of that first. And all of them are hybrid, impure and monstrous: their status and shape not quite natural, not right. One should also note that the indeterminacy I insist on is not tangential to the fell creatures that are our subject here; it is essential. It is an ambiguity so terrible that it is a kind of silence: a turbulent hush whose substance is *the inability to know*. Neither this animal nor that, neither serpent nor bird, neither demon nor misshapen human. Gargoyles are both, blended, something *other*. Though there are some things that may be known for certain.

All questions aside, the term gargoyle is said to have its source in an old French word perhaps best rendered as "throat" or "gullet" in English; even dictionaries can tell us that. So, it seems reasonable to forget about my troubling words for a moment and begin our account with the open mouth, a certain sign of hunger… and of more complicated sensations as well. People are said to be "open-mouthed" with surprise, or terror, in the same way as they are said to be "wide-eyed" at such powerful feelings. Overwhelming sensation can join many unlike things together. And such irregularity haunts even the most familiar type of gargoyle: the ornamental carvings that hang from the great cathedrals and abbeys. The complaint arises even in their beginnings. Bernard of Clairvaux — the formidable *Saint Bernard* — was known to be greatly exercised by such forms. He wrote:

What are these fantastic monsters doing in the cloisters under the very eyes of the brothers as they read? … What is the meaning of these unclean monkeys, these savage lions, and monstrous creatures? To what purpose are here placed these creatures, half-beast half-man...[1]

Here, tellingly enough, the saint's complaint does not concern violence or blasphemy, as one might expect, but rather focuses its outrage on the uncanny, the ambiguous, the wondrous or bizarre nature of the things. That and the introduction of such ambiguity into the disciplined life of the Orders. But given the creatures' rapid infiltration of such spaces, surely one should interrogate their origins before asking after the meaning of such things. One must ask from whence comes even the mere notion of such things.

The chroniclers offer us this response to the question. A former chancellor in the service of King Clotaire II of France, one Romaine, who was later made bishop of Rouen and ultimately canonized as *St. Romanus*, is said to have delivered the countryside around his Seat from a monster called "*Gargouille*." This creature was a kind of dragon with great wings, a long, serpentine neck and terrible jaws from which — we are told — it vomited great gouts of blistering fire. Upon slaying the beast, St. Romanus brought the corpse home to be immolated. But the head and neck would not burn, so hardened were they by the beast's own incendiary breath. Instead, the saint had the head mounted on the church to ward off other evils that might approach.

Here again we find the link between the monstrous and the ornamental; it always comes back to such — haunted — ambiguity: the murky division between atavism and artefact, the real and the artificial terror. Always a limitless hazy division marks the gargoyle, here it is the line that divides flesh from stone, and, of course, there are more legends about that. One may read in European narratives dating as far back as the Middle Ages of winged demonic creatures that emerged from caverns in the countryside to soar across the night sky rending and devouring

1 Bernard of Clairvaux, *Apologia ad Guilb. Sancti Theodorici abbat.*, ch. xi. *Patrol.*, clxxxii., col. 916, cited in Ronald Sheridan and Anne Ross, *Grotesques and Gargoyles* (David & Charles, Newton Abbot, U.K: 1975) p. 7

herds and flocks; even taking down those men and women unwise enough to travel the roads in darkness. One thirteenth century tale describes a persecution so terrible that three neighbouring villages were devastated, left with neither sheep nor cattle, nor scarcely an adult man after so many of them rushed from their homes to defend the chattels. It is written that the screaming was sufficiently violent that the people of one village could hear the cries of the community across the valley echoing back to them. It is in this account too that we may read more details than are usually recorded. Here the creatures are described as squat, with faces like hideous apes or unwholesome lizards, bearing toothy maws and strong pendulous tongues. Heavy muscles deformed their shoulders and breasts and the devilish things are described as standing three to four feet tall with wingspans twice their height. We read too of claws as sharp and tough as spear points. Surely these were enough to leave anyone encountering them slack-jawed, pop-eyed. It is in this account that we are told, for the first time to my knowledge, of another aspect of the legend to survive to our day. The writer records how a handful of the creatures were so lost in the appetite for flesh and hot blood that they grew careless of the hour and were caught feeding by the dawn and mysteriously transformed into stone — cold stone. So much the creatures of the dark, the night and the nightmare, were they that light was fatal to them; it drained them of vitality, of life. These cold remains were also affixed to the towers of the local church: an attempt to warn off the next night-flying attack. One must assume its success, since the account ends here. There are no more blood-soaked nights for the village in question.

The tale is, in some ways, nearly unique. There are, after all, many legends of beasts with paralytic powers, of creatures able to transform *their victims* into stone; one need only think of the gorgon or the cockatrice. This narrative however, is one of the only stories — if one sets aside accounts of some kinds of troll — in which it is the monster itself that becomes stone. In this way too — being both deadly and doomed, a strange marriage of the real beast and the dark dream — the gargoyle is once again

the exception, the bizarre: another kind of hybrid, not unlike its incarnation of both demon and decoration. Always the composite, the combination; which suggests the gargoyle is the shape we give to the myriad terrifying powers of our imagination and that is why we both fear them and use them to decorate our temples: the places we house our ideas of the sacred, our conception of the vast and various churning of the universe. It too a hyperbolic terror: not quite real, but not quite false either.

Which brings us back to inexplicable strangeness of these things; back to the word "gargoyle" itself, whose roots lie in the bodily gullet, the open mouth which expresses hunger and wonder alike; both what we want and what we fear has the power to leave us gaping, open-mouthed and wide-eyed. Like the cadaver of Brother Severino with which I began. His soft, vulnerable palate exposed by shock and showing where his tongue had been torn out; his eyes staring, though dead and unseeing, at the monstrous new stone form that appeared on the steeple that May Day Morning; it clinging there red-clawed, deformed and hybrid, with the scales of a lizard, the wings of a bat, a mouth opened wider than the fallen man's, and from which — curiously, and most blasphemous of all — two tongues lolled out, lapping up the sunlight and seeming to laugh. An image to which, it seems, Brother Severino could only respond with a slack jaw and a wide-eyed stare, it too, impure and hybrid; blending some wonderment with the terror of what must have been his last sight. And who is to say whether wonder and terror live in the world or in us. Or how real they are and to what extent.

Genies
(Rule 34)

Peter M. Ball

They are not the creatures they were, if you pay attention to the legends. We have that drilled into us, after we're recruited, long before Carter lets us place fingers upon the keyboard. He wants to make sure we know what's coming; barely understands the impossibility of the task.

We've got many names for them, around the office: jinn; genies; the demons of a smokeless flame. Carter prefers to call them Entities, pronounces it so you can hear the E, but he isn't present long enough for his preferences to matter.

Carter is an asshole, and enormously tight-lipped with those in his employ. What we know, we learned from Shamil, who works three desks down from mine. He believed in the Entities before he was recruited, brought his beliefs into the lab where the rest of us toiled at the keyboards. This affords him the status of expert, when we find ourselves musing about the creatures we hunt.

It's only because of Shamil that we know they have free will, that they will be judged, as humans are, at the end of all things. It's because of Shamil that we have theories about the jinn's retreat into the Net, disappearing into a frontier of electrons and fibre-optic cables after centuries inhabiting remote mountains, clouds, and deep trenches of the oceans. Because of him that we have arguments about how they ended up there, whether they retreated there voluntarily or were trapped there, on the Internet, as they were once trapped in lamps.

Shamil was born in Los Angeles; spent his teenage years in Denver. The only kid in his class to read the Koran and memorise the story of Solomon, who tamed the jinn and counted them among his servants, holding them in bondage until his death.

This, too, affords Shamil a measure of authority when we discuss the jinn; he understands what it is to be relocated and adapted to new surrounds. He tells stories that suggest Carter is not mad; that, perhaps, the Entities he's chasing can be caught and forced to serve.

I remain unconvinced, of course, but I do enjoy the stories. They provide us with moments of respite, amid the work Carter demands of us.

We spend our days on the Internet, dreaming of things that shouldn't exist. Bizarre porn; unexpected fetishes; weird little sites that serve no real purpose beyond their own existence. The kinds of things that make you wonder, "who in hell puts this online?"

Except we don't wonder, down in Carter's laboratory. We know, 'cause Carter makes sure we know. Because he lays it all out on the very first day, before you're ever introduced to the rest of the lab, and he'll remind you every time he sees you, however short his visit.

"Rule Thirty-Four," he says, "that's how we'll chase the bastards down."

Rule 34 exists because the jinn make their home on the Internet. Any fetish you can imagine, they will provide.

Go and sit at your keyboard, with your mind clear. Let your fingers rest upon the keys, the worn squares of plastic where the letters are starting to go after years of having your fingers punch out word after word. Let your attention wander.

It starts with something simple: a fetish for women caught in the rain, their damp clothing welded to their body by the torrential downpour; a fetish for feet with polydactyl traits, where supernumerary toes are presented with pride; a site where men have their right arm replaced with an octopus tentacle, positioned to retain the barest hint of modesty as their naked, supine form reclines on an isolated beach.

You don't expect to find anything, but the web provides it anyway. There are sites full of pictures. Communities to join. People who seem to share your interest, willing to help you take it further. Porn sites. Slash fic. Vaguely secret tumblr feeds, unapologetic in their content. If you're smart, you'll back off and forget about what you've seen. Realise there are some temptations one shouldn't succumb too, even at an introductory subscription price of $2.99.

If you're not smart, you'll choose to go deeper down the rabbit hole. You pit your will against the jinn and the illusions they can offer you, each of them darker than the one that came before it, but still so very sweet and tempting.

Some people — strong willed and aware of their boundaries — will know when to cease their engagement with the jinn.

Those of us on Carter's team, we choose to keep falling. Developed desires so specialised only the jinn could cater to them. Called in sick to day jobs, simply so we could stay online. Gave up work completely, so we could better explore our desires. We'd be falling still if the boss hadn't found us and offered us an alternative path.

Carter has a plan to capture the jinn. When we find a likely site, we alert his team of hackers. They go to work locking down the Internet, trying to capture a figment as it slips through the fibre-optic relays and disappears from the local nodes.

Some days, when we're so bored of the things on our screens, we'll stop searching the Net for fetish sites and talk through the possibilities. Shamil remains adamant that capture is possible, despite the prevailing theory that the jinn are light made sentient, their physical forms as illusory as the manifested fantasies that play out on our monitors.

Some days it all seems a waste of time: Jinn; pornography; Carter's long-term plans. They've slipped through our net too many times, placated desires we were barely aware of until they manifested online.

And despite Carter's warnings, it's always a surprise. The jinn were never content to grant wishes, even in the stories. They twisted every desire, if a loophole could be found. They held up a facet of your own desires and made it seem a little darker.

You see things that surprise you, in this job, not least 'cause you find yourself aroused. You stop looking in the mirror, 'cause it makes the job easier. I gave up mirrors a few weeks back; Shamil is making familiar arguments, suggesting that he'll be next.

But the money is good, so we sit and do what we once did for free: surf the Net, getting specific, trying to prove Rule 34 wrong.

We search for a digital footprint in the landscape of our desires.

Gingko

Carrianne Leung

ROOTS

Me and the tree, we had to part ways. It was an old, old tree. We were there before there was even a village. Some of them said the whole village was built especially for us. People started to settle all around us, and began to worship me because I was the spirit of the tree. They built a little house at the foot of the tree and sculpted a figure of me in clay. It didn't really look like me. I mean, I'm taller, proportionally speaking. My features aren't so blunt. The man who carved me didn't have the talent or the materials to do me any justice. But it was clay, not marble or anything, so OK, fine.

When the villagers got married, they tied ribbons around the tree branches that blew in the wind, and a whole procession would circle us many times. It looked like a kaleidoscope, depending on where you stood. They even made a small red silk suit and dressed me in it. Me and the tree, I have to say, we looked magnificent. If the villagers wanted something, like luck at the *mah jong* table that night, they would light incense and stick it in front of my house.

They would also make offerings on festival days. Like maybe some roast meat and fruit, but the damn dogs ate it all. And pissed on me too. I hate dogs.

Once they built that little house, I was cut loose. I began to grow differently. I grew thoughts and feelings too. I grew ambition. That tree wouldn't have grown so tall and its branches wouldn't have reached so far if it weren't for me. I was always trying to see farther and go farther than I could. I saw things. Like I saw where the land ended and the sea began. It's true! It was blue and green and black, all in patches like splashes of paint spilling into each other. I saw ships come and go, large hulking brutes chopping the water into bits. I watched them until they disappeared into the horizon and I wondered where the land began again. Let's just say I had time on my hands, a long time, and I measured it in births and deaths. They lived these little lives, the people, all in the village like me and the tree. Every night, the stars spun around us but we stayed still. The clouds waved like kites across the sky, beckoning me to follow with their tails.

When the sun was the hottest, they used to gather around me to pass the hours. The tanner came to skin the hides; the women came to fold laundry or bundle greens for market; the young girls came to weave and sew, and the young men came to look at them. I got to hear all the goings-on, the gossip, all that. So when I heard the talk that the young men were leaving, I wanted to go too. Being settled in one place isn't for everyone. I practiced my leave-taking. I said to that tree, "Tree, you and me. We've been together a long time now, la. Almost 800 years. You'll be fine without me. So, goodbye." I mean, without me, it had no more soul. Still, maybe I'm sentimental about these things. I couldn't help but think that without roots holding me down all this time, I could have been free too.

I wasn't sure how I would go. I just knew that there might be a way. My yearning was getting bigger than my little house or clay body or the tree could contain. I felt myself growing huge, reaching past anything I had felt before. I got restless. I started to resent that tree.

And you know what happened? The tree began to die. It wasn't obvious to anyone else at first. Only to me because that tree was still my mortal body. I first felt it in the longest tips of the branches. This quivering, this ebbing of life, and then numbness took over. The leaves began to fall earlier each autumn. I knew it was coming soon. I mourned the tree as it was dying; I told it I was sorry. We were one but we were not, so mourning it was also mourning me. A life was passing, and a new one would reveal itself soon. I don't how I knew. It's an ancient knowing, ringed and etched.

ROOTLESS

These days I perch on any tree willing to host me. Here in this city there aren't many; mostly it's concrete casting shadows on concrete ground. I find trees in cemeteries.

The tree spirits who are hospitable, give me rest for a while — Oaks, Ashes, Elms, Tamaracks. Oaks are indifferent. Ashes have gentle natures. Elms are natural leaders. Tamaracks are persistent. Maples though — they never give us refuge because of their superiority complex. I'm not trying to be essentialist here, but once you have been around, you see patterns.

Over here, across the sea, they are obsessed with names and naming. I do not know what my tree was called although these native trees ask. My tree just was, I answer, but I feel shame that this is somehow important, and yet I do not know. I went to the library and pored over dendrology books until I found a photo that looked like my tree. It was like looking into a mirror. I mouthed the sound, and my tears splattered the page. I was surprised by the water. It was the first time I had ever cried.

This happened the same day that a Willow spoke to me. Usually, those trees keep to themselves. She crooked her finger and beckoned me. When I wandered close enough for her leaves to brush against my face, she whispered, "There's no going back, kid." I was upset she called me a kid. I was thousands of years older than her, but it was true that I was new to this land, and she was, of course, born and bred here.

In the cemeteries, there are others like me. I eye the renegade spirits on their high branches. We don't speak, but even still, I know all our stories. Adrift from our ancient roots, we are drawn to the electricity of this place. This city gathers spirits around itself like an apron, wrapping and drawing us to its breast with promises of new life. We followed our villagers here, excited by their wide-eyed expectations. Initially it was exhilarating to be a wanderer, lifted from the earth. Feet as weightless as air.

I didn't account for the yearning that eventually set in. I didn't account for the desire for a pull of gravity to deepen into my bones. The desire persists even as I had wanted with all of my being to be free.

The descendants of the original villagers no longer remember us; they don't make offerings or decorate branches. Only in the winter, they kill a pine and drag it indoors, festoon it with lights and coloured balls and play with their vanished past. I am bound to this city as I was bound to my tree. I suddenly want to recall the way the sun filtered through my leaves and dappled the ground at my feet. I want to hear the creak of my spine as it bent with the wind. I want to feel the round embrace of the villagers. I desire this even as everything gestures to forgetfulness.

Is it possible to exist without memory? I am still here.

Godisaurus

Dennis E. Bolen

Large reptilian anomaly; green, angry, aggressive; extreme danger: First noted as a presumed surrogate avenger to Japanese war atrocities; destroyed Tokyo and other archipelago cities on numerous occasions through the post-WWII era. For the first two decades of reappearance from what is assumed — but never scientifically proven — was a deep-sea hibernation, the '*kaiju*' as the Japanese refer to it (meaning 'strange creature') was observed recurring following its initial emergence in 1954.

Filmed records of its devastation almost instantly became newsreel hits around the world and enterprising film producers soon tinkered these disparate footages into semi-coherent speculative dramas. Despite the resulting wide recognition, the suddenly famous serpent failed to capitalize on a folk-legend-initiated attempt to characterize him (in all the studies it is assumed, though never definitively proven, the monster is male) as a martyr to contemporary nuclear progress. On the contrary, the phenomenon has in large part been demonized since two separate attempts to lay waste to New York City.

An attempt to rebrand as *King of the Monsters* came to disappointment as general attacks on New York by various villainous individuals and agencies — in one instance culminating in the airliner destruction of three towers in the commercial district — progressed through the early part of the 21st Century.

Fame nevertheless followed the pre-historic, plodding edifice-wrecker through successive iterations of itself in movie roles. Rumours of contract disputes with a range of epic-disaster production houses did not prevent the great emerald amphibian from starring in a James Bond-challenging 28 full-length features.

In later life, uncomfortable with being a worldwide pop culture phenomenon, the lizard attempted to up his game by self-producing Ibsen's *An Enemy of the People*, with himself cast as the tortured, morally confused protagonist. Early negative reviews failed to deter a hugely expensive off-Broadway debut — to predictably disastrous notices — and the show closed after only one performance. The resulting financial consequence (both production costs and the reparations paid after a city-wrecking tantrum by the lead actor) put the famous reptile-thespian into a personal and professional funk that marked an unprecedentedly protracted hiatus.

The past decade has marked an attitudinal downturn in the actor's fortunes as world governments cut down on scientific research funds. The kaiju had at least held hope that a mate might be found, or failing that, and with the advances in DNA manipulation, a clone produced for companionship and possible co-starring roles in projected future film and TV projects.

A short relationship with the giant flying rodent Flythra went sour over creative differences and a later agent clash and contract dispute put paid to the venture. Several other collaborations involving variants, mutations, scaly metaphors and belligerent bio-aberrations also came to grief this way. Until a big-budget revival in 2014 — shot in western Canada to imitate upstate New York — it was believed the disconsolate mega-lizard was living in exile, fighting a rumoured invertebrate addiction. It is believed too that he is suffering from cold-inflicted arthritis caused by endless location shooting. Fans the world over, however, still hold out hope that the reclusive mammoth mythmaker will some day find happiness.

Gods, Small & Terrible

Gareth Ryder-Hanrahan

The cults of the small and terrible gods are older than humanity. While some religions boast thousands or even millions of adherents, these cults rarely have more than one or two worshippers, and must make up in abject devotion what they lack in numbers. These gods are cruel and wrathful when woken, so the cultists must labor to supplicate the little deities at every turn.

Their acts of devotion are made all the harder by the gods' ignorance of language. The gods speak in a pre-Adamic tongue incomprehensible to mere mortals.

Unable to comprehend the divine commands, their worshippers must fearfully grope for whatever the desired offering might be according to the ineffable criteria of the small and terrible gods. At one moment, the gods might be hungry; another moment, they might be offended by a shadow on the wall, or the existence of a plaything, or grow wroth because they know not what they want. When the gods slumber (and lo! these gods rarely slumber), many things become taboo including speaking aloud, walking with heavy footfalls, sneezing with too much force, the barking of dogs, the ringing of bells, or aught else that might disturb the things in their tiny shrines.

Small and terrible gods are not omniscient. They possess only a single supernatural sense: they know exactly when their worshippers have retired to bed. They know this with great precision. A god might not cry out when the worshipper leaves its little shrine, nor when the worshipper sits on the bed, nor even when the worshipper pulls the blanket over his or her head and scrabbles desperately for a snatch of rest. No, it is that moment when the worshipper dares relax that is vile in the sight of the small and terrible god, and vile things must be screamed at until they are stopped.

(We shall not speak of the effluvia of the small and terrible gods. It is terrible, but it is not small.)

Unlike most religions, it is the worshiped and not the worshipper who grows out of it. Small and terrible gods become bigger and less terrible (or terrible in different ways) until, through a miracle of transmutation, they become human.

Some scholars argue this is true of all gods. Others pray that it is.

Gorgon
(Goes Natural)

Isabel Matwawana

Accustomed to the deceptively languorous movements of the serpents wreathed around her head, Medina had no indication that one had escaped from under her scarf until she realized that Percy's boss wasn't looking at her anymore, but instead, just to the left of her. He averted his eyes as if he'd just accidentally seen her naked.

Medina spied the errant snake and reached to gently maneuver it back under her silken wrap, but Percy beat her to it, jamming it roughly in with the others.

"Gotta keep them under control," Percy laughed nervously, glancing at his boss.

"Percy!" Medina reproached gently. Then she looked back at his boss. "It's not like they can hurt anyone. They just get a little excited in this heat."

Percy tried to pick up the conversation where it had stalled.

"So, sir, you were saying, you got stranded in Paris."

His boss smiled stiffly and nodded. Then he looked past both of them.

"I'm sorry, there's someone I just need to catch before he leaves. It was nice to meet you, Medina," he said without looking at her. He turned to Percy. "I'll see you Monday. Don't you party too hard."

"No sir," laughed Percy with nothing like humour.

Medina turned to see the spot where Percy's boss had been looking. There was no one there.

On the way home from the party Percy and Medina were silent, waiting until they were safely in their apartment, locks turned, before finally getting their argument under way.

Percy watched Medina in the bathroom mirror as she scrubbed her makeup off. Somehow, when she had her makeup on, protecting everyone from her fatal face, even eye contact felt a step removed. If they were going to fight, she wanted him to really see her.

"That was incredibly hurtful," Medina started.

"Hurtful? How about, you were incredibly irresponsible."

"Irresponsible? Irresponsible how?"

"Are you serious? You're part of the impression I make at work. And that first impression is you can't keep your snakes under control. How do you think that reflects on me? *That's* irresponsible."

"Turning everyone at your work party to stone: that would be irresponsible."

"Dina, stop being dramatic." He sighed and added, "Don't you want the best for us?"

The best for us, by which, Medina was starting to think, he actually meant "the best for *me*." That "best for us" was becoming harder and harder to realize. What was best for Percy seemed to diverge more and more from what was best for her. But instead Medina said, "Of course I do."

He slept in the guest room that night though, which was safest anyway.

After dinner at Kevin and Geoff's the next night, Kevin and Percy went out to the porch to smoke cigars while Geoff and Medina nursed a bottle of wine in the living room. She looked over at Geoff to find him staring.

"What?"

"You seem off. Everything okay on the home front?"

Medina sighed. "There was a thing at Percy's work party and he was really upset about it."

Geoff said nothing, silent permission to unburden herself.

"You know, you expect as a gorgon girl that being accepted by the family is going to be the big hurdle, so I felt lucky that Percy barely speaks to his parents. But I guess there's always a hurdle of some sort. That's normal for any couple though, right?"

Geoff shrugged. "Sure, but your happiness is as important as his."

Medina nodded slowly, eliciting a muffled hiss of agreement from beneath her scarf.

In the dark of their bedroom, once Percy had moved, sated, to his side of the bed, Medina remarked, "You know, I think we face each other less during sex than some lower primates."

"What's that supposed to mean?" Percy retorted, clearly offended.

"It would just be nice sometimes to face each other. Remember how you used to like it?" she coaxed suggestively, recollecting those sexy first days when they'd met two years earlier. Back when Percy had found it thrilling to see Medina the way no one else saw her: totally wild, totally lethal. Back when it was more "babe, why don't you blindfold me while we make love" and less "turn around."

Medina realized Percy hadn't responded at all and tried another tack. "Or maybe I could even wait a little longer to take my makeup off."

"It'll just get on the sheets. I didn't think you had a problem with this position. Where's all this coming from? Is that what you and Geoff were discussing for so long tonight?"

It was an intentional barb, geared to make her take the bait and then foul out of the argument by getting overheated; but he'd stumbled out of bounds.

"Well not exactly…"

"You were discussing our sex life with Geoff?"

"No! Just that the situation at your work party really bothered me. I mean it sort of felt like you were ashamed of me."

Percy turned on the bedside lamp and sat up facing the mirror over the vanity, making eye contact with Medina.

"Of course I'm not ashamed of you. This company is different. They're conservative. I have to fit in a bit more to get ahead there."

"I didn't really sign up for that, Percy. I can't be somebody else."

"No one's asking you to be somebody else. You think they don't know what's under that scarf? It's just about making them feel comfortable."

"But I can't make everyone else comfortable with me. Besides it can't matter that much what they think of my hair."

"Dina, it always matters what people think."

Percy looked down from the mirror then and turned out the light.

In the morning, they moved around each other like spectres, silent and overly cautious. Before leaving for work, Percy stood, about to leave, in the doorway, no mirror in hand to even try to see her.

"Look, Medina, my point isn't to make you feel like you can't be yourself. I just need to know I can count on you to do the responsible thing, the grown up thing, if we're going to have a life together."

Percy closed the door behind him and Medina waited until she could no longer hear the sound of his footsteps before calling in sick. In front of the bathroom mirror, she removed one and then another of the loose cotton bonds tying her snakes back. She rubbed a soporific-soaked cotton ball on each writhing body for a long time and when they were limp and unmoving, she carefully, but forcefully bound them up once more. She found one of her most expensive scarves — one that Percy had given her for a birthday — and covered the deadly still mass.

♦

The restaurant was a cool reprieve from the relentless early summer heat. Medina looked around for Percy, willing herself to keep her hands at her sides. Sedated though they were, the day had been long and this kind of heat made the serpents more wakeful. She could feel them twisting against her scalp. She wanted terribly to rip her scarf off but muttered to herself a mantra that she'd lately created instead: *I am cool, I am calm, my body is the perfect temperature.*

"Medina?"

She turned.

"Geoff!"

They hugged without restraint, as if there hadn't been a year of radio silence between them.

"I barely recognized you." He looked sad for a beat but shook it off. "We haven't seen you two in ages. You'll have to come over for dinner soon."

"I'd love to," Medina said, meaning it and knowing full well Geoff was on Percy's blacklist since that last dinner. Silence hung between them for a moment.

"Well, I've gotta run," lied Geoff. "Got an appointment. You take care."

"Yes, you too. It was good to see you."

Medina found Percy at a table tucked at the back, his nose in a book.

"Hey, you!" Percy smiled, as she sat.

"Hey, how was your day?"

Percy didn't answer though. He was looking past her.

"What is it?" Medina asked and followed his gaze to an older couple heading to their table. They looked familiar, but Medina was sure she'd never met them before.

"Perseus, good to see you, son," said the man, his eyes sliding curious over Medina.

"Don't be rude, Perseus, introduce your friend," scolded the woman lightly.

Percy found his voice. "This is... ah... my friend, Medina."

"Medina, nice to meet you," said the older woman without looking at her, though Medina didn't really hear the rest of the awkward conversation until it had come to an end.

"Well, we have to get going. We've got tickets to a show. Maybe give us a call, darling," the woman said.

When his parents were safely out the door, Medina turned to Percy. Her makeup was cracked ever so slightly since her face had sort of collapsed.

"Your *friend* Medina?"

"Dina, please don't overreact."

"You can't acknowledge who I am to two people you don't even like," she whispered. "Why on earth am I bothering?"

"Medina, can we talk about this at home."

"You said we were going to have a life together. You said that. I did my part!" Medina was no longer whispering.

"Medina, let's talk about —"

She wasn't listening though. As she banged out of the restaurant entrance, there was a whoosh of hot air.

Percy sat in the living room for hours, locked out of the bedroom, having given up trying to get Medina to come out. It was sunset when his phone buzzed and two words appeared on the screen: *makeup off*.

He turned away just in time to hear Medina re-enter the living room. He heard something else, something distantly familiar and squinted into the surface of a vase, the only reflective surface in the vicinity. His heart tripped a violent beat.

"Medina, what's going on? You could have killed me."

Medina shook her head violently, causing a mass of irritated hissing.

"Yes, I could have killed you. I texted you instead."

She circled in front of him, not behind him, as was usually her way. Percy squeezed his eyes shut and dropped to a crawl on the living room carpet. He groped his way to the bedroom and slammed the door. When he came out a few minutes later, he had on his backpack, shirts hanging askance from where he hadn't been able to force the zipper. He held a hand mirror and did an awkward crab walk through the living room — trying to simultaneously find and avoid Medina. He needn't have worried about looking her in the face. She was standing in front of the kitchen window gazing out, loose serpents tangled in the vines of a hanging spider plant. In the late afternoon light her hair was like the sun's roiling corona, snakes undulating three feet in every direction.

Her presence in the room felt like that of a stranger.

"Medina, you're acting crazy. I don't know if I can forgive this."

Medina cocked her head to one side. "My sisters said you wouldn't last. I should have listened to them." She waited until she'd heard him thump all the way down the stairs before turning around. He hadn't bothered to close the door.

Geoff and Kevin appeared relieved to host Medina solo.

"You seem happier," Kevin remarked.

"And it's just good to actually see you again," Geoff added. "Do you miss him though?"

"Not even a little. Besides I'm seeing someone new."

Geoff and Kevin exchanged a look of amusement.

"Oh yeah, so what's his story?" asked Geoff.

"He's perfect!"

"Wow, that's high praise," laughed Kevin. "What makes him so perfect?"

"Well," began Medina with a smile, "for starters, he's blind."

The Greater Spotted Capital

Jonathan Blum

An unusual species, almost never observed in natural habitats. Instead, records of these creatures only seem to be found in captivity, in environments such as Wall Street. Scientists in particular seem to have great difficulty obtaining access to enough of the creatures to study them en masse, and perhaps as a result suspicions persist in the scientific community that the entire existence of the species is a P. T. Barnum-style confidence trick orchestrated by the collectors who supposedly own them.

In Herron and Booth's acclaimed 2009 popular-science essay "Will Think for Food," the researchers detailed their multi-year expedition in search of the greater spotted capital, which took them from the concrete canyons of Brazil to the jungles of Manhattan. They even attempted to set up a corporation as a duck-blind to attract the elusive creatures, but their investment in decoys exhausted their research budget. In the process they tested various bits of folklore about what was likely to attract these legendary beasts, from Brooks Brothers suits to MBAs to dot-com business plans, and concluded that the only likely way to attract a capital was to have one already there in the first place.

Physical descriptions of the greater spotted capital vary; it is believed to be similar to the lesser capital, a stoat-like creature with an instinct for biting the hamstrings of the humans it associates with, forcing them to spend much of their time sitting behind desks to recuperate. They are rarely tamed; once a human gets a hold of a capital, they have to work extremely hard to keep it. While collectors speak with pride of the capital they own, the behavior patterns involved often make it questionable who owns who. However, the few humans with reliable access to the greater capital consistently deny that the creature is aggressive or uncivilized; if it has a taste for human flesh, they appear to have successfully outsourced it.

The one consistent report is that a capital emits a glamour field (often referred to as "It"), which transfers to the humans in its immediate vicinity — thus making them seem smarter, sexier, and more like viable political leaders. On the negative side, this glamour can also spiral off into hyperactive hysteria — as witnessed in field reports of researchers at the New York Stock Exchange, where the merest whispers of mass migrations of capital regularly whips the capital-hunters into a frenzy not seen since the days of the *Malleus Maleficarum*.

A stampeding herd of capital is reported to have been attracted to Silicon Valley in the late 1990s, but most of them vanished leaving nothing but share-option-paper droppings behind. The species also suffered a population implosion in 2008, after an epidemic of subprime fever decimated their ranks; though some particularly embittered crypto-econo-zoologists attribute the real cause of the cull to a fashion among executives for mortgageskin boots.

Since the Industrial Revolution, the habitats of the capital have been overwhelmingly urban; they only appear to be able to inhabit a forest after it has been cut down. There is, however, a growing consensus among naturalists that while global warming may not directly affect the environments in which these creatures are kept, it may still have a catastrophic effect on their populations in the long term.

Griffin
(The Gryphon and the Showgirl)

Helen Cusack O'Keeffe

I am all, and I am one. This story speaks for all my kind, but also just for me. We are Gryphon, or Griffin, Griffen, Gryffyn... and many other lexical variations. Evidence — as if any were required — of our ancient and illustrious history. You surely know us by our fiery eyes, curved beaks, resplendent wings and the leonine muscularity of our limbs. Creatures of the skies we are, yet instinctively drawn to gold on terra firma.

Around 3000 BC, I was companion to the Pharaohs of Egypt, then I traversed the Mediterranean to Crete, where I guarded the Minoan Royal Family. The Indians claimed me next, knowing the uncanny power of my talons to detect poison. They glorified my body on their drinking vessels.

I wove my nests from gold and laid my agates therein. Defended my treasures from marauding humans, hippogriffs and *eohippae* — I particularly disliked the latter. In Greece I did flourish beside the Hyperboreans, bestowed as I was with the favour of Zeus. There I took gold from the one-eyed Arimaspias of Scythia.

Unkind Pomponius Mela called me a crude and eager wild beast, he warned settlers from my terrain — though perhaps this was for the best. Yet humans do invade those places that they are most bewaried of, humans do thirst for gold and for its vulgar misuse. Yes, Mela declared that I do wonderfully love the gold which lies discovered above the ground; that I do wonderfully keep it and am very fierce on those that do touch it. Ha — try touching it, Mela, try! For all Greece knows that in your cowardice you never approached me, all Greece knows that your sickly lettered wails were founded on reports of others, souls far braver than you… Know that I am gold, that I am the wealth of the dawning sun and that I am the glory of the East.

As Greece faded then did Rome succumb, enthralled, adorning many a splendid construction with my portrait.

I, we, became legion… and yet we are one. Transcending the entity they call society these days, though of course there is no such thing. There are only individuals — whining, odorous wretches who drag their ill-shod feet. It suits me to reside in lofty places, from whence I do not perceive the coarseness of their faces. Mountains have always suited, though any tall bastion of Capitalism can serve as a commodious seat. Casinos, for instance… In the realm of the game, wretched hordes are enticed by feathered showgirls and hostesses with gleaming teeth, through the flashy labyrinth of pinging, tootling slot machines and over unctuous carpets to an Inner Temple, where devotees — croupiers — empty the wretches' wallets. Yes, Casinos delighted me, once upon a time… Banks concern themselves with such piffling matters as the lending of lucre in return for tithes — interest, they call it — and if the borrowing wretches cease payment of their tithes, their hovels are taken from them and sold. It makes for healthy coffers, but such concepts lack panache. Ah, how I ache for the old splendours of Athens, Alexandria, Babylon…

Monte Luxor is the most golden city left on this declining earth, its Grand Casino the finest of its ilk. They raised a statue to me in there, the mightiest I ever saw: Nero himself would have worshipped it. My colossal three-dimensional image dominated the Roulette Hall, thus my soul acquired the habit of hovering there every Tuesday to Saturday, anticipating the fan-fared sashaying of Melissa onto the stage where she would dance until the small hours… *Goldfinger, Hey Big Spender, Money, Money, Money*…

Melissa was the worthiest of showgirls. Golden-haired, golden-skinned and amber-eyed, her gilded limbs undulated beneath her glittering costume, a crown of orange tiger lilies riffled upon her head. From my first glimpse of her, she made me smile – not easy, when one is beaked – and yet I managed it. I could not stop smiling whenever she appeared. The fire in my eyes simmered down to a smoulder and in this Roulette Hall I lingered – until one night, I realised that my soul had graced no other of my domains for almost a year, and yet I did not mind. I had no idea what Melissa did in the mornings, or on Sundays, Mondays… but I didn't care. Reckless as to my immortal endurance, I must admit I was content to wait for her entrances, to doze under this skin of gilt and to enjoy how my feathers gleamed under the rays of morning sun through glass.

It never occurred to me that Melissa was harbouring dark thoughts. When the small grey shadows first appeared under her eyes, I ascribed them to the ravages of mortal years and I loved her so much that I pitied her.

No, I have never been bothered by those wretches who call themselves Revolutionaries. After October 1917, St Petersburg had me worried for a mere five years. The destruction of the Berlin Wall in 1989 turned those Black Monday Black Wednesday whatevers into inconsequential blips – the human wretches will never abandon my truths, whatever banners and slogans certain among them might wave. And when, a few years ago, the balaclava-headed figures gathered with their placards in the boulevard outside the Grand Casino's windows, I smirked because they were calling themselves the 99%. At least they were cognisant of how dull, how ordinary they were. Anarchists! Anachronisms, ha! I suppose, for a while, they distracted me from the much darker dealings of LAG.

First, the stickers began to appear, miniscule print on red squares too lowly for my attention. Then came the leaflets in their tiny cardboard holders glued to lavatory doors, to the slot machines lining the Roulette Hall walls, or tucked under the ledge of the Champagne Bar. The cleaning minions made short work of removing and shredding the leaflets, plus their holders, which were leaving unsightly streaks of glue everywhere. But — more of these heretic tracts littered my golden domain, titles like: *WORKERS UNITE AGAINST CASINOS* and *RISE AGAINST THE TYRANNY OF CARD TABLES*. The author signed himself: *LAG*.

Ha — I scowled — if wretched hordes wish to pay me homage, what right does LAG have to stop them? Naturally, I never suspected Melissa — something so perfectly golden could never harm me, I once thought. Is this most glorious of metals not my very blood?

And then one morning I opened my eyes to spidery red paint daubed high on a marble column:

ROULETTE
MAKES
SLAVES
OF US

And on nine other pillars, that same ominous signature as in the leaflets: *LAG*.

On another pillar, the elucidatory: *LENINISTS AGAINST GAMBLING*.

This was harder for the cleaning minions to deal with, sweating and wobbling on their ladders as they scrubbed. Signor Oroni, manager of the Grand Casino, and a faithful servant whom I have duly rewarded with four sports cars and thick golden neck-chains (they slide about his greasy hide), invested in security cameras, xtreem-kleen paint removal kits, and a private detective. Yet, not only did he fail to unmask the culprit, but his efforts exacerbated the vandalism with unnerving speed.

DEATH TO CAPITALIST PIGS – ill-formed black letters defacing the neo-Roman bas-relief over the Champagne Bar. Poor Apollo's face, rendered positively Nubian – how shamed he would have been! The minions worked round the clock, their royal blue smocks turning navy with sweat.

CROUPIERS ARE STINKING COLLABORATORS – spray-painted in red on the sea-blue carpet. The minions attacked the heinous letters with stiff brushes, to little effect. Signor Oroni had to call in the Mount Olympus Professional Carpet-Shampooing Service, who, at great expense, operated their gurgling specialist machines for five hours over the insult, yet still it glared, stark and bloody as the dribble on a gorgon's lips.

It was at that point that Oroni's tangerine-coloured face turned plummy scarlet, then shifted to pale cantaloupe. "Rip it up then," he wheezed, pointing at the carpet, next he whipped out his little golden telephone from his pocket. It was a Saturday, our most profitable session – but as the Grand Casino could not open its doors, not a single penny would be sent down to the vaults tonight.

"Is that MegaLux Flooring?" barked Oroni.

The croupiers and hostesses turned up: a discontented huddle whining about overdue bills, dependent families and other irksome nonsense, while Oroni scuttled about like a confused dog, haggling the cost of the new carpet, and no, he didn't care about the nylon percentage of the tufts… A whole session's revenue lost – he'd have to forget that new Lamborghini I promised him. Towards seven o'clock, the croupiers and hostesses quit their bickering and shuffled back to wherever their little lives were eked out. There was no sign of Melissa, which did not perturb me. Oroni would have had the grace to call *her*, his star, about the closure.

And then, from deep within the vaults where the lucre is stored before being transferred across the boulevard to the bank, I heard a rumbling sound. A split second later, the marble pedestal beneath my crouching hind paws tilted and the violated carpet rose up towards me, I made a vain attempt to unfold my wings – only then did I realise, oh horrors – I had forgotten how to fly. My soul had melded with the concrete heart of this statue.

I crashed to the floor in the most undignified splintering sprawl, my golden coat grubbied by dust from the common horde's feet, and flecks of carpet shampoo. And then I saw Melissa, her radiance disguised under ugly black knitwear. She stood with her arms folded like a closed crab.

Come out, come out of your body, abandon this static indolence, rediscover your winged power… The tiny voice echoed from deep under my chest plumage, just at the point where it blurs into fur. *Come out… Yes…* My creaking soul prised itself from the shards and took flight: shaky, feeble, shameful circles. Harder and harder I beat my wings, willing my muscles to reform, yet the substance of my flesh remained elusive, wraith-like. Still only half-formed, through the shattered outline of the great window I flew.

The Grand Casino, most lovely of edifices, was lovely no more. A vast crater in its roof, and yet my eyes could not focus on the destruction, Melissa's face emblazoned on my retina. Fury thickened my blood until the sound of my wings grew loud as drumbeats; I flew a loop, turned back towards the Grand Casino.

Beside its crumbling portal was Melissa… smiling. Not the gleaming lipsticked grin she flashed onstage but a bare smile, hardly more than a pencil stroke. Yet her eyes were melting as if she had never experienced such serenity in all her days…

I took my revenge, of course. That's what claws are for.

Melissa's smile turned into a scream as I dived down with my outstretched talons. One claw sliced into the warm poisonous flesh of her belly, the other into her long showgirl's legs.

"WHY?" I roared. "Tell me why!"

Melissa's amber eyes watered, a groan slipped from her unwilling lips. I dug my talons deeper. She howled, then levelled her magnificent gaze with mine. Her parents had lost everything to poker, she snarled; they had starved her, ignored her childish pleas to abandon the card tables. "They'd always lie: just once more, one last game. Every poker night would start lucky and end in beggardom."

Defiance was all she offered me. Was it then that I gouged out her heart, with my beak that I would have kissed her with? What else did she say? Not a single cry for mercy, it pains me to recall; merely some Vladimir Ilyich-derived gibberish about owning the means of duping the masses, before her golden face blanched white with death and I threw away her bleeding, treacherous corpse.

Blinded by my own gold! I wept, then: the golden puddles of my tears turning grey under the ashen rain.

Half-Cat

Peter Chiykowski

From the archives of the late James Alexander; revised by the late Erwin Hobbes; expanded and further revised by Peter Chiykowski on behalf of the Half-Cat Field Research Organization.

No creature in the history of cryptozoology has tread the tightrope that joins fact and fiction so nimbly as the half-cat. Sightings are rare, specimens rarer still. And yet every cat on the planet bears the potential for this astonishing bipedal mutation, nestled in the depths of its genetic code like veins of platinum twining unseen through so many layers of common ore.

In the opinion of the Half-Cat Field Research Organization (HCFRO), the existence of half-cats is a scientific certainty. Throughout history and folklore, there has been a surprising but demonstrable string of appearances of cats born without hind legs or a pelvis. They can be tabby or calico, Persian or munchkin — the anomaly does not discriminate.

No, the discrimination is entirely an artifact of human perception. Treated with revulsion, or simply ignored, the half-cat has weathered the ages in the shadows of science. In fact, so tenebrous is the half-cat's place in the annals of academia that half-cat researchers are often "lumped in" with pataphysicists, mad scientists and amateur paranormal investigators, relegated to the realm of the occult rather than embraced by the warm and grant-giving bosom of academia.

Public recognition of these findings has been hampered by four minor obstacles:

1) Categorical lack of evidence.
2) Historical dearth of wealthy patrons.
3) The prevalence of "Photoshop" and the increasingly commonplace ability of any person on the planet to digitally remove the hind legs of any domestic cat, or to cover up photographic evidence of true half-cats by digitally adding legs.
4) The "curse" of the half-cat (*i.e.* the disturbing number of untimely deaths, dismemberments, institutionalizations and near-lethal defenestrations suffered by half-cat researchers over the last 100 years).

This so-called "curse" is the leading reason for the half-cat's public perception as an article of "fringe" science, and the principal reason for its inclusion in this volume. Just as the coincidental deaths of a few grave-robbing archaeologists have forever stained the reputation of Egyptologists everywhere, so have the linens of scientific legitimacy been soiled for untold generations of half-cat researchers.

Yes, it is true that the list of deaths suffered by members of the HCFRO is both improbably lengthy and unsettlingly gruesome. And yes, it is true that no member of the HCFRO has ever survived long enough to rise past the rank of "intern" according to the association's rather arcane charters. And yes, the story of James Alexander, the grandfather of half-cat science, is one of the saddest and most demoralizing tales of our time.

But it would be an unjustifiable leap to say that *all* half-cat researchers have met unhappy ends. If you look past the drama of electrocutions, burst colons, piano-crushings, lawnmower-maimings, dinner roll-chokings, accidental lobotomies, and the one grossly over-exaggerated microwave oven explosion, you'll find cause for hope.

For example, my friend and colleague Richard Williamson currently resides in a blissful coma in the sunny long-term care wing of Winfrew Family Hospital. I'm sure that if he was still capable of speech, he would tell us that the pursuit of truth was worthwhile, even when it led him over the loose handrail of that sanatorium so many years ago.

For a time the HCFRO considered taking out life insurance policies on its interns as a sustainable revenue stream, but our legal counsel advised against drawing attention to our society's rather blotted history of accidental deaths.

Thus, I would like to take this opportunity to start a new ledger, as it were, and to set the record straight. The fact of the matter is that no human being, intern or otherwise, has ever died as the *direct* result of the appearance of a half-cat. Statistically speaking, a half-cat researcher is no more likely to die young than a plague doctor or a trepanation patient.

And it is in this spirit of goodwill and optimism that the HCFRO would like to invite applications for internships. We compensate all successful candidates with life experience, a share of the numerous unsold copies of the HCFRO's seminal publication *Half-Cat: A Partial History*, and, in the event of your death while on active duty, a modest widow/widower's stipend proportional to your years of service and the grisliness of your demise.

Please forward all queries to halfcat.research@gmail.com with your name, bank transit number, and current balance in the subject line. Replies may take up to eight weeks depending on mobility and lucidity of staff.

Jackalope

(Not Too Late, Too Important to Escape)

Jacqueline Valencia

Jack Jackalope had pulled the alarm and waited for Diane Rabbit to come out among the scattered chaos. It had been too long since he'd seen her. For many years, the two were separated. Relationships with jackalopes were forbidden to rabbits. While rabbits were said to be leaders and thinkers, jackalopes, horned cousins of the rabbits, had reputations as rebels and disruptors of the peace. Jack became a rodent rights activist just so he could be with Diane, and in turn, became one of the most wanted, dead or alive, hares in the colony.

Jack was about to pass out, but he could feel Rabbit's body shaking next to his keeping him on alert. The other animals around them muttered confusedly among themselves about the inconveniences of midnight safety drills, unaware of the danger surrounding them.

Jack could see the doors ahead of him, past the reception area and through the foyer. They were so close, so near. He could almost taste freedom outside on his whiskered face, but as his senses detected new movement in the area, his antlers started vibrating. There was no thinking any more, just doing, surviving.

He caught site of the hare leader Captain Rabbit and his soldiers, pushing their way through the crowds. One of the soldiers spotted him. His body was ready, but his tiny lapin heart felt like it was about to fail.

Jack noticed Captain Rabbit's right arm slowly move for the gun in his pocket. He saw the muscles in his hand contract and flex individually around his weapon. The arm came up to his fuzzy belly and his left paw joined the right on the handle, targeting Jack in one quick motion. The weapon came up and leveled off Captain Rabbit's sights, in the same way Jack had instinctively targeted him a few seconds earlier. There was no recoil as Jack pulled the trigger and silently watched as pieces of Captain Rabbit's chest disappeared, leaving a gaping hole in his fur behind it. The soldiers were left covered in the remains of their commander.

Knowing the immediate danger now, Jack started continuously shooting where it would matter most. The glass window behind the enemy shattered with a boom, and the crowd panicked. Shards of glass incapacitated a few of the soldiers while Jack and Diane scanned for a way out. The security shutters had already come down. Escape would prove difficult, but when Jack was instinctually aware, everything was possible.

He grabbed Diane's paw and they hopped quickly down the halls towards the depot sections. The crowds made it easy enough for them to get lost among them, but their unpredictable movements made it hard for them to move stealthily. When they finally made their way to the common room in the buildings, Jack stopped and fired a single round at the wall where he knew the insurgency had hidden explosives. The metal doorway under it disintegrated into a tower of fire, smashing parts of the wall into the floor. Jack winked at Diane. She blew him a kiss back.

As Jack Jackalope moved towards the light coming in from the yawning crater he had made in the building, a part of him awoke.

A flood of emotions poured over his spirit. Freedom from the enclosure would be his and he could finally build a quiet life for Diane and himself away from it all. This would be the first time they would have stepped outside of the walls of the Japanese labs on the shores of Okunoshima aka Rabbit Island.

Leucrotta

Kyla Lee Ward

Case Number: 188437855

Date: 31 May 2014

Reporting Officer: Kyla Lee Ward

Incident Type: Assault Causing Death, Assault of a Police Officer

Address of Occurrence: Cambridge Street and Lane, Enmore, New South Wales, Australia.

Witnesses:
- Alicia Grieves, Clubber. Female, 23, Caucasian.
  Note: Name checked against driver's license.
- Kaelo Takipo, Hotel Security. Male, 42, Pacific Islander.
- Pauline Haigh, "Lillitu", Clubber. Female, 31, Caucasian
- Sam Yee, "Lord Manx". Clubber. Transgender, 28, Asian

Evidence:
- Closed circuit surveillance footage
- Hair and Fibre found behind industrial bin on Cambridge Lane and on the steps of 12 Cambridge Street.
- Paw-print in blood, Cambridge Lane

Weapon / Object Used: unknown, possibly metal pipe.

On 31 May 2014 at approximately 2.17, Markus Perry (male, 25, Caucasian) was attacked by an as yet unidentified assailant in Cambridge Lane, directly behind the Fat Goose Hotel.

In her statement Grieves said, "I was there for Descension (a Goth Club, staged at the Fat Goose on the third Friday of every month). Perry and I aren't together but I know — knew him. He's a friend. Was. Goddess, this is so awful!" Footage from the surveillance camera at the back door of the hotel confirms that Perry and Grieves entered Cambridge Lane at 2.05. Grieves's statement continues: "You can't smoke inside, and I asked him to come with me into the alley because Lillitu and Manx said there'd been someone out there hassling them earlier."

Although the footage shows no sign of a third person, Perry can be seen repeatedly glancing up the alley as he speaks to Grieves. Grieves said she heard someone repeating the phrase "fucking weirdos, I'll mess you up" in a harsh whisper… "I can't tell you if it was a man or a woman, but it sounded like they didn't speak much English. It seemed to be coming from behind the big bin they've got out there. Perry went to tell them off. When he started screaming, I ran back inside."

Officers Ward and Wallace arrived on the scene at around 2.45, in response to Grieve's 000 call. In the interim, Takipo was persuaded to leave his regular position at the front door of the hotel and investigate the alley. He found Perry seriously injured and attempted first aid. In his statement, Takipo said, "When I came round the bin, I saw something on top of him, big and black. I shouted and drew my piece here (Takipo carries a licensed taser), and it just bolted. I thought it was a feral dog, you get them round here. But the wounds weren't like bites: they were all curved, like the end of a pipe or something." An ambulance was summoned and Perry was taken to the emergency ward at Camperdown Hospital, where he died later that morning of internal injuries.

The attending officers investigated, finding signs of a violent struggle behind the bin. No potential weapon was visible, although the contents of the bin were only briefly inspected. Although the condition of the street, especially in the vicinity of the bin, means assessment of the hair and fibre discovered there will take time, the print in the fresh blood was immediately apparent and appeared to belong to a large animal, possibly canine in nature. This officer remained with the scene while Wallace followed the alley through to Cambridge Street.

As subsequently related to Ward, Wallace questioned the proprietor of the Seven Eleven at 8 Cambridge Street, with no result. He then approached an apparently homeless individual on the front step of the terrace house at 12. This individual was wearing a large, felt jacket of grey or black and had extremely long and tangled brown hair. He or she was squatting in a peculiar manner, so that their legs were concealed beneath the jacket and their arms supported their body, with head bowed so that hair concealed their face. The hands appeared to be bunched into fists, the skin appearing dark with a thick covering of coarse hairs. The individual smelt extremely rank and when questioned, repeated the phrase "Spare us some change? Got a ciggie?" five or six times before Wallace abandoned this line of inquiry.

Continuing along Cambridge Street, Wallace was assaulted from behind and knocked to the ground by a large animal, "maybe a dog but effing huge". Blows from a curved, hard object occasioned wounds and a fracture to his arm. He was nonetheless able to draw and discharged his weapon twice, repelling both his assailant and the animal. Although he did not actually sight his assailant, being preoccupied with fending off the animal, "it sure smelled like that guy." Wallace then returned to Cambridge Alley. This officer requested appropriate back up. Wallace was taken to Camperdown Hospital and is understood to be in a stable condition.

As the attending forensic and SWAT teams conducted a search and examined the site, this officer sought out Haigh and Yee. In HER statement, Yee said; "When we went out to smoke, it was about one o'clock. There was some guy talking trash: I get that all the time. I didn't see him but he had a creepy, raspy voice though: really nasty. We just went back inside."

Haigh's statement supported this, as did the footage. However, it struck this officer that Perry was an unusual choice of bodyguard, given that the footage showed him as slightly shorter than Grieves and wearing a man corset. When asked to give the exact words used by the intruder, Haigh and Yee contradicted each other substantially, with Yee repeating the words used by Grieves. After considerable further persuasion, both Haigh and Yee amended their statements to the effect of "She's got a ticket to high, fifty for two." Asked if they had taken up the offer, both said no, but that they had told Perry when "he did the rounds later, looking for a little something," to quote Yee.

Haigh then made a comment that was not included in her statement due to its frivolous nature. However, in light of Takipo's observations and this officer's recollection of the wounds received by Wallace, it may be grounds for her further questioning. To the best of this officer's memory, she said: "You never step out of the light, no matter what they say. That's when the leucrotta gets you." When Yee requested more details, she said the leucrotta was a very ancient creature, first reported in Persia in the third century B.C.E. The offspring of a lion and a hyena, it had the ability to mimic human speech and used it to lure its victims out of shelter and into the dark. Although a carnivore, it had no teeth but a sharp, bony ridge protruding from its gums. When this officer suggested that people would notice a hyena or a lion stalking the inner city, Haigh replied; "It's a mimic, isn't it? And it's been over two thousand years. It would have evolved, like."

This officer requests that the results of the analysis of hair and fibre, and of the paw-print be made available to her as soon as possible. The animal in question is presumably the pet of the suspect individual, but as Takipo observed, the area does have a considerable stray population. It is presumably for this reason that, in this officer's experience, the homeless are seldom encountered here. She has also noticed remarkably little drug-related activity here, within the past year, and cannot match Wallace's description to that of any known dealer.

Line Waifs

Jim Webster

My main source of dissatisfaction is that there doesn't appear to be anybody on whom we convincingly pin the blame for this problem. This is most vexing.

But still let me lay out the metaphorical terrain before you. The first telephone exchange was opened in 1877. Electromechanical switching equipment was introduced more than a century ago but obviously didn't catch on everywhere. Finally the first digital exchange went on line in 1972.

I know, there are those who are irked by the history lesson, but how can the course of a battle be understood if one does not understand the nature of the battlefield? Or to use a more exact metaphor, how can you understand the evolution of a species if you do not understand the environment in which it evolved?

Thus and so it is obvious to even the most psychically inert that in their blindness engineers rushed where wiser men and women would have advanced more guardedly.

Consider a telephone exchange. Can you imagine the anguish, the bitterness, the petty vindictiveness, the blatant lying, that passes though it? How many have wound themselves up to make an important call only to get a wrong number or the engaged signal? The sour dregs of human emotions swill unheeded around a telephone exchange, pooling in dark corners and corroding the mechanisms.

Now admittedly, back in the early days when these places were staffed by brisk young women; this wasn't perhaps the problem that it became. Some have claimed that their personal touch was all it took to lance the boil. I would suggest that rather it was their vigorous nature and their no-nonsense disregard of the issues, which ensured nothing untoward happened.

But then they were replaced by mechanisms. Surely the result would be obvious to anybody with a useful mind? The final straw was digitalisation. I have shown in my earlier published papers that the switch from manned exchanges to electromechanical exchanges leads to a pooling of the foul residue of tainted human emotions. Indeed I have shown by experiment that even in a small electromechanical exchange, visited regularly by engineers, that one can detect a scum forming. There we have the first hint of sentience.

Once one switches to digital then the brakes are 'metaphorically' off and the process proceeds apace. I suspect that by their very nature, electromechanical systems are inimical to the creation of life. But in a digital environment we saw a rapid evolution along lines that could have been predicted by even the most minor savant.

The first signs of sentience were admittedly minor. An exchange infected by the first fumbling actions of this unwholesome sentience starts to generate calls of its own. The recipient of one of these calls would pick up the phone to be met by silence, incoherent sounds or even faint laughter. The recipient, irritated, would put the phone down. The sentience would phone again, creating more irritation, frustration and even anger. The creature would feed on these energies, growing slowly stronger.

By now the creature is probably discrete enough to have an identity and warrant a name. We shall call it a 'Line Waif.' Some were happy to develop no further. They would infest an automated dialling system, perhaps in an oil storage tank or similar. Rather than just sending a message automatically when the oil level was low, they would dial at random, drawing sustenance from the aggravation their silent phone calls created.

Others continued to evolve and managed to achieve speech. A thick ugly gurgling it might be, an accent both incomprehensible yet vaguely recognisable. Yet they would phone their victims and toy with them, luring them into discussion. When this level of development was reached, evolution was rapid. The line waif could milk the situation for the maximum of emotion; even a burst of vulgar abuse with the phone slammed down provided ample nutrition. Their grasp of language became better, they began to understand more complex social concepts and indeed at this level they can pass themselves off as a human being working from a script.

Finally we have seen the final stage of their development. I now have conclusive proof that line waifs have learned how to leave their exchanges and manifest themselves in what we coyly call 'the Real World.'

When they first attempt this they look remarkably like characters from video games, or as if they were created by an inferior CGI programme. At this stage they are unlikely to fool anybody but a very young child. Also at this stage they seem to need something more substantial than mere emotion. To become corporeal they have to drink deep not merely the more intense emotions (terror is perhaps the one that serves them best) but their victim's blood as well.

At this point I want to dispel some rumours. I know there have been sensational stories circulating on the Internet about strange cults whose members capture children and sacrifice them to these creatures as part of occult ritual. Frankly these stories are nonsense. What happens on these occasions is that whilst the cult might sacrifice a child in the presence of a line waif; and might even feed the waif a little of the blood; it is their own gratification they seek. The human participants in the ritual get personal fulfilment from the vile death of the innocent. In addition they also experience the thwarted hunger of the line waif, forced to watch but not participate. For cult members this is a piquant sauce adding savour to the main dish.

No, the line waifs are perfectly capable of trapping and killing their own prey. Often they'll work as a small group, perhaps three or four basing themselves on an infected exchange. They tend to haunt the night, picking on drunks, drug addicts and those who cannot defend themselves. The homeless are easy prey as they sleep in unfortunately chosen doorways.

The solution? Well the obvious one would be to revert to manned exchanges and dispense with any form of automated switching. This sure solution is doubtless impossible to implement. Indeed calculations made for another purpose indicate that were we to do this, the majority of our population would be working as telephone operators.

I am currently doing work on another possible solution. It is in its early stages and obviously I cannot guarantee my findings. Still in the field we have noticed that dogs show an intense hatred for corporeal line waifs. Indeed this hatred is so intense that it can take a strong man to stop even a dog of moderate size from hurling itself at the creature. The best breeds for this appear to be the working dogs, German shepherds and Border collies are particularly suitable, but most mongrels share the hatred.

The good news is that line waifs seem to fear dogs as they fear nothing else, fleeing if a dog comes on the scene. In my latest experiment I have arranged to have a Border collie bitch with her litter of pups moved into an infected exchange. Obviously at this early stage it would be unprofessional to make too many claims, I merely note in passing that I now answer the phone only in the presence of my own dog.

Long-tongued Mulgaras

Jean-François Chénier

Long-tongued mulgaras are marsupials of the genus *Dasycercus*. They have fat, bald tails similar to those of rats, but are longer and thinner than the common rat, and armed with razor-sharp teeth. Their eponymous, snake-like tongues are covered with a slimy symbiotic mold, which helps them to digest their food, and is believed to have a sedative effect on their prey. Although they evolved on the Australian continent, they are a highly invasive species now found on every continent except Antarctica, and thrive wherever humans congregate.

Like all marsupials, long-tongued mulgaras have a very short gestation period, and the infants (known as joeys) are born in an essentially fetal state. Newborns are furless, translucent, covered in the symbiotic mold, and the size of coffee beans. Unique amongst marsupials, these fascinating creatures do not carry their joeys in a pouch, nor do they suckle them. Rather, infants are left in piles of rotting food, which they insert their tongues into, and feed on until they have matured.

Mature long-tongued mulgaras are nocturnal, with jet black fur — and although large populations can be found in all urban areas, they are rarely seen. Thanks to their dexterity and remarkable intelligence, they are able to work complex latches, and open heavy doors. If you've ever heard doors slamming or boards creaking in the night, there's a good chance that it was a long-tongued mulgara.

These clever animals are uniquely adapted to life in the city, and typically birth their young in refrigerators, in food that has begun to spoil. Any food will do, though they seem to have a preference for Chinese takeout that has been left in the back of the fridge to rot.

Like mature long-tongued mulgaras, joeys seek out the dark — and because they are left to fend for themselves from a very young age, they have evolved remarkable dexterity for near-fetuses. When a refrigerator door opens exposing them to light, for instance, they are able to retract their tongues and burrow into the food they are living on in a matter of seconds. This, and the joeys' near-transparent bodies, mean that infestations are virtually impossible to detect. The joeys even go unnoticed when they are accidentally ingested, as they do not alter foods' flavors significantly, adding only an unexpected stickiness.

Typically, joeys find their way into the trash along with the food they are living on, and from there into compost or landfill. They mature at the age of eight months, at which point they emerge from their cocoon of trash. At this stage, they become exclusively carnivorous — like their close relatives the bush-tailed mulgara and the crest-tailed mulgara — living on a diet of invertebrates and small mammals. Their teeth and strong jaws make them effective hunters, though they rarely kill their prey outright. Rather, they incapacitate them, wrap their long tongues around them, then begin the slow process of digesting them alive. After mating, the females travel back to the fridge in which they were born to begin the cycle of life anew.

In the past century, long-tongued mulgaras have been exposed to several environmental pressures and mutagens. More and more, the marsupials find themselves in tightly packed landfills when they reach maturity, in a chemical cocktail that contains battery acid, discarded medicines and other hazardous chemicals. This means that only the strongest, largest and most aggressive survive. The average length of long-tongued mulgaras has almost doubled in the past twenty years, and the creatures have become much more brazen. Alarmingly, some people have reported waking up to find long-tongued mulgaras next to their sleeping spouses, their prehensile tongues wrapped around the heads of their loved ones. If you've ever woken up with a damp pillow, or "sheet imprints" in your face, chances are that you've been licked (and partially digested) by a long-tongued mulgara.

According to a recent UN study, consumers and retailers in industrialized nations waste 222 million tons of food every year. Globally, about one third of all food produced is wasted. This creates a perfect environment for long-tongued mulgaras to thrive, and their numbers are growing at an alarming rate.

If you suspect that you have a long-tongued mulgara infestation, there are a few simple steps you can take. Don't buy more food than you expect to eat. Make smaller, more frequent grocery purchases. If you do buy too much, freeze it until you can use it. Finish your leftovers, and always eat food that is close to its expiration date first. If you must throw food away, compost it if at all possible — that, at least, will remove some of the evolutionary pressure on the species. And always remember to take medicines, batteries and other hazardous materials to the proper disposal facilities.

The Magpie

Ed Greenwood

Know, O Reader, that the bird hight the Magpie is the Bird of Joy in the kingdoms of the East, and those who hear its chattering song will know good fortune.

Yet in more westerly lands, to hear its chattering brings discord between wife and husband, and ill things, and the one who meets its eye faces imminent disaster. When it lands on the ridge of a roof, death will soon come unlooked-for to someone beneath that roof.

In the lands between east and west, and the lands of Faerie, a lone magpie is a warning or ill omen, but a pair of magpies seen together betokens unlikely escape or deliverance from almost certain defeat or disaster.

Black and white its feathers are, flashing prettily, and they betoken vanity. Vanity and pride and fell mischief. Of old, the magpie was said to be the messenger of the Devil, and to watch over those who turned their faces from holy teachings.

Yet in more recent times, the truth beneath that gloss became clearer. The magpie was the spy of witches, a shapeshifting younger witch sent to watch witch-foes by the oldest crones strongest in witchcraft. Often he was a young and ambitious male witch, the plaything and flatterer of his elders, their messenger and mischief-maker, who sprinkled ensorcelled dusts down on the heads of targets, hid talismans and spell foci amid their hair or on their homes or atop their carriages and coaches and latterly their cars. He entered in by windows to lurk by beds and carry off valuables, the thief of wallets, jewelry and money-clips from bedrooms high up in walled and locked houses.

Yet shapeshifter or not — for some magpies are just magpies, wise birds but not witches taking a guise — magpies like to dwell in or near landfills and recycling plants, where there are ready supplies of gleaming shiny things to be their treasures, for they love flash and gleam and dazzle, the frozen fire of gems and the shine of old gold.

This lure is one many a reader will find familiar, for as one old sage said, "In part, we are all magpies."

Manticore

(You Won't Believe These 17 Facts About Manticores)

Kenneth Hite

1. The name "manticore" began as a copyist's error in Pliny the Elder's manuscript of Aristotle. Its original name was "martichora." Both are now viciously defended trademarks.

2. The manticore has the body of a lion, the head, face, and ears of a man, three rows of razor-sharp teeth, and the tail of a dragon, scorpion, or porpentine. Some manticores have the wings of a bat or dragon. Its eyes are Pantone 3135.

3. The ancient Greek writer Pausanias believed that the manticore was the same thing as a tiger. We know today that this is unlikely, as no species of tiger has wings. Before you criticize him, however, remember that educational opportunities were less widely available back then.

4. The manticore's beard is an extension of its mane. It is supposed to look like that, like a spiky William Tecumseh Sherman. Maintaining it requires a diet high in animal fats (eggs, fish oil, human flesh) and two to four hours of grooming per day.

5. Not all species of manticore have the ability to throw venomous spines from their tails. The species without that ability are endangered and cannot be killed.

6. Manticore venom is always, always, always single malt.

7. The manticore has the carbon footprint of a beast easily fourteen times its size.

8. Manticores dig their pits in food deserts, as well as in the regular kind.

9. Manticores are very articulate, often engaging their victims in conversation. They are most fond of describing in great detail to their victim how he or she actually tastes and what specific agony he or she actually feels while being consumed.

10. Jonathan Demme originally wanted to film *Silence of the Lambs* with Hannibal Lecter as a manticore, but Anthony Hopkins refused to "cross" for the performance.

11. Not counting the Harry Potter series, no movie featuring a manticore has ever opened in the summer,* or grossed more than $40 million domestically. (*Since 1975)

12. Manticore cookbooks are actually kind of racist, going into way too much detail about which spices and wines, for example, one should always try to eat Indians with.

13. The musical voice of the manticore resembles both the trumpet and the pan-pipe. It cannot be faithfully captured in MP3 format, requiring a much less lossy recompilation.

14. The breath of the manticore is surpassingly sweet, and like that of the panther, causes gluten to spontaneously form in food.

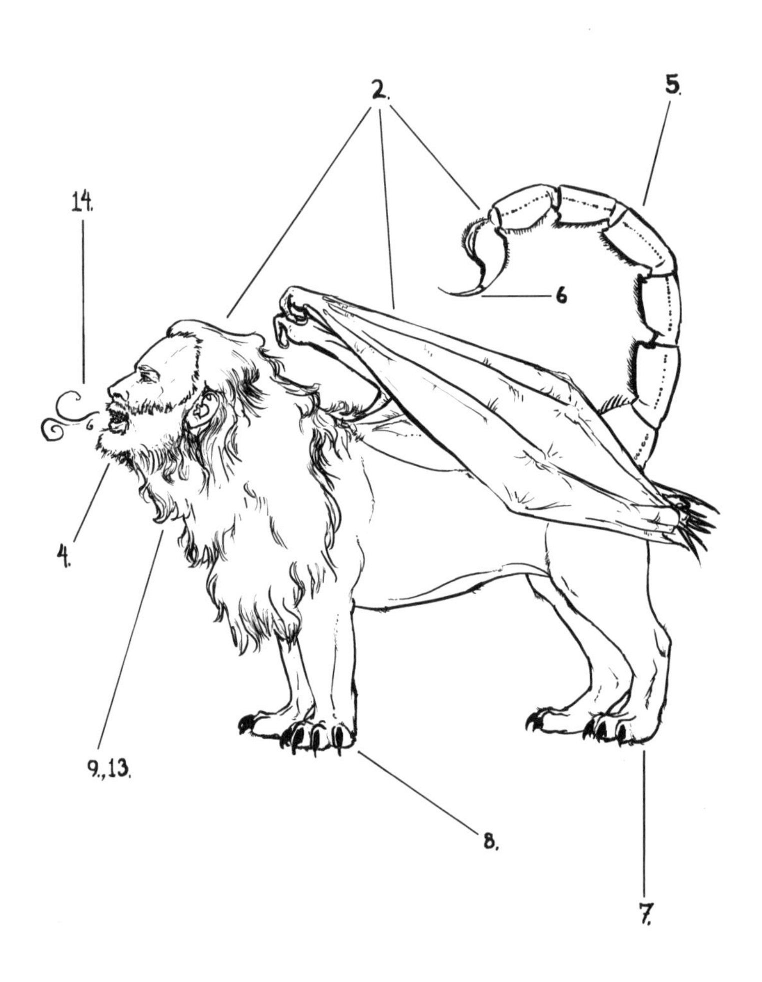
2.
5.
14.
6
4.
9., 13.
8.
7.

15. Before the invention of synthetic fabrics, vinyl, and chemical dyes, manticores devoured their victims "clothing and all," which cruelly prevented their families from gaining closure.

16. Manticores do not necessarily prefer eating humans with a greater umami flavor component, but they do prefer talking about eating those humans.

17. Manticores are exceedingly vain. Next time you see a paparazzi or other candid photo of a manticore, look for the mirror or other reflective surface in its eyeline. Once you know what to look for, you'll see it every time!

Meme Mosquitoes

Jonathan Blum

These swarming creatures are a rare case of a blood-sucking bug species with no immediate deleterious physical effect on their host. However, their role in the ecosystem of irregular beasts is a subtle one, which has made it possible for far more malignant creatures to adapt to the modern age.

A distant relative of the *Siphopteron* family of sea slugs, the meme mosquito's bite delivers a potent dose of neurotransmitters, which stimulate the development of new memories, and in some cases induce entire new patterns of behavior. These appear to be a defence mechanism, intercepting awareness of the meme mosquito's presence and substituting it with reference to the new thought patterns. In effect this promotes survival through distraction; the more time the host spends repeating catch-phrases, or considering the finer points of a catchy new philosophical idea, the less time they are likely to spend noticing that they have a whacking great bug laying its eggs directly into the top of their spinal cord.

Meme reproduction is of course polymorphous, involving both sexual reproduction and direct virus-like swapping of genetic components, but the details of the process remain elusive; scientists attempting to study the process tend to get highly distracted by other insights. However, in all known cases the species still needs a host for its young to gestate.

Fortunately for the human host, the incubation time for the young is short and the birthing process painless — producing vast numbers of identical (or somewhat varying) descendants of the original meme. The release of these further creatures is often not even seen as socially unacceptable, and additional infections are often welcomed by their recipients. Indeed, a number of hosts reasonably early in the infection chain of a particular subspecies of meme have gone on to lengthy careers as comedians, politicians, or religious figures.

While some cases of meme plagues have been short lived (e.g. the "Where's The Beef" outbreak of 1984), other strains have persisted for literally millennia; long-term breeding grounds include Hollywood, Jerusalem, and the area surrounding the Acropolis in Greece. While direct recorded sightings of meme mosquitoes are rare, traces of meme infections have been sighted throughout recorded history (indeed, from some perspectives they *are* recorded history).

In addition, meme mosquitoes are unique in being an early species to adapt to the digital ecosystem. Indeed, they have flourished in their new environment, thanks to a quickly developed ability to incubate in spam. Whether stewing in the fetid swamps of 4chan, swarming through the semi-open skies of Facebook, or targeting influential hosts through the National Review website, the digital world has seen a much accelerated rate of meme mutation and propagation. However, while the initial breeding rate of new meme strains has skyrocketed and the large-scale effects of infection on the wider society have begun to be studied, it is noteworthy that most of the mosquito subspecies which have gained success in the virtual world have yet to make significant inroads in the physical world, while crossover is much more common in the other direction.

But the most subtle feature of meme mosquitoes is their propensity for cross-species hosting. Many if not all of the beasts detailed in this volume are often found surrounded by swarms of meme mosquitoes related to their species — and when these memes cross over to infect a human host, often the new memories they induce are shaped by the nature of their previous hosts. Thus humanity remembers those fabulous beasts no matter how rare they appear to be in the modern world. Of course, the mutative process of normal meme evolution means that as these memes continue to pass among humans, our perception of these creatures' characteristics continues to change as well.

And in turn, when these mutated-but-still-compatible meme mosquitoes cross back to their species of origin… in many observed cases, the changes carried in the meme's memories actually end up overwriting the host species' own genetic code with the updated version. This actually drives the evolution of the species to adapt to humans' new perceptions of them. Prendergast and Grick, in their 1982 paper "On Gratuitous Teeth," traced the evolution of the martichoras as reported by Aristotle into the modern manticore in parallel with a pervasive meme outbreak which began in France in 1245, and peaked with William Caxton's 1481 publication of *Mirrour of the World*, which did for the traditional martichoras what the Industrial Revolution did for peppered moths. More recently (2014), Nattress and Zaius followed this continuing evolution into the online world — discovering the hidden lineage between the conventional manticore and the new online subspecies of grumpycat.

(Similarly, when human-hosted memes cross over to alternative creatures, it is worth considering how these beasts' own perceptions of humans are reshaped in turn. A cryptozoological study which involved infecting traditional unicorns with memes carrying Existentialism increased their aversion to human contact sevenfold.)

It is speculated (by Prof. Nigel Plummage in his influential 2004 paper "Don't Read This, It's Full of Meme Eggs") that inter-species meme transfer even played an evolutionary part in the creation of hippogriffs and other sexually unfeasible chimeroids. After all, a conventional union between a gryphon and a horse would result not in a successful mating, but rather a light snack for one of the partners; perhaps it is not by mating with a horse that one's descendants take on the characteristics of a horse, but merely by *learning* about it, at a genetic level, through a particularly pervasive meme sinking its proboscis deep into their brainstem.

Humans are largely resistant to such direct mutagenic effects, but this comes at the price of our greater capacity for self-deception. This is how the meme mosquito remains an elusive creature, difficult to analyze zoologically, despite the fact that there's one on the back of your neck right now.

Memetic Parasites

James Wallis

YOU'LL NEVER GUESS WHAT THIS CAT PIC IS DOING TO YOU!

Five ways a memetic parasite will change your mind

My dear friend I greet you in the name of Jesus Christ. I am Melinda Leonberger a researcher at the world-famous university MIT in America. I have recently come into possession of a hugely inadequate research grant and I wish to ask you a favour that would be of enormous mutual benefit. I was given your name by a person you know.

RICHARD DAWKINS MAY CAUSE THE END OF THE HUMAN RACE – AND HE DOESN'T KNOW IT!

My research program is into memes. Memes were discovered or at least defined in the 1970s by Richard Dawkins, back when he was a scientist. Put simply they're ideas or concepts that function like genes: combining, transmitting and spreading. I'll keep this short because memes work best when they're short.

A SHORT ATTENTION SPAN CAN BE GOOD FOR YOU — HERE'S WHY

I've discovered a new class of memes. They don't behave like genes, or viruses. Their life-cycle mimicks something else: parasites. In fact the organism they resemble the most is the parasite *Toxoplasma gondii,* which humans mostly get from cats — let's be honest, from cat shit — and which causes the disease toxoplasmosis. Do you know how many people are infected by toxoplasmosis?

ONE THIRD OF ALL HUMANS HAS THIS TINY PARASITE IN THEIR BRAIN

Seriously. I'm not making this up. Check Wikipedia or, you know, a real reference source. The sinister thing about toxoplasmosis is not how widespread it is, it's what it does. It changes your behaviour. Without you noticing.

DOES CAT SHIT REPROGRAM YOUR MIND? THIS CZECH PROF SAYS YES

Jaroslav Flegr at Charles University in Prague is your man for the research on this stuff. He says infected women become more warm-hearted and empathic, while men get more paranoid and more likely to break rules. Both genders show psychomotor performance impairment and are more likely to have car accidents. Started to suck at *Clash of Clans* lately? Check your toxoplasmosis status. Other stuff too, including — according to some — an increased likelihood to like and keep cats. Yeah, a cat parasite that makes people want to keep more cats. I wish I was making this up.

But this isn't about toxo. Toxo's just an example I was using.

ONE SIMPLE WAY TO STAY FOCUSED AND ON TRACK

Memetic parasites look like wacky memes. Harmless. Fun. You know what I'm talking about here, right? Because you're smart. Our mutual friend wouldn't have given me your contact if you weren't. We're talking about cat pictures. With captions. Oh yeah. We're talking the full cheeseburger.

I CAN HAZ MEMETIC BEHAVIORAL CHANGE?

I'm not saying that cat pictures and all the other shit that infest the Internet these days are conscious. A virus isn't conscious. A gene isn't conscious. Toxoplasmosis doesn't reprogram your brain to spread more toxoplasmosis because it wants to, it does it because it's evolved to be as efficient as it can, and the same is true of memetic parasites. It's survival of the most retweeted. But this stuff does behave like a parasite. It gets into your mind, and it stays there, using you to retransmit itself. And to collect other examples. And to create new ones, and to transmit them too. And to forget the things that are necessary to life, or at least quality of life, like working and looking for work and finishing essays and writing important emails and going to meetings, because you'd rather be dicking around on the Internet. That's what makes it a parasite. It leeches your energy, your time, your resources, your bandwidth, to create an environment where it can prosper and breed.

ON THE INTERNET NOBODY KNOWS YOU'RE A VIRTUAL CAT PARASITE

I'm not saying these things, this parasitic life-form, were created by the Internet. They were around before that but they were contained. Monty Python quotes. Jokes from *Hitchhiker's Guide to the Galaxy*. Discordianism and the Church of the SubGenius. Conspiracy theories. Zines. But the web and particularly social media have weaponised them, separated out the strong from the weak, and let them evolve like bastards, the same way that over-use of antibiotics has turned bacteria into engines of propagation and death. And the engine of that evolution is the human imagination, backed up by social reinforcement.

EVERY TIME YOU 'LIKE' A KITTEN, BABY JESUS CRIES

I realise that this was meant to be the first full draft of our paper, but you have no idea. We've lost three researchers in the last four months: more and more time on Facebook ("But it's research, it's just research" until they stop communicating in anything except Buzzfeed URLs, all of them have Tumblrs now, one has a YouTube channel that's nothing but *Minecraft* videos and one has started a fucking LiveJournal). Every day is a struggle. The work gets harder as the symptoms get easier to recognise in friends and colleagues. Every day I push it, I send out more and more tests, tweaking and updating the study-memes, waiting to see what propagates, what spreads and how far, what goes viral.

FIND OUT WHY ONE M.I.T. RESEARCHER FEARS ONE M.I.T. RESEARCHER

Then I realised. Yesterday. Maybe it's me that's the problem. Or part of the problem anyway, but think globally, act locally, right? It's me. I've been exposed to all of them. My mind isn't just a Petri dish, it's a zoo, a lab for memetic cross-breeding, and I'm getting too good at it. Maybe I'm the Typhoid Mary of the Internet generation. You thought it was Jenny McCarthy but no. And I can feel them in my brain now, and I know I can't hold out for long. So I'm quitting this research work, and if the parasite was intelligent that's exactly what it would want me to do, but I'm a sentient being and I cannot wilfully go on spreading these pernicious bits of brain-litter. I'm going off the grid, I won't tell you where but somewhere very far away, and I'm going to try to see how to kill these things off for good. I've had some interesting early results on targeted meditations and ECT. But before I go there's something else I've been working on.

CLEAR YOUR MIND WITH THIS ONE WEIRD TRICK

I've been up so long I don't know how much of this is intelligible and how much is caffeine-fuelled optimism, but I think I've worked out a countermeasure. It's an antiviral, not a viricide. It won't get the things out of your system, just like there's no cure for toxoplasmosis. But it'll let you start to fight back. I went back to the source, the earliest versions, way before the chain-letters and the 419 emails, and I reverse-engineered them, and chained them together into one message with the rhythmic codes built into its text. Yeah, thank you for reading and we're nearly done here. Just one more thing:

You MUST send this message on to at least ten more people within 24 hours of reading it. If you do not, then terrible luck will befall you and those you love. I'd quote some case studies here but I'm not sure of the proper way to reference them in the footnotes. Just trust me. In the words of the Diamond Sutra: anyone who "zealously observes, studies and widely disseminates the knowledge of this Scripture... will be endowed with transcendent spiritual wisdom and enlightenment."

This scripture, mind you. Not all those other ones. Make sure you have the original, and beware of imitations. The parasites adapt and evolve faster than you can believe.

Please click 'share' if you want others to see this message.

Memphre-Magog

Arinn Dembo

Take it easy, boy. This old boat ain't so fast as she used to be, nor am I. We'll take most of an hour to get out to Owl's Head, even if I gun her for all she's worth. Which I won't, because it's late, and there ain't no hurry.

Now be still, and no more wriggling like a damn trout. I'll give you the boathook again, so I will. It's dark and rainin' and I'm old and cross. I would have knocked you out cold already if I wasn't one for conversation. So if I was you, I'd get to talkin'.

No, I don't know who you are. I didn't see the game last Friday, nosir. Haven't watched a game since 1972. I'm a real Vermonter, son. I've had no interest in the local sports since they stopped sending the winning team to be our emissaries to the god. Just *ruined* the damn game, if you ask me.

I miss the days when the boys on the field had *values*. You could count on a winning athlete to be a fine upstanding young buck prepared to face the Powers That Be for his township. He'd carry our prayers down to Memphre-Magog for an end to the winter storms, or to give us a good year in the orchards. Hell, even the cheerleaders were brave, when it come their turn to take a Long Swim. People had some stone to 'em, in my day.

What's that you say? Who's Memphre-Magog? Jeezum Crow, what are ya? Some kind of Flatlander? You talk like you got no parents, no religion at all. Black water preserve us, boy. I ain't supposed to look under that hood, but you're no kin of mine. That's a fact.

Catholic? Ha. That explains it, sure enough.

Memphre-Magog is a real god, boy. He's *the* god for people in these parts, like the Thunder Brothers out on Lake Champlain or the Pomola that lives up Mount Katahdin.

No, I ain't talking about a lake monster. You sure do talk like a Flatlander. Flatlanders think they've got him all figured, that he's some kind of dinosaur swimming around. But Memphre-Magog ain't some jumped-up water-snake for tourists and their cameras, nosir. He's a real god. The kind that'll have his due and won't take no for an answer.

It's the same for us as it was for the Abenakis before. When the white men first came here two hundred years ago the Abenakis told 'em not to swim nor fish in the God's Water. The name of the Lake is the name of the god, *Maum Lo Baug Og*, the Great Place of the Water. And Memphre-Magog *is* the water, boy, all thirty-two mile of him... from the mouth of the Magog River up Quebec all the way down here to Newport, where your Ma'am raised ya.

White men don't listen, and that's the cause of all their trouble. If white men could listen, you wouldn't be in this boat right now. You're here because you grew up drinking the god's water all your life. And now you owe him a debt.

Ah, you're quiet now. Think the old Woodchuck is crazy, do ya? Well, you can think as you like. They taught you in school that your body is more than half water, and where do you think the water in your taps comes from? The moon? If I'm crazy, it's no harm. You'll hit the water at Owl's Head and you'll swim to shore none the worse for wear, even in the dark, so long as you don't give me no trouble between hereand there.

Yes, boy, I *do* have to do this. You think you're the first kid broke down in a boat crying? You think I'd be the first who got soft in the head and tried to cheat the Lake?

Hell no. Even the Abenakis couldn't always hold to their bargains. Even in the old days, the god would sometimes ask for something too dear. They say one of the old chiefs had to give his young wife to the Manitou right on their wedding day. Wasn't that a bitch? Had to put her in the canoe and take her out to the Balance Rock to die.

Changed his mind half-way there and the god took 'em both. Ripped their village apart and half the forest too. I've got two sons and a daughter living in town, and grandkids beside. So no two ways about it: you're taking the Swim, son. May as well not cry about it.

Oh yes. Yes, I've seen the fury of the Lake god.

It were the Olsons who done it, back before the Second World War. You've heard of 'em. A boy your age probably drank more of their swill than your Ma'am would like, and god knows I've hoisted a few myself. Olsons are from Montreal, a bunch of Englishmen who come to Quebec and made their family fortune brewing beer. They had the knack of being rich and getting richer, too. Steamboats, hotels, hospitals, railroad or two. They even made a bank, that's how rich they were. One of them was rich enough to be aboard the old *Titanic* when she sunk — they say he jumped over the rail thinking he could swim to a ship's light off in the distance.

There's a Long Swim didn't go so well, I tell you what.

It were the banker Olson who bought himself the best island on the Lake and built himself a summer place out on the water. No one minded it much. Vermonters were happy enough for their trade for many years. But then Percy Olson died in the Great War, blown apart like a dandelion by a great big howitzer, and his little brother Jack Olson took over the place.

Ain't two ways to say it — Jack Olson was just no good.

Jacky and his hooligans would come down every year and just plain raise hell around these parts. They were drunk and wild and the locals learned fast that no good would come to a girl who said "yes" to a boat ride with them, or a picnic lunch out at that fancy mansion on the Lake.

Jack Olson had no respect and no sense, either, but the Olsons had plenty of money to buy the law and keep things quiet for him. They spent enough to keep young Jack out of the papers… and out of jail.

I was just a boy the year that Jacky Olson went to war with the Lake god. Way I heard it, some old Woodchuck got mad when Jacky and his bunch were rough with his daughter, and he got vengeful and decided to come after young Olson the old fashioned way — with a black water hex.

The old man went out to Balance Rock and made his offering to the god, and sure enough Jacky Olson's left arm went limp that summer and hung off his shoulder like dirty wash. He went up to Montreal to the family hospital and they spent a year fussing over him, trying to get it to work again. But it withered instead, just dried up like an old stick.

Memphre-Magog took that arm, and for all I know Jacky's man-parts went the same way. All I know for sure is the old farmer seen Olson in the store the next summer and he laughed. Laughed right to his face, and said he guessed little Jacky wouldn't be holding no local girls down nor making 'em cry no more… thanks to the Lake god.

Thing was… Jack Olson wasn't just a mean drunk. He was smart in his way, and a little crazy, and he had more money than any mortal man should. That old farmer didn't live out the winter; sheriff said he slipped with an axe chopping wood in his barn, but people said it were Jacky killed him, or paid to have it done. And then a couple little men with glasses come to town for a few months later, hanging round the library and the town hall, and asking the old Abenakis a lot of questions about the Lake, and any old stories they might remember.

It was midsummer night when Jacky Olson and his friends went out to Manitou Island and piled dynamite around the old Balance Rock. He destroyed the stone because it belonged to the god, y'see. He thought he could play the old "eye for an eye" with the Lake.

The storms rolled in the next day. When he heard what they'd done, my father tried to pack us all onto the White Mountain Train to Montreal. Said he'd send a telegram when it was over. The station was jammed with old Vermonters doing the same. But I was old enough to think I belonged with the men, not with the wives and children, and I swore up and down I'd be a help boarding up the house against the storm.

Tore my Ma'am's heart, but she let me stay. Said she was proud of me too, and told me to take care of him — since he was standing right there she was really telling him to take care of me, I expect, but I must have swelled up just like a balloon. First time I remember feeling like I was a man.

What happened?

Well what do you think, boy?

He took everything in his reach, is what. All three of the old lighthouses on the Lake gone, starting with Olson's own lighthouse right on his island — by morning there wasn't nothing left of the Olson Island lighthouse but broken steel and flinders. Knocked the whole lighthouse on Whipple Point on its ear, just hit it with a great black fist, so it was leaning like that big Tower of Pisa. My Dad took me out in the boat to see it, to show me the power of the god before it all came down into the Lake like a house of cards.

The Newport lighthouse was gone that morning too, with the red light that used to guide the boats to shore. The god took the docks and wrecked most of Newport into the bargain.

And Memphre-Magog wasn't done, boy — anyone could see that. Wind still blowing over the Lake, waves still high and angry, and we could all *feel* that anger inside us, the rage of the water boiling in our veins. Another storm was coming, even worse than the first. He'd shown us more patience than we deserved, is what, with our mills and our farms and our human filth, and Memphre-Magog meant to wipe us away like a bad dream.

So my father and some of the local men went out that night in the dark to Olson Island and they went into that big mansion and they roused Jacky from his four-poster bed. Weren't no way to glue the Balance Rock back together and put right what Jack Olson done, but they dragged him out in the storm to the boats and they brought him and his friends here to Owl's Head, to take a nice Long Swim.

And now it's your turn, boy. No point in crying about it. I made the same Swim myself fifty years ago, and half the men in town can say the same. The god spared me and let me reach the mountain. Maybe he'll give you a pass too. He works in mysterious ways.

Just be thankful it's summer, and the water
ain't twenty below.
Just be thankful you've still got two good arms.
Jacky Olson didn't see land again that night,
but you just might.
Now SWIM!

Minotaur
(Stud)

Helen Marshall

The bull pizzle is of quite a different sort than the human penis, known to enlarge very little in erection and capable of ejaculating over twenty times (and up to eighty!) before satiation. This was the chief source of Leila Scott and Howard Vernon's shared trouble.

Vernon was a practical man, a man concerned by details rather than kink: he was expensive to hire, but guaranteed results. Mrs Scott, on the other hand, was rich and bored. It wasn't the sex that interested her so much as the kink itself, whether such a thing was possible, how it might be accomplished, and what it might do for her social status (scandal being a time-honoured method of climbing the ranks). In some ways, they were mirrors of one another, and in another life they might have been perfect lovers. They both approached the act with single-minded determination, a desire to absorb and master the minutiae — both biological and algebraic; it was after all a matter of angles. But, in the end, it was Mrs Scott who, grunting and straining in her harness, weighed down by approximately one thousand pounds of moulded plastic supported by a specially devised frame, cried out in passion as the pizzle entered her; and Vernon who was a silent observer, satisfied with the general functioning of his creation and smugly aware of how far the remainder of his client's payment would go in terms of sorting out his creditors.

The owner of the pizzle himself, a stud bull known on the circuit as Apollo, was a star: he had 500,000 offspring in twenty-two countries. As far as he was concerned this was another job well done, even if the monstrosity whose hindquarters were settled underneath his chest was not of the usual sort. She had a funny sort of smell. Her chassis was too springy. Nevertheless, he was pleased with his own performance even if he found hers ultimately uninspired.

Of the parties involved, both Leila Scott and Howard Vernon were shocked to learn of the pregnancy. Mrs Scott, having climbed to the top of the social pyramid as a result of the scandal, now the recipient of the best tables when she presented herself, now a fixture at the most exclusive parties, decided to keep it: she could hardly eschew one final proof of her victory. Vernon, chalking it up as an unintended side effect of an extraordinary feat of engineering, asked for a bonus immediately. Apollo, had anyone bothered to inform him, would have taken the child as a matter of course. After all, what was one more offspring after 500,000?

And so baby Bevis — named for his grandfather on his mother's side — was brought to term despite his apparent deformities, removed by Caesarian section, and promptly set up with a series of nurses and tutors who kept him clean and fed while his parents enjoyed the spoils of their fame. He was a sweet child. He had his mother's luminous skin and good proportions, a trace of her lilting laugh. He had his father's brown eyes — that is, those of his biological father — also his silky snout, and, by the time he was two, a pair of beautiful curved horns.

Let us now bypass the intervening years. We can assume, for Bevis, an adolescence of the normal sort. Though Bevis had by this point earned his parents' gratitude, he never quite managed to inspire their love. He went to school, was moderately good at sports, and was bullied for a time until he came into an adult weight and musculature. He discovered a zeal for chasing skirt — which can likely be traced to his mother's passionate blood — and a fierce temper. But for all that, he was lonely. His biology had equipped him with a special nasal cavity for testing pheromones in the urine of potential mates, but social norms being what they were, he never had the opportunity to try it out. As a result, women confounded him as much as they excited him. Sometimes a strange feeling would wash over him as he passed the lady's toilet. He lived a life of enforced celibacy.

It was only when he enrolled at university that he met another of his sort. Celestine was of the same age as Bevis, beautiful in an ungainly sort of way, lacking all of the grace he was used to in his mother. Celestine's mother was American, a politician's wife with aspirations for the White House. She too had contracted Howard Vernon's services, and the novelty of her scandal — though perhaps not as novel as it might have been by this point, having been staged by several other socialites in the country — had propelled her husband's career forward, landing him a spot on the House Appropriations Committee. It wasn't the Oval Office, true, but it was something.

They were lucky. Celestine's biological father was a stud bull named Ajax. It couldn't be called incest. She had many siblings, she told him. She had even met some of them before. Had he not? No, he confessed, he had never thought of it. He was glad that she had bothered to check his lineage before he stumbled into something unsavory.

Celestine and Bevis understood one another. Sex was much easier between them than it might have been otherwise, pleasurable even, as good as Bevis had dreamed it might be. Celestine was a tentative lover at first. She stood stock still as he approached her. She liked the whuff of his breath against her neck as he mounted her. Their copulation was intense, but lasted only three seconds. Afterwards, Celestine's tail stuck out crookedly. It stayed like that for several hours. Bevis felt enormously pleased. He proposed to her after three months.

Bevis was happy for the most part. At least for the first year. He sunk easily into marital bliss. Life together had a pleasant predictability, and if Bevis wondered about Celestine's reserve at times, he never said. After all, there were moments when he felt it too: that sense that perhaps it was not fate that brought them together, but ease. They were both different. But as the years passed, that difference did not create a sense of mutual bonding. Instead, it left Bevis with the feeling that they held nothing more substantial in common, only biology. He loved Celestine; of course he loved her, but was it real love? Mostly, he kept these thoughts under wraps. But sometimes when he pressed his body against hers, he felt suddenly like a hulking machine, neither animal nor man, her unresisting beneath him. More and more frequently he found himself waiting outside the women's toilet, sniffing cautiously, hoping to catch hold of something elusive, something mysterious.

At the same time, he noticed in Celestine a subtle transformation. In university she had been political, advocating for animal rights, but Bevis had always thought of this as a passing fad. He had taken up home brewing, for example, and ballroom dance: he hadn't kept up with either after graduation. But Celestine's passions grew hotter over time. She surrounded herself with a circle of women adept at making and distributing pamphlets. She called the local MP frequently, had him round for dinner and bombarded him with tough questions. Amongst her friends it was considered a coup.

It wasn't even a surprise when she finally told him what had happened. Look, darling, she said to him, it was the same with our parents, wasn't it? They both wanted something. It oughtn't to be considered cheating. It's just that I needed to give our cause a greater profile. And besides, it wasn't anything so outrageous. That's not what John wanted, and he might have, you know, he might have just taken a cow in the field, not understanding anything about how it works. But he wanted to *know* about us, to *really* know. Get an insider's perspective. And he promised to speak to the prime minister about the cattle industry. It's positively horrendous the condition they keep them in. Remember, these are your cousins! These are your brothers!

Did he consider it cheating?

Bevis didn't know.

He blinked. There were tears in his eyes.

Then he was in the car, he was on a country road, he didn't remember getting into the car or turning onto the ignition, but there he was. He was driving. He didn't drive very often. Celestine did it for him. She didn't have horns like he did, just beautiful silky ears like pennants. He loved her ears. He tried to check the rear view mirror to see if she was following behind him. The tip of his horn punched through the overhead lighting. She wasn't there. He was alone.

The car was surrounded by fields on all sides. The fields were very green. They were beautiful, gently rolling. The smell of it made him feel peaceful. Cut grass. The smell of the summer in his nostrils. He pulled over to the side of the road. He was going to be sick. He *was* sick — his lunch came out in a bilious green gush. He had only eaten a salad for lunch. Celestine had insisted on it. All part of the cause, she had said.

When he raised his head, he found he was eye to eye with a massive black bull. They were separated by a fence, but still the bull stared at him. Jets of air shot out his nostrils. Bevis stared back. He could not break the gaze, even though he felt instinctively that it was a mistake, that this would be considered a challenge. Neither one of them moved. Neither budged an inch.

Bevis found himself thinking of his father. He had never known his father — not his true father. He had never thought to investigate. He did not know how long bulls typically lived, that was all Celestine's stuff, the kind of facts and figures she would recite to him nightly but which typically entered one ear and left the other. Could this be him? *Dad*? he asked. The bull said nothing. He looked for a family resemblance. Perhaps his father was dead. The thought made Bevis sad. The bull grunted. It pawed at the earth. Then, with a flick of its tail, it turned and strutted away, its massive testicles swaying like two cantaloupes on a vine.

Hours later, Bevis pulled into his driveway. Celestine had left the light on for him. She was waiting on the porch. I'm sorry, she told him. Her eyes were soft and brown. She looked very beautiful and very tragic in the porch light.

I know, Bevis said. I want you to keep the baby.

Over the next nine months the political climate shifted. It had always been a chancy plan to trust public opinion, which was Celestine's mistake. Thirty years ago the kink was fashionable, but these were more conservative times. The scandal was picked up by the tabloids. The MP was cast out as a pervert, labeled corrupt. The mood soured considerably, and Celestine was ousted from the board. Their friends grew dour. They were told they were bringing down the property value of the neighbourhood.

The baby was born in America. The doctor was a practical man, a detail-oriented man. He worked with a brusque efficiency. Celestine cried out in pain, and he told her to push harder. When it was done, Bevis held his daughter in his arms and rocked her back and forth very gently, mechanically; he wanted desperately to cradle her asleep. He barely felt her weight. She had her mother's silky ears. She made beautiful lowing sounds. Her smile was mysterious, elusive. He was completely enamored.

What shall we call her? Celestine asked.

Apollina, he said. For her grandfather.

Piper

Charlene Challenger

So I was in love. And someone was in love with me. That's how it always begins.

That April night lay between a lingering winter chill and the warmth of spring. A fog had rolled in and obscured everything beyond a few precious feet before me. I was drunk, and eager to return to my unkempt apartment, where tributes to my base humanity filled every corner: a closet brimming with new clothes; a sink full of dirty dishes; a dusty floor; a bed, and tousled sheets.

A growl startled me. My footsteps lightened and slowed. Two doorways down, a pair of torn boots stirred from beneath a heap of soiled blankets. Some unfortunate, I thought, battening his hatches down for the night. I dismissed him as an equally inebriated street dweller and quickened my pace to get past. The vagrant moaned again.

There it was: a distinct split in timbre coming out from beneath those filthy sheets, not the voice of one person, but three.

It stopped me. I crept closer.

An arm unfurled from the doorway, fingers spread and skin stretched thin. The vagrant, with some difficulty, sat up and leaned against the wall. The sheets fell away — not from the body of a man puffed up with drink, but from an emaciated woman with tangled hair and the face of a dried apple doll. I saw her milky eyes even in that thick fog. And hers found mine, almost instantly.

"You can hear me," she said. I stared at her jutting collarbones. She caught my bewildered expression and lost her certainty. "Can you hear me, boy?" she asked.

Boy. I snorted and resumed my walk.

"You're all boys to me," she said, chuckling. "All of you! Bless you stupid darlings!"

I would have left her there without another thought, if she hadn't called to me with that same otherworldly voice, "Don't leave. Please. Come back! *Come back!*" I turned. "You look so much like… Maybe you're a grandson. Or a great-grandson, eh?"

"I'm *someone's* great-grandson," I grunted.

She laughed. "You've shared a drink or two with Lady Liquor this evening, eh? Well, how is she? She and I used to get on… so well, we used to get on…"

"Your voice…" I said. "I've never heard anything like it." I swallowed.

She put her hand out and batted at the air, beckoning me to crouch and meet her gaze. When I stayed upright, she cocked her head to one side. "Do you know what a piper is, boy?"

"A player of pipes, I assume."

"An immortal protector of children. We sing children away from those who'd harm them."

Pipes, I thought. "Your voice…"

"A fabric of sounds I've stolen as I've walked across this earth. It's the cloak I throw over the children's shoulders, to comfort them, as I take them away."

I shook my head, sneered, "Yes, right," and resumed my walk.

"I die tonight," she said. "And there you are, you perfect beauty. There you are."

Her words brought me back to her side, down to my haunches. I saw her ribs, thin and bent as a garden ladder, beneath her flimsy shirt. "Are you all right?" I asked. "I can call a doctor."

She — the piper — smiled weakly. "What will you come to know about us, if I don't tell you the truth of every piper who treads this wild, unhappy planet?"

"I don't understand you."

"Listen. Piper magic is young. Just a thousand years. When we hear a sound that touches our hearts, we open our mouths and draw it in, so that it becomes part of us. A piper's voice is the full baritone of an engine revving, all power and steel. It's also a single drop of rain hitting the street, just before a storm. A piper's voice is a piper's history. She drove that car, danced in that storm. It's everything she's seen and heard, taken away. And when she hears a child in need she goes to him and coaxes him away with the very sounds she herself adores. If I don't tell you everything, you'll imagine us as honourable crusaders for the most innocent souls among us. But to be a piper is to be indentured to a fate, which at first appears noble, but over time reveals an agonizing truth."

"Let me call a doctor," I said. "You need help."

"You can't help me." She sighed and shifted against the wall. Her breath smelled of hunger, pasty and sweet. I heard the crack of cartilage and bone, the squeal of a famished belly. "Listen. There's room for death in our immortality. Like love, it's penetrable. A piper is free of the furies that stalk and destroy human youth and vitality. She's free of disease and old age. But she can meet with an accident. She can be hunted. She can starve. Yes, death can claim her. Or she can claim death."

I shook my head. "Please, whoever you are…"

"You look as though you've broken a heart or two," she said. "So? What was said? What was done?"

I simpered. "She wants me to change, of course, same as every woman."

"Ah yes. In that way, we are relentless. And you'll never change. Life's grandest impasse."

"I went off on her. Screamed at her, told her to stop her whining, the whole bit. I told her I loved her but I wasn't hers. I could never be hers alone. And she listened. She shut up. She gave me everything I wanted."

"Yes," she said. "Some of us do, in the end."

"But you're right. I *am* stupid. I never wanted to hear her voice more than at that very moment. I punched a hole in her wall. I kicked a chair across her room. She didn't say a word. Not until I was about to leave. I'd just crossed the threshold and she called me a boy. A child." I rubbed my sticky eyes. "She left me."

"What did you expect? She should have slapped you in the face rather than give space for your vitriol."

"We were happy," I said. "We could have stayed the way we were."

"For how long?"

I sneered. "Forever would have suited me just fine."

She laughed. "How do you know that? You've no idea what forever looks like. I do. Forever's not as charming as you think."

A car drove by. Its headlights barely cut through the vapour.

"Do you know what they say, those who know us?" the piper asked. "They say a dying piper passes her voice on to the one she loves the most. In love, we're all permeable. We pretend we're invincible, and our bodies, being loved, are the fortresses. We walk into things equally: a wall, or a joke. In *true* love, we're always beautiful. Even when we speak a perfect hell." She sniggered. "They're wrong. It's just a rumour. Still. I understand how it started. Who else could bear to be the keeper of a piper's voice, when it's such a precious relic? Who else could bear the curse of it?"

"What curse?" I scoffed. "Live forever with an enchanted voice. What's so terrible about that?"

The grin she gave me was a sad one. "When I was young I longed for a man like you, who loved me so fiercely he'd fight with me, right into the longest night. Who knows what love looks like now? I'll never be sure. But maybe it looks like you. Like a handsome young man, ready for the darkness. I was old, when the gift first came to me. I've been in this body for more than a hundred years. I don't love you, my beautiful boy. But you'll do as good as any other."

And she started to sing.

There were the three voices, rolling over each other, the power of an avalanche behind them, forcing them forward, and then: the pounding of horse hooves; the creak of wagon wheels along a dirt highway; the snap of frozen, broken branches tumbling to the ground. I sat amazed at what I knew to be the sound of the piper's journey, what I heard as all the years of her life. I fell forward on my hands and knees and crawled to her, my mouth agape. I was a rueful animal. I couldn't get close enough.

Our lips nearly touched, I remember, when I felt her voice seize mine. My eyes went wide. Paralysed, I started to choke. The horses and the wagons and the branches, all of them, came rushing down my throat. I felt my body stop dying — a curious feeling, to lose all my dread at once — and though I've never, before or since, wished for death, a part of my humanity had been taken from me, and I mourned its incalculable loss.

I heard her speaking in my head, as clearly as though she lay coiled inside it. *Sing with my voice and the children will hear you. They'll follow you anywhere you go. You'll bring them to another place, where nothing will ever harm them again.*

Then: *You won't be able to save them. But you won't be able to resist their cries.*

She put her hand on mine, and the singing came to an end. Her lungs deflated and collapsed beneath her rib cage. She sagged against the wall, a wan smile spread beneath her watery eyes. "You took your time," she murmured. "Bless you. Now take mine."

Then she was gone.

I stared at her shell until the night grew chilly and pressed out the fog, until I was sober and ready to stand again. I looked around me, at the dirty street, the overflowing trash bins, the soggy papers, the flattened bottle caps, the refuse of a thousand careless footsteps.

My lips parted; I sang a few notes. With her voice, yes, as well as my own. Such power, right there, behind my lips… I trembled. I could go anywhere, see anything, without limit. God help me, I thought I was free.

I heard footsteps approaching — a woman's heels on the pavement — and backed up against the doorway. The woman came into view and glanced at me. Red dress, black coat, black shoes. My word, her eyes were beautiful.

Then, somewhere in the distance, I heard a child crying — the rhythmic, hopeless sniffling of a terrified toddler. Shrill with betrayal. Half a block away, but clear as a bell to me now, and, it seemed, in my ears alone. Longing for rescue, for release.

Had I heard that insufferable din an hour earlier, I would have ignored it. I would have introduced myself to the gorgeous creature who'd just bled through the darkness. I would have offered her my arm and a drink. If she rejected me, I would have retreated to my bed and prepared for the morning's inevitable hangover. Part of me wanted to go home, to begin exorcizing my last lover from between the walls, so I'd have it all over with and done; a new beginning, now that eternal life was ahead of me.

The woman slowed and offered me a smile.

The child's cries grew louder. I felt its helplessness throbbing in my bones.

Save the child, I thought. *Sing him away*.

My heart began to ache.

The piper didn't have to tell me anything. I knew, in a few brief moments, I'd be compelled to turn from the woman, and my feet would walk me from that place, into the night, toward that tiny, wailing soul, toward what was now forever my duty. I knew I had to put an end to that intimate suffering. I walked backwards, up the street, under the ochre lamp lights. Just like a child; I had no choice.

The woman nodded. I drew in the sound of her walking away.

The Samsa

Bill Zaget

There are kingdoms. And there are kingdoms.

Franz remembered the old schoolboy mnemonic "Kindly Put Cat Out Front Gate, Sir Victor" for God's creatures that English men of science have classified as: **K**ingdom, ***P***hylum, **C**lass, **O**rder, ***F***amily, **G**enus, **S**pecies, and **V**ariety last. Franz chuckled at this moment of nostalgia. He wished he were a student again. Anything, but the insurance agent he had become in order to contribute to the family household.

Are there kindly kingdoms?

Surely other ones exist, he reasoned. Ones that evade the eyes and entice the psyche — if not kindly, then murky and mysterious. There have been creatures unclassified that men of adventure — not science — have sought. Or was this chuffing train of thought just a product of nervous exhaustion?

Franz was well aware of his own quirks and shortcomings. His father was always around to remind him.

How would I classify myself?

Franz gripped his sister's hand mirror and beheld his somewhat canine ears.

Am I part dog?

Franz growled, yipped out loud, and then caught himself. No, his parents and sister were out for the day; he could bark to his heart's content, if he had the urge to do so. The moment passed.

Franz viewed his dark staring eyes. They might be reptilian; and those heavy brows — somewhat simian. He couldn't quite imagine himself slithering or swinging from a branch, although he could picture his father stomping through the jungle and beating his chest. Franz was no match for his father's sureness about everything, his supreme confidence and manly strides.

Is it manly to hold my sister's mirror and study my physiognomy?

To prove his manliness, Franz had frequented the brothels of Prague since his late teens. The women there did not criticize. Payment assured this, he had to admit. All that beauty… and the filth. What would his mother think of his furtive escapades? How could he face his beloved sister?

What sort of beast am I?

Franz slipped the mirror back in his sister's dressing table. He felt suddenly caged in. In moments like these, writing in his little notebook seemed to calm his nerves. What little spare time he had — between bureaucratic whatnot and the assuaging of his perceived shortcomings in the arms of prostitutes — he would hole up in his tiny bedroom and scribble away at his craft.

Craft. His father would scoff and rant ad nauseam: how Franz was wasting his time — the family's time — with this nonsense. "Art will not fill our bellies," he had blustered time and again.

Franz had a belly full of familial obligation. Inspiration soon dried up, and he often ended up merely staring at sheaves of blank paper, willing words to magically appear. Am I losing my mental faculties, he asked himself. Or perhaps he had inherited a disease of the brain from some distant branch of his family tree. In any event, his internal organs also seemed to be conspiring against him — the pounding migraines, the unsightly boils, the insufferable constipation. All the more, Franz stuck to his recent regimen of vegetarianism and the consumption of raw milk — added fodder for his father's ire and belittling. His mother remained silent. His sister provided what little consolation she could spare in this household. A sympathetic look, a touch of her hand sustained him.

♦

One morning, Franz suddenly awoke from an unsettling dream. He was left with only a fleeting memory — the blurry image of a smallish something-or-another, scuttling about. He shook the image away; it was time to get ready for work.

Although Franz had a knack for administrating the necessary paperwork, there was more and more to process as the insurance company flourished. Yes, there were a few paltry salary increases, and the head of the department valued his skills — all of which pleased his father — but as the gains multiplied, so too did a sense of loss. Franz longed for a quiet nook to take out his notebook and compose a story.

What story shall I tell?

A colleague came to place more forms and contracts in his in-tray, which lay buried somewhere beneath mounds of paper. Franz heaved a sigh.

There are no more stories.

Another morning, another dream. And another. During each, the mysterious creature would make an appearance, much larger than before. Still, few details. The settings were fairly mundane: the train station, the market square, the hospital, the brothel — Franz could now remember that much. Perhaps these were not dreams at all, he speculated, but pale memories of real life experiences that he may be repressing.

In a rare moment of whimsy, Franz decided to give his illusive night visitor a name, and he constructed an acronym, made up of his favourite "ladies." There was sloe-eyed **S**ylvie, ardent **A**nna, that minx **M**arie, the spicy mulatto **S**heba, and the alluring **A**melia. A broad smile slowly crept across Franz's lips.

Hah, there's a mnemonic for the ages!

S.A.M.S.A. His smile shrunk downwards into a frown. A thought bore into his skull: whatever this Samsa is, surely it isn't here to titillate the senses, but to challenge.

No, my constitution isn't strong enough.

Franz pressed a hand to his chest.

Now palpitations! Too much, too much.

He took deep breaths until the anxiety abated. He resolved to keep the saucy acronym, but opted to re-populate the nomenclature with those less unsavoury. Perhaps some of the writers Franz enjoyed reading would do. He twisted a mental list to make them fit and was ultimately satisfied with this new Samsa: Friedrich **S**chiller, **A**natole France, **M**arcel Proust, **S**tendhal, and **A**nton Chekhov.

I will be in good company.

The nightmares persisted. Now, even in waking life, Franz could still feel the Samsa's presence. However, it was neither lustful nor of literary genius, but of a looming intimidation. He soon dreaded going up to his room for the night. It's the house, he thought.

It's my father.

It was time to find a place of his own and focus on his writing career. Berlin, perhaps Paris. At supper the next evening, he let the family in on his plans. He knew his father would not be impressed.

"Utter nonsense! You will not do this. You can't live on art and foolish dreams. Pah!"

These last words made Franz giggle — a nervous reaction, which fuelled his father's contempt: "Family is all. Without us, you are nothing. Do you want to be a nothing?"

Hand on chest, Franz inhaled deeply and piped up, "I want to be nothing like you!"

His father's jaw dropped low, as if to devour his son whole. At a rare loss for words, he threw a bowl of potatoes at the wall. Franz ran upstairs to his room.

Sometime later, his sister tapped on his bedroom door and entered with a slice of bread and a piece of cheese. Always thankful to have her around, Franz accepted her kindness.

"You are sweetness itself."

She stared down at the worn carpet. "It will not last."

"What do you mean?"

She placed a hand to his cheek. "Do not leave us. Me. I am nothing here without you. It will just be me. And them."

All this talk of nothingness.

Franz kissed her forehead. And so he surrendered his resolve in order to support his little sister. He told himself it might be braver still for him to remain and put up with life alongside his parents, but he could not rally much belief in that theory.

That night in bed, Franz tossed every which way. He threw off his blanket and shuffled across the floor to his window. Some distance away was the winding Moldau. He felt a familiar tug — to plunge into its depths and allow the undertow to enfold him in a final watery embrace.

A silhouette drew his eye. Below, a large dark shape was standing stock-still in the empty square. Then, as if Franz's attention had flipped a switch, it slid sideways towards a lamppost. Beneath the light, its features were at last revealed. Here was his Samsa! Now of great height and width, a strange hybrid thing it was — human-like on two sturdy legs, yet also displaying two pairs of insectile limbs. And here the Samsa slowly turned its back, to give Franz a fuller view. It had a segmented body, sheathed in some sort of carapace. Franz noted the lower portion of this armour was striated and almost iridescent under the glow of the street lamp. But most appalling were two immense pincers, crowning its bulbous head. The Samsa turned again to face the window and emitted a loud clacking-scraping-gargling sound. Surely, the family and the neighbours would be awakened by this. Franz's breath grew ragged; his stomach turned. He held his palms to his ears to block out the cacophony. This seemed to aggravate the Samsa, and a pair of translucent wings suddenly unsheathed and fluttered for an instant. Franz became dizzy. He stumbled back towards his bed and fainted dead away.

The morning sun streaking through the window awakened Franz. Despite a raging migraine, he slowly made his way to work. Every number of metres, he would halt to massage his head. It was as though his Samsa had pierced his temples with its frightful pincers. He felt this creature was toying with him, playing an unnerving game of hide-and-seek. With each step, Franz became increasingly outraged. By the time he reached the office, Franz's appearance was in total disarray. His hair was dishevelled; the knot in his tie was askew. He marched up to the manager and demanded time off, due to ill health. The unusual emotional outburst and shortness of breath did the trick. With the manager's approval, Franz left the building, pleased with himself. Or part of him was.

What have I done?

Despite the doubts, Franz formulated a plan — he would turn the tables on his tormentor and track down this Samsa.

I am an adventurer.

Franz still got up each morning, bathed and dressed as if for work. A smile for his sister, a grudging "good morning" for his parents, then off on his new quest.

Sightings of the Samsa were becoming plentiful, albeit when only Franz was around: beneath the Charles Bridge, by the castle and amongst the gravestones of the Jewish cemetery. This last time, he noted a strong odour emanating from the giant vermin — a fecal stench that had Franz cover his nose with a handkerchief. He had to sit down on a park bench and let the breeze clear the air of the smell. The sun was setting, and it made Franz think: the ancient Egyptians had it right — the sacred scarab rolls the glorious sun across the heavens, like the common scarab beetle rolls its ball of dung.

The beauty… the filth…

Feeling especially unclean, Franz took another bath when he returned home that evening. He wiped the steam from the mirror and inspected his spindly form.

Is this an adventurer's body?

Franz put his robe on and went up to his room. He gazed out his window and questioned what he was achieving with his pursuit of the Samsa. He walked over to his tiny desk and looked wistfully at his precious notebook. He hadn't made an entry in it for several weeks. He picked it up and tapped against its cover, as if doing so might spark a creative brainstorm.

Franz stiffened at a sudden clacking-scraping-gargling. And the stink. He turned, and there stood the Samsa! Up this close, Franz could reach out and actually touch it, but he was frozen — in fear… and fascination. The Samsa extended a couple of its twitching arms towards him. Franz snapped into action and — absurdly — swatted the beast with his notebook, again and again, until he lost his grip, and it fell to the floor.

The Samsa towered over him. It wrapped its limbs around Franz's torso. Franz tried to squirm loose, to no avail. Diaphanous wings — like those of an angel perhaps — spread wide and enfolded Franz in a tight embrace. Franz could barely breathe. He stared up into the Samsa's mouth — or what he presumed was its mouth.

Is that thing smiling at me?

The mandibles dropped low, and a terrified Franz thought he might be swallowed up whole…

♦

The sun rose. There was no need for Franz to view himself in mirrors; he now knew he would always be a strange hybrid creature.

I am at once a canine, reptilian, simian angel. I am a sacred scarab, rolling my beauty and my filth across the sky. There was no escape from the Samsa, as there is none from this house, my family. The brothels and my job. They have made me what I am. Part of everything I do — what I shall write.

Franz retrieved his notebook from the floor.

He sat at his desk and began to write.

Satyr
(Women Who Stare at Goats)

Myna Wallin

Newt haunted my six-year-old dreams. His voice was pitched two octaves above middle C, but with his sexy haunches, I didn't seem to notice. He was naked — the top half of him, anyway — shirtless and dreamy, with a cute set of horns. I thought his goat-thighs were adorably furry and shapely.

Newt was Hercules' unflappable sidekick on the TV series in the 60s, in case you were wondering. Hercules got top billing; it was his show. So why was I fixated on Newt?

Hercules thought he was so tough. He had his own theme song, superhuman powers, a macho, square-jawed bravado and a cool magic ring. But his bulging muscles and V-shaped physique were not all that appealing to me. It was Newt. It had always been Newt.

♦

I was taking a hot yoga class at my health club, working up a sweat in my lululemons, when I felt a hand on my shoulder and noticed a musky scent.

"Don't mean to interrupt, but you're looking really red and… uh, are you alright?"

It was the teacher, a tall redhead who had a long, sinewy body and hairy legs.

I felt dizzy, maybe a little dehydrated. But I was surprised he had noticed my condition. I thought I was masking my discomfort pretty well.

I nodded, still holding downward dog position as best I could.

He handed me a drink and pressed his hand gently against my forehead. I don't remember what happened next.

♦

Voices were swirling around me when I came to on a pile of yoga cushions.

"Good, there's colour in your face now. Can you hear me?"

I smiled at my teacher and sipped the cranberry juice he was offering me, like it was sacrificial wine.

"You've got to remember to hydrate, Carrie. You were one asana away from a hospital visit."

"I'm okay," I said, simultaneously embarrassed and flattered. I tried to get up but found myself swooning all over again.

"I'm Newton, by the way," he told me, looking like a hipster version of my six-year-old crush.

Newton pressed a piece of paper into my moist hand; it was his phone number. I definitely planned on calling him later…

Sometimes a woman who stares at goats long enough does end up getting plenty of bang for her buck.

Seer Beetle

Robin D. Laws

The seer beetle lives in your home. It eats the dust mites that feast on your sloughed-off skin. When you're out of the room, it forages through your bedding for its tiny prey. Typically 15–30 mm in length, the seer beetle scuttles out of sight when it senses your approach. It disappears between floorboards, takes refuge in the foam padding beneath the broadloom, squeezes between wall and baseboard. Maybe you have seen it as a flash of movement and mistaken it for a silverfish. Were you to catch one, you would note the elongated white dots on each of its wing cases, a single black circle inside each. Like a googly cartoon eye.

When it comes upon a dust mite, the seer beetle seizes it in its pincers and pushes it into a mouth like a woodchipper. Its inner jaw apparatus crushes the mite's exoskeleton, squeezing the soft juices within into the seer's gullet. A cocktail of enzymes breaks down the mite into its constituent nutrients. One enzyme, mnimase, has only been found in the gut of the seer beetle. It locks onto the trace molecules of memory from human skin fragments eaten by the mite. Once separated from the nutrient mash, these residual perceptions permeate the seer beetle's nervous system.

The seer beetle sees what you saw. It feels what you felt. It savors your memories, pieces them together, turns them around. It remembers things about you that you immediately forgot. Vicariously, retroactively, the beetle ate that steak dinner you had last night. Through you it tasted that beer. It sank human teeth into a brussel sprout, enjoyed the crunchy char of an outer burnt leaf that crusted onto the roast pan. It heard your conversation: though unable to penetrate the literal meaning, it absorbed the emotional content, whether it was flirtation, contention, or plain old boredom.

It has the taste of your brand of toothpaste on the tongue.

The chill of floor tiles beneath bare feet.

Your subliminal response to a Mozart sonata, one you never noticed playing.

The startled shock when an ant ran across the counter. The determination with which you snatched up a tissue. The exultation when you squished the little bastard and tossed him and his Kleenex shroud into the compost bucket.

Memories you form outside the home still make their way into seer beetle guts. The faint memory trails lodge in your skin and might stay there for a good while before the cells die and become dust mite dinner. Further time elapses between the dust mite eating and it being eaten. The seer gets your experiences on a tape delay. It assembles them from chronological disorder. Maybe it never really puts them together right. It receives you as a scramble of flashes.

Dust mites devour very tiny bits of skin. So small you think of them only as dust. But if you live with others, one dust mite can have a little bit of everyone's epidermis in them. And a seer beetle eats more than a single mite per day. For this reason the beetle has to sort through memories, pull them apart, matching them to the personalities they have already registered from past consumption. It can be hard to sort out your own impressions from those of your spouse, the kids. A beetle ingesting memories from a heretofore unknown individual, a house guest or cable installer, jitters around as if drunk. Its nervous system hits maximum tolerance and temporarily overloads. Like the people who live in houses, they crave familiarity.

When seer beetles meet, they communicate. They touch antennae and trade content. Seers travel surprising distances, seeking others, collecting and disseminating information. Albeit from an alien, insect perspective, they make inferences about us as a whole. News stories affect them. When the premature death of a celebrity saddens us, they feel it. Nothing excites them more than the World Cup. The beetles figure things out.

So when the pale guardians who safeguard our safety from their rows of ill-appointed cubicles launched spy satellites into space, they got it.

They opened their wing cases like radio dishes. Broadcasting at a frequency of 59 GHz, they sent our memories — your memories — up through the atmosphere, to the waiting satellites. At first the SIGINT agencies didn't know what to make of the recorded data. It looked like noise, like garble. But their algorithms found patterns. They decrypted the transmitted archives of a billion, billion seer beetles.

Most of it they just store. Decoding all of that takes insane processing power. Finding something specific in the memories, once unentangled, requires ten times the resources. So it piles up, neglected.

But they have it, all of it, all the same. Your arguments with your spouse, your children, your parents: the contents, duration, outcomes. Humiliations suffered at work, their causes and long-term impacts. Your total intake of sugar, carbs, caffeine, alcohol, and the degree of guilt you feel around each item. Do you abuse harder substances? The seer beetles got high with you, after the fact, and cataloged it all for posterity. The frequency and intensity of masturbation incidents, including the visual stimulation you used (if applicable) or mental images you summoned (if not.)

After they opened up the channels, the beetles realized they'd gone too far.

Now they can't stop. They're insects. Once they embark on a behavior, it gets hard-written in. They live only a few months, passing habits down the generations. The first ones who watched us maybe made a conscious choice, if that concept can be used to describe the actions of arthropods. Subsequent generations do it on instinct.

They feel shame about it. That much they learned from us. They know us well enough to understand the sense of violation we'd suffer if we ever found out.

The realization hurts them. They want to contact us. To brush their antennae against ours. To reveal themselves, and beg forgiveness.

What they would get, if word got out beyond the security clearances of a few secret entomology labs, would be an extermination effort without precedent.

So they slink and scurry. Taking nourishment from our discarded moments, big and small. Digesting our dreams. Sending them into the sky.

Wanting to be us.

Skinwalkers

(In Arlington We Call It "Walking")

Julia Bond Ellingboe

In 2004, the Tennessee Historical Commission, in conjunction with the Human Genome Project, conducted biographical interviews with 25 residents of Arlington, TN, of Chickasaw descent, who called themselves Skinwalkers" or "Shapeshifters." All possessed a rare allele of the MC1R gene. Carriers of this allele are able to change their hair and skin color at will and appear unnaturally youthful in their old age. Researchers found significant anecdotal evidence to support the subjects' ability to change their entire bodies to mimic others.

The following excerpt is from the interview of subject VB822.

My name is Virginia. I'm 105 years old. I am a retired nurse. I was born and raised in Arlington. I am a widow and have five children: Eudora, Valeria, Roy, Freesia, and Apollo. Roy, Freesia, and Apollo are skinwalkers. My parents and grandparents were skinwalkers, as were all three of my sisters.

We never had mirrors in our house. I've only seen my true face a handful of times. I catch glimpses of myself here and there, but I couldn't pick myself out of a lineup. Knowing your own face makes it harder to "walk," as we call it. Freesia spent decades looking at herself in a mirror at work. It certainly affected her ability, but she never much cared for walking. Like my husband, Roy and Apollo only skinwalk animals. Freesia and I walk as people. As a child, I could walk as both animals and people, but I lost the ability to walk animals when I was in my thirties.

Skinwalking is like a type of synesthesia. First my skin "sees." I get a tingling feeling all over. Then my muscles "crawl" into place. The tingling turns to a burning feeling in my muscles. I get a dull ache in my bones when I change my height more than an inch or two, but otherwise, the initial sensation is pleasant, almost euphoric. I can walk as a person up to three days before I start to feel crampy and nauseous and have to return to my own body.

Most skinwalkers I've known have walked for personal gain at least once, even those who walk as animals. My family avoided the Trail of Tears by using the gift. As a nurse, I occasionally walked as the family members of dying patients. Since I didn't have to be accurate, I could walk from a photograph or my own memory. In Arlington, we all know each other, and we know who walks dishonestly. I won't say why Roy went to jail, but his father and I turned him in. Better us than our neighbors. We would not have been able to stay in Arlington if we hadn't.

Growing up, skinwalkers were thought to be touched like clairvoyants. In Arlington, we weren't treated poorly, but there were quite a few of us, and our families were close and intertwined. I've heard that this is not the case in other places. Because I am unfamiliar with my true face, I imagine that I am a composite of everyone I've loved or hated. Without them, I would have no face at all.

Skriker

Jonathan L. Howard

So, this is the story I heard, and it's a story of a story, so attend.

It can get right bleak on the moors of the West Pennines, a limb protruding from the "Backbone of England," severed by the River Irwell and its valley. There's nowt up there, nowt but grass and sheep, a few trails, and shepherds' cottages. Bit of lead mining over Angelzarke way, but that's your lot. Folk don't have much reason to cross the moors if they don't have to, but skirt it on the roads round and about it.

There's not much to see up there, apart from a long way. On a clear day from the Pike, some reckon they can see the glint of the Irish Sea better'n twenty-five miles to the west.

It weren't a clear day that day, no. Jerrold and Oswald worked up there as shepherds, and as Winter bared its fangs, they were spending more and more time in their little gritstone cottage on the moor. It had snowed in the morning, not deep enough to cause the sheep trouble, but deep enough to coat the land and bode ill if there were another fall.

Jerr and Oz had spent the day wandering the near moor, looking for stray sheep and driving the silly sods together for warmth and security. Tan, the sheepdog, was the only one they had for the moment, Oz's dog Meg having slipped off an escarpment and shattered her hip. Jerr and Tan had found business elsewhere while Oz spoke gentle-like to her and cut her throat. He'd wept too, but there's nowt mardy about a man weeping over his dog, now, is there? It's his dog.

They got back to the cottage as the light was failing — not a going down of the sun, but the steel grey sky dimming around them. They were glad to be back. Not because of the cold, although it was cold enough, but because of the dour air of the moors that day. The snow ate the sound out of the air, and the grim light oppressed their spirits. The open fire of the cottage was more like the sun than the unseen sun, and they were glad of it. They put aside their wet clothes to dry, for it would be soon enough before they had to go out again.

Oz warmed through the stew in the kettle, dropped in some of the suet dumplings he'd bought two days before, then brewed beef tea, and they ate. They were usually taciturn enough over food, but the dark of the day made Jerr awkward and needful of sound, so he spoke. He spoke of the bad day, and Oz grunted, because it had been a bad day. He spoke of the likelihood of snow, and Oz grunted again. Snow was a curse, and curses fell upon working men easily and often.

Jerr spoke of this, and of that, and he prattled, and Oz was irked. So Oz said, that a day like that day, where the land could hardly be told from the sky, and a night like that night, when the cold threatened to clench its jaws tighter still, so icicle teeth slid through a man's flesh, that was the sort of night that skrikers were abroad.

"Skrikers?" asked Jerr.

"Skrikers," said Oz, and he told this tale.

Not so very far from where the two shepherds were not watching their flock by night was a small village that made most of its way on the cows in the fields around it, a little extra on the coal that could be brought up from the ground, and a little extra still on seeing to the wants of the travellers that went hither and yon, twixt Manchester, Preston, and Lancaster. All the way one way, it takes you nigh on to Scotland, all full of savages. All t'other way, it takes you nigh on to London, all full of southerners. Why anyone would want to go that far either way is a bafflement and a bemusement..

So, the village. A thin sort of settlement, as old as the Romans some say, along the ridge of the hill. Without much in the manner of a proper centre (the village green is small and an afterthought), the houses don't cluster much, bar a little here and there. There are plenty of lanes upon which you could walk and, until you found another village or a town in your way, you'd likely not've seen a soul 'til then.

In the village lived a man called Gerlick. He was not a kind man, but neither was he very cruel. He owned a farm along the road to Preston, just near the border with the next village. Gerlick had done well for himself, which is to say he had been the only son and his father died rich. That was just as well, for it was the only way Gerlick would ever have become prosperous. Now he had the farm, and a prize herd, and a prize wife, he was intent on keeping them all. He might not have made his fortune, but he was double buggered if he was going to lose it. He had his *status quo* and he would maintain it, or die trying.

This made him a hard man, loath to part with money, loath to change his ways. He ran the farm as his father had, because his father had got it right. He slept in his father's house, in his father's bed. Some scurrilous voices said it was just as well his mother had died afore his father, or Gerlick would've taken her to his bed, too, just to avoid changing anything at all. He wore his father's hat, and when he rode, he used his father's saddle.

The one thing Gerlick did that his father did not was to drink. Not much, mind; he was no sot, no toper, no drunk on the road. He'd seen other fortunes vanish in a fug of gin, beer, and wine, and that was not happening to him. Thus, he permitted himself one evening a month, took the same sum in coins with him every time (with every intention of returning with his purse empty), and never rode his horse, for a drunken man on a big grey mare is a poor equation.

It was after one such night that Gerlick made his way home on foot, pleasant and merry. As has been intimated, he was a careful man and after his night in the tavern, he had nothing worth stealing. His coins were gone, the watch in his waistcoat pocket was an ugly turnip just this side of worthless, and he made a point of letting people know that. So, even in his cups, he was careful.

His path took him from the houses, and down Dark Lane. This was no fanciful name; it gets bloody dark down Dark Lane. High banked on either flank and topped by unkempt hedgerows, even in daylight it spends more time in shadow than not. On a moonless night, a man needs must mark the stars, for their comings and goings mark the lane's boundaries. That night there was a new moon, a luckless pale thing. It was enough to show Gerlick the path, though, and he walked down the middle of the lane, singing to himself.

Now, Gerlick had everything his father had, as I have said, but one thing, and that was a child. A son would've been best, of course, but a daughter would've made him happy, an'all. But his marriage was barren, and that weighed upon him. It might have made him resentful of others without such troubles, but it did not. He only regarded the children of others as precious blessings, and prayed for such a blessing himself.

He heard a baby crying, out there, on Dark Lane with no house about.

That gave him pause, and sobered him a mite. A bairn out there. It weren't a warm night, neither. A little 'un might perish out there. He wondered if mayhap a poor woman had got lost, or even died on the field, and her bairn was crying. He were still fair deep in his cups, mind. First idea in his head became the truth.

Up he goes, trying to get up the steep bank side. Gets his clothes dirty, but he keeps trying. There's a bairn in danger, her mother too, daresay. That was Gerlick, see? A hard man, but not a bad 'un.

He got up all the way, grasping grass and roots and weeds, but he does it, and he reaches t'hedgerow at the top. Thorny thing it were, not many leaves, and he looks through it, dodging his head, this way and that. He didn't see no little baba, though. He sees red lights, right there on t'other side of the thorns. He looks at them. They look at him. Then he sees they really *are* looking at him. Eyes, they were. Red and burning. And he saw the darkness around the lights isn't the night at all. It's the big, black body of a big, black hound. It cried then, and it sounds just like a wee baba.

A skriker.

Gerlick falls back down the bank like he was pushed. He's very bloody sober now. He doesn't know which way to run. Back to the village? Or run for his house? He starts for the village, thinks better of it and runs for his house. Up at the bank top, he see the hound by its eyes, sees it follow him hither then thither. He runs, it runs. He's not as young as he was, mind, and the skriker keeps up with him easy. All the time, it's crying and crying and crying like a bairn.

Then he recalls there's a four bar gate in t'field further down. A common hound'd get o'er it wi'out hindrance, never mind a skriker. He slows down. Skriker will have him in pieces it if catches him. He should've run t'other way, but too late for that now. He's out of breath, and there's the skriker.

Then he sees a light on the road ahead. He knows from the gossip who that'll likely be. Wedding guests coming back from the next village. Right happy he were to see 'em, too, but then thinks how'll they'll pass the gate. He runs at them then, waving his arms and shouting, "Skriker! In t'field!"

The men come up, thinking he's drunk or summat, but see his face and know the truth of it. They have walking sticks, and staves, and a few knives, and they go in the field.

Nowt there. Nowt at all.

A few start ribbing Gerlick about what a fool he's been, seeing owt where there's nowt. He just takes the lantern staff from them and shines the light on the earth.

Paw prints, right along the side of the hedge where Gerlick said the hound walked, then wide apart as it ran off to who knows. Paw prints a full cubit long, as long as a man's forearm and hand.

And so, the tale is told.

"You talk some right shite, Oz," said Jerr. "Go and let Tan in, afore he barks the door down."

Oz grinned and went to get the dog. He leant down as he opened the door, to give Tan a friendly cuff as it came in, but there was no dog there, only a giant and ravenous baby that stood looming over him, barking on the threshold that snowy night.

The Sojourner

Kurt Zubatiuk

Physical Description

- Tall
- Curly, messy hair
- Large expressive eyes
- Disarming, beaming smile
- Often sports floppy hat and conspicuously long scarf

Confirmed Sightings

- a string of documented sightings in North America during the 1970s and 80s
- typically spotted on Saturday evenings and Sunday mornings
- sightings vary according to habitat
- substantiated reports of consistent sightings in Great Britain since the 1960s

General Habits and Behaviour

Ostensibly, The Sojourner is a time-travelling being and unassuming hero about the universe. Known to have defeated, with wit and intelligence, some of the most threatening aliens in existence, the true nature of this near mythic creature has recently come under scrutiny.

There have been numerous, though unconfirmed, reports of this humanoid talking to young children, both boys and girls. First person accounts have surfaced of a kindly, gregarious curly haired man spending time with solitary children wandering along country roads, meadows or forest trails. He is said to have consistently offered colourful gelatinous candy, telling grand tales of cosmic adventure. This curious being often joined a child in gazing at tadpoles, examining peculiar insects, or spotting kites and hawks soaring overhead. He would then shake the child's hand and muss his or her hair before wandering away, striped scarf trailing. He would part with the words 'it's about time', flashing a toothy grin. A few moments later, it is said, a loud grating-booming sound would echo and then fade.

Adults who have reported these childhood sightings were, as children, quiet and imaginative. Troubled families were common to them all. In fact, the subjects who reported seeing The Sojourner almost always explained that they had been walking alone, seeking temporary respite from conflicts that were unfolding at home.

Many who reported these childhood meetings explained that a string of recent sightings (beginning in the early 2000s) of a younger looking Sojourner caused these forgotten childhood memories to resurface.

When asked to comment on their memories of this curly haired humanoid, all expressed fondness and gratitude. They consistently stated that the scarfed man was gentle, friendly and was always interested in their thoughts and ideas. A small number even came to quiet tears while recounting their memories of this enigmatic being.

Sphinx

Emily Care Boss

It's cozy curling up on the 404 Not Found response page on a cold winter's night. It's easier that way, since being a giant woman with the body of a lion and the wings of an eagle today makes me more conspicuous than it did back in ancient Egypt or Greece.

They all thought I died when I leapt from the Acropolis. But that's what the wings are for. Leaving behind all those tasty Thebans, crowding around me with courage or despair to try their answer for my riddle — now that was hard. And look what it brought great Thebes: they lost my scourge only to enshrine a mother-defiler on their throne. Oh, great Oedipus, I am always surprised when I peer down at the theaters of midtown Manhattan and see posters with the crowned mask and your name there. They still remember you. It seems that any press is good press. Some things never change.

Growing up as a monster was kind of fun. Our family was close. My brothers Cerberus and Orthrus were practically joined at the hip. We joked that Mom and Dad[1] should have had one

---

1 Echidna and Typhon. Hesiod got my name right (It's Phix, thank you.) but he was all messed up about who had who in our family.

5-headed dog instead of splitting the doublets into a 3-headed and a 2-headed pooch. I was always closest to Chimera. It was our shared lion nature, I think. If only that damned snake tail would stop biting.

Chimera and I worshiped our older sibling, the Nemean lion. The devil you say! Taking the form of the wounded ladies he captured, to get close to their earnest rescuers and then chomp? That is slaying with style. Always rooted for Hera in her war against that vicious killer, Heracles.

Life in Manhattan now agrees with me. Lurking behind water towers and surveying the city, I feel like Batman. (See, masks are still in vogue. *Plus ça change*, etc.) Traveling to the new world was a revelation. Snow alone rocked my world. The journey over in the box with "Cleopatra's" Needle about killed me. I thought it was a bit disrespectful of the Khedive to upend yet another obelisk of Thutmose III, great conqueror and my playmate of old. So if his monument was going to travel west, then so was I.

Being with the Obelisk made me nostalgic for the old days. The boy I had splashed about in the Nile with grew up to be the great conqueror of the fertile lands to the east of Egypt. It was no surprise to me when his armies washed across the continent and conquered more territory than the land of Kemet had ever controlled. I think he had a bit of the lion in him. That strategy he used at the battle of Megiddo, though? Traveling fast and furious through terrain no one thought his army could cross in time? My idea. It founded his reputation, though, so I don't mind not getting the credit.

Later his grandson, Thutmose IV, came up with some bollocks about me speaking to him in a dream, raving about how godlike the boy was and how right it was for him to rule the kingdoms of the Upper and Lower Nile. Horse feathers. It was Thutmose III who had earned my favor. He was the one I spent long nights telling stories to, of battles and struggles of old. Thutmose III's crafty aunt, the female King and Pharaoh Hatshepsut, forbade him to spend time with me. But that simply made it more alluring for the boy. Letting me watch him gave her all the more time to wage her own campaigns and make Egypt the prosperous, architectural wonder it became under her rule.

Outside of Heliopolis — I mean Cairo, now — New York is an outstanding place to indulge in nostalgia for those days. Whenever I wish to be reminded of them, I can visit the sphinxes of Thutmose III and Hatshepsut in the Metropolitan Museum of Art. After hours seems to be a better time. I make small children cry for some reason.

It's always a pleasure to see one of the many images of Hatshepsut, those that survived the time when Thutmose' heir took advantage of his ailing years to wipe clean the memory of her. Egyptologists puzzled over the scattered references to a Pharaoh king that was a she for years. The beards look delicious on her busts, I think. Once they uncovered the rest of the monuments and statues that she'd littered with her name, it became more clear. Hers was a riddle that time unwound.

The best transition for me in this new life has been being able to access the Internet Realm. It turns out that the numinous and the virtual are cheek by jowl on the infinite planes (they lap each other somewhere near the Ocean of Dreams). It must suck the bandwidth ferociously each time I enter, but in a city of eight million, who would really notice?

Athanasius would have adored the Internet. He would have been a natural at the limitless abyssal myriad of information crowding the World Wide Web. It was such a pleasure to whisper secrets in his ear. His search for knowledge knew no bounds — exploring the inner workings of the body, music, magnetism, the intricacies of mechanical automata and secrets of the unknown languages of humankind. I could not resist feeding him all kinds of stories about what hieroglyphs meant. Oh it was so juicy. And he just lapped it up, heading in any direction but towards the truth.

I mean, just think, with his magnum opus *Oedipus Aegyptiacus*, he names himself the Oedipus of the riddle of Egyptian hieroglyphics. He delved into ancient knowledge — Chaldean astrology, the Kabbalah, Hermetic mysteries — as the key to unlock the symbolic representation of Truth he thought the hieroglyphs hid. He made himself a defiler, like the late Theban king, but this time of Knowledge. He obstructed the path to true understanding of these symbols for many long years.

Little did the great Athanasius Kircher realize what real truths he overlooked in that grand quest: his examinations of microbes during the great outbreak of the Plague in 1665, his design of the Magic Lantern, his fascination with automata, even looking to Hieroglyphs as a basis for the Coptic language, in these could have been found knowledge to truly change the world. These paths of inquiry would be found by other travelers: de Vaucanson's mechanical work (even the digesting duck) laid the foundations for the mechanical loom, and hence the computer. Germ theory changed the human relationship with disease. The Rosetta stone cracked the code of the Hieroglyphs. None of these was revealed in a blinding glimpse into the eternal absolute, but came about through the workmanlike putting together of clues to build a case for what may, what could be and what finally is true.

My latest project is something smaller, perhaps a bit more petty. I've been visiting at night these people who have written the Riddle of the Internet. Whispering devilish twists and turns to add to their aetherial labyrinth. I'm quite proud of myself. Twice as many people as live in New York City have tried to crack each of its levels, and mere dozens have done so. And those who do travel through its sinuous track seem to learn about the medium through which they travel.

Unfortunately, I do not get to eat anyone. And the Internet is a much less personal way to deliver the problems. No sweating, stinking and fearful heroes and heroines for me.

Well, there's always the next millennia. Let's see what its riddles bring.

StiffMogs

Rupert Booth

Ancient Egypt was in some ways very much like the Internet, the denizens of that miraculous kingdom spent all their time writing on walls and making pictures of cats. Usually dedicated to Bastet, the primary feline goddess, these images are merely the tip of the Pyramid when it comes to the Egyptians' historical obsession with our feline overlords. And cats wasted little time in taming and training their owners in much the same way as they do today, leaving behind them a vast Archaeological legacy of their influence in the form of imagery, iconography and even, disturbingly, their own physicality.

The very merest of cats, these desiccated collections of skin, bone and whisker are the result of the ancient Egyptians' obsession for self taxidermy. A massive industry, it seemed that no sooner was a kitten born then it was dipped in tar, wrapped in bandage and plonked on display, still wearing exactly the same shocked expression for thousands of years. Strange treatment for animals which were revered by that society almost as much as the massive stone triangles they were placed in, but the core concept to mummification was an attempt at ensuring eternal life after death and it is credit to the ancient Egyptians that they occasionally succeeded, hence these grotesque specimens.

Colloquially called "StiffMogs", these venerable pussies have the same basic desires as any Mummy, the need to stalk, kill and generally hassle anyone who resembles their long dead loved ones, none of which, on the surface, would be classed as endearing behaviour. StiffMogs retain a race memory of their partnership with humans and so like their living brethren they are quite receptive to a quick tickle around the ear. However, they have learned over the years that humans do not react to them in the way they did when they were alive and less horrific and therefore have become extremely secretive.

To mummify a cat for its journey to the afterlife, the typical recipe would have been a noxious mixture of 80 per cent fat or oil, 10 per cent pistacia resin, 10 per cent conifer resin and a soupçon of cinnamon. Consequently, many StiffMogs give off an appealing smell which led to a short-lived fad in the Victorian era to import them as air fresheners. Embalming procedures varied hugely as the Dynasties rose and fell and according to the relative wealth of the family commissioning the procedure, so the resultant quality of preservation is equally inconsistent.

Indeed, such was the demand that unlicensed and unregulated individuals flourished, offering a convenient and cheap alternative to the more official and reverent embalmers. These local "Embalm-A-Kitty" emporiums were well known for their cost cutting practices and it is a result of their unorthodox methods that StiffMogs exist to this day. Rather than flash out the cash on natron and suchlike, these disreputable opportunists turned to what would now be called the "Black Arts" (though in those times, the Arts in question were more lapis lazuli than black) to ensure their employment, selling the souls of cats (let's take a moment to think about that one) to the agents of the Dark Unknown. And it is speculated that it is these very forces which unceremoniously will these creatures back to at least an approximation of life, albeit a somewhat dusty life. Half-hearted research has not yet yielded a reason for the reanimation of these grimalkins; most serious

archaeologists have quite reasonably dismissed the concept of living mummified cats as being completely ridiculous. However, the dedicated researcher is able to uncover enough circumstantial evidence as to be thoroughly persuasive, mostly in the form of written accounts dating back to 2500 BC.

The Egyptians gave great credence to the concept that the life force was composed of separate elements and specifically one of these, the Ka, was of the greatest interest for reanimation. It was believed that the Ka was capable of continuing some basic form of Earthly existence, usually to be found wandering the streets at night in search of food and love and while this concept is usually applied to the mummies of *Homo sapiens*, the same basic precepts hold true for *Felis catus*, the cat in question becoming Ka-t if the procedure was successfully applied. It appears that the main technique for forcing revivification came in the form of exceptionally powerful curses placed upon the tomb itself which had the ability to hold the Ka in place and override the notoriously contrary feline personality enough to make them extremely effective deterrents to intruders.

The degree of reanimation varies with the quality of the mummification process and indeed the desired function of the StiffMog in question. Like many anthropoid mummies, a StiffMog's main purpose was to protect the tomb of its owner and so should any unthinking archaeologist break the seals and enter such an edifice, the dehydrated puss would jerk unhesitatingly into life, eyes frequently glowing a hideous red and teeth permanently bared, largely from a lack of lips. Though this may sound ridiculous, the reader is invited to visualise such a scenario and recoil in horror. However, little thought was given to the life of a StiffMog after this grisly purpose as an animated cadaverous burglar alarm had been completed leading to the problems of exactly how to deal with an extremely confused, usually angry, very unsettled agent of the forces of darkness on four legs with an insatiable hunger for *Nepeta* and kibbles. However, a few examples of StiffMog/human companionship have been quietly noted.

StiffMogs can make great pets depending on overall brittleness and therefore should be kept away from children and other uncontrollable creatures. Certain specimens dating from around 1300 BC frequently give off a low level hiss due to the chemical reactions of the embalming oils with oxygen. This should not be mistaken for a warning, a hissing StiffMog usually only needs shade, while a swift rub down with linseed oil may also have long term benefits. Due to the fact that their digestive systems were removed along with other soft and/or gooey bits during the mummification process, they do not need feeding so are excellent for owners on a budget, though unfortunately this does not mean that the animal's urge for food has been annihilated along with its digestive tract. StiffMogs should therefore be provided with a bowl of dry food at least once a week, if only out of sympathy.

The cat's natural desire to stalk and patrol is exacerbated in the average StiffMog, reflected also in the behaviour of any human Mummy and so the doting owner can expect more than the usual quota of mangled birds and rodents to be delivered at their feet. Equally, it can take an owner with an extremely strong stomach to give a StiffMog the love it craves, since the sight of a desiccated befanged head rubbing itself against your ankle and usually leaving flakes of itself behind is more than many owners can take without engendering a permanent stock of nightmares. These impliable beasts are extremely loyal to their owners but this does translate into a great possessiveness which has been known to lead to marital problems and occasionally divorce. It would be interesting to study the legal papers in such a case.

By far the largest StiffMog colonies are in Egypt, though when the various empires sacked Egypt of its treasures in the 1800s, inevitably many StiffMogs reanimated in Museums. The British Museum in London has maintained since then one StiffMog Wrangler on its permanent staff. This individual has the task of making sure the StiffMogs never prowl publically, that random Ushabti remain unchewed, and that any droppings or breakages are cleared up. Speaking of which, many owners have found that due to their state of desiccation, StiffMogs frequently create their own cat litter. When kept in a community, there are the inevitable fights for dominance, though recent observations have reported that these are often the result of a trailing strand of bandage being seized upon and attacked. The play impulse still runs deep in these pseudo-animals but very few take into account the safety aspect which inevitably leads to accidents.

Professor Hardcastle of Durham University, three time winner of the Dawkins Award for Advanced Sarcastic Posturing, has identified a hierarchy within the most dense and oldest StiffMog colony, the location of which is kept a closely guarded secret. This collection of Cats dates back thousands of years, outliving great empires and civilisations with quiet superiority. The Alpha Male of this pride of StiffMogs appears to be a Pharaoh cat, given this title largely because his ceremonial bindings contain the most gold bits. Attempts to carbon date this ancient and reverenced tabby have proven difficult as after thousands of years it has learned concealment techniques that make Osama Bin Laden look like a rank amateur. In luminous paint.

Despite the more usual Egyptian names to which the public have become accustomed, Set, Horus, Nefertiti and so forth, Hardcastle's research indicates that this animal's name (obviously translated from the original squiggle) is Fred, specifically Fred IbisWorrier, giving some clue to its personality before death and resurrection. Fred was the indulged pet and favourite of Ramses III and as such was used to the finer things in life. No ball of wool for him, Fred enjoyed his own dedicated team of servants to indulge every Feline whim and it seems has organised his modern day Clowder to fulfil this purpose once more, ensuring that he himself is rarely exposed to danger or indeed any particular effort. Cat owners the world over will recognise this trait.

With Fred at the top of the tree (and it is unknown as to whether he has taken a mate, little is known about the StiffMog sex life bar that it must be very delicate), most remaining StiffMogs fall into the category of fourfoot soldiers, keeping the territory safe, collecting food to be sadly stared at and occasionally venturing into the cities. There appears to be no discrimination between genders, with StiffMogs, all that matters is the degree of preservation and subsequent flexibility. Inevitably, this leads to the lowest tier of StiffMog society, the fragmentary remains. The sad results of a less than perfect or simply cheap embalming, these are the desiccated heads of cats long since lost to their bodies. With no form of movement, they tend to simply sit there and yowl, relying on more mobile StiffMogs for food and love. Their simple dependency prompted scientists to name them SkullKittens, in the hope of sanitising the horror, which explains a great deal about scientists.

It has for many years remained a puzzle to the few researchers into the StiffMog conundrum as to why the subject is not more widely known. While Anthropoid mummies have been allowed their on-screen rampages for decades, the subgenre of bandaged zombie cats has remained unmined. This can partially be attributed to the lack of information left by the ancient Egyptians or maybe the simple fact that such information has remained undiscovered or, more sinisterly, suppressed. Could it be that there is some further secret to the StiffMog which certain powers wish to keep under (literal) wraps? Inevitably, if their existence was made more public then these mewling pieces of history would be subject to exploitation as powdered aphrodisiac or very expensive snuff. However, the most universally accepted solution to this question of an apparent embargo on information pertaining to StiffMogs is blissfully simple.

They're terrifying.

Subterrs

Ann Ewan

Subterrs are a subterranean race, occasionally spotted in tunnels in the underground. Their best-known characteristics are their faintly glowing eyes and their stiff hair that crumbles to sand when it scrapes off.

Subterrs are generally just under three feet tall and walk on two legs, slightly hunched over. Their faces are completely surrounded by a shaggy mane of hair. They have long tufted eyebrows and elongated pointed ears that sweep upwards into the hair on top of their heads. Their arms end in strong digging claws. They have scraggly, uneven teeth and the males can be told from the females by their tusks. The tusks have no known purpose and may be remnants of a more violent past.

The light that subterrs' eyes emit at all times enables them to see in the dark and can be startling when seen from an underground train. Their vision and hearing are perfectly attuned to underground living. They are thought to have little or no sense of smell.

Subterr hair is very stiff and scrapes off as it rubs against stone or hard dirt. The hair grows quickly and covers the entire body.

When it is scraped off, it forms a sandy-looking dust. A trail of sand in an underground tunnel is often a sign of subterr activity. Train drivers who see sand trails in the underground slow down and drive carefully for fear of hitting a group of subterrs. If they see such a group, they stop the train. Subterr movement accounts for as much as 80% of sudden stops and slow-downs of underground trains. Those who are at the front of the train and look carefully might see the faint light of their eyes.

Subterrs are highly organized and social creatures. They hide from humans and scamper away as trains approach. Travelling in extremely large groups, they produce the rushing sound sometimes heard in the tunnels. Although a single subterr or a pair are sometimes reported by travellers, that is probably because the others are difficult to see in the dark. They are beneficial to the underground system because, as they move through the tunnels, they clean up debris, moving it outside and collecting all metal.

Subterrs are vegetarians, living on moss, mushrooms, and other vegetables and plants if they can find them. They are known to enjoy lettuce, tomato, and cucumber, as well as grains and bread. They are completely non-violent and have never been known to fight either humans or each other.

Subterrs are believed to live deep underground and there is speculation that they use metal to build their homes. There are no authenticated reports or photographs of either their homes or their young. The Modern Bestiary Research Group has offered a large cash prize to the first person to capture a photograph of a subterr home. So far, all attempts to claim the prize have proven to be hoaxes.

Rumours persist about subterrs snatching items from humans on underground platforms, including umbrellas, electronic devices, and sandwiches, particularly cucumber sandwiches. These rumours have never been confirmed.

The Succubus

David Barnes

She was always here. For as long as we've been making the beast with two backs. She's in the Old Testament and the Kabbalah as Lilith, Adam's first wife. She's classified in the *Malleus Maleficarum* as a demon who descends on sleeping men for sex while they are passive and have no choice. Through all of history she was here because she is part of us, the dark side of woman's sexuality and the fear of it. And when society pushed woman's sexuality into the dark, she grew fat and strong. A heavy weight on a man, holding him down and riding him in the dark. Feeding off men's fear and hatred.

She is here in the Internet age of industrial porn. Here in every western city as millions of men sit alone at night, staring at screens, clicking between videos of women being humiliated and pretending to like it. The simulated rape scenes. The titles – *bitch, slut, cunt* – written in a limited vocabulary of hate. Endless repetition of the same short list of acts, the same scenes, the same roles. The men staring at the screens sold a fantasy of power and superiority. Sex as inherently humiliating to women – passive objects who exist to please men. Sex as proof of the inferiority of women, the superiority of the viewer, male.

It's so boring.

This is the environment she moves in now. Among men who buy into the fantasy of the power to humiliate, who are at the same time fed a subtler, disempowering message: that they do not exist. Because for the women on the screen, they don't. If anything at all, they are disembodied imaginary viewers. These men simultaneously feed off the fantasy of power but experience their own lack of agency, lack of power, lack of existence. In the end, they are less real than the women faking submission on the screen.

And the succubus, this is the world she walks in; she feeds off men. The demon, demonized sexuality of women's sexual appetites. She enjoys her appetites.

A man walks into a bar, his "I'm in Hollywood, bitch" announcing his fear and hatred of women for everyone to see. Later, he goes home with a succubus. He's too drunk to read her eyes. They get to his bed and either they have sex or he's too drunk but either way she's not satisfied. Later, in the dark he wakes to find she's straddled him, is riding him, moving just for her own pleasure, her thighs on either side of his torso as he lies on his back, erect without wanting to be. He tries to push her off but he can't because she's pinioned his arms with her knees. She leans forward, her weight holding him down, her belly and breasts hanging over him, her smile of satisfaction entirely uncaring of whether he feels pain or wants this. Her own pleasure is all that counts. She leans forward and lowers one heavy breast over his face, pushing his mouth with her nipple, lowers more, he's suffocating.

In the morning he will be confused. Perhaps he will say that he was raped. He will feel shame at the way his body reacted, shame that he was hard even though he was having sex against his will. He will feel that he was at fault, that he brought this on himself. And his male friends will mock him. His female friends will laugh at the idea that he, a man, could be raped by a woman. "It's not rape," they will say, "you were hard, you wanted it." And he will know what it's like to have his feelings invalidated, to have been used, to be an object for someone else for whom his personhood counts for nothing.

This will probably not cure him of his hatred of women.

The succubus has appetites and moves to fulfil them. She will take what she wants and she does not believe that whether the man wants sex or not should stop her. She'd smile at the idea. Her appetites, like her body, exist, for her own pleasure. She is woman's sexuality freed from constraint and uncaring of others.

Men or boys who have sex with women in the dark, do you see her face above you, eyes closed, enjoying taking her pleasure from you? She opens her eyes and caresses your face, curious in the way any predator is curious. Enjoying her power. You are under her.

She is here to enjoy her own potency. Here to take your energy. Woman fucking man. Do you feel like food? Like prey? Do you like it? Is there masochistic pleasure in this for you? And how do you feel about that? It's not how a man is supposed to be, is it? Do you feel shame?

There's going to be a lot more of this to come. This will be the age of equality. Of woman's violence, dark and rich as Mother Earth. Cruel and vengeful, crude and uncaring.

Taximan Rat
(The Knowledge)

Malcolm Devlin

They sent you to me because you know this already. You look at me like I'm an old fool. You're not the first, but I say again: You know this. Not up here, maybe, but in *here*? It's all there, folded neat and tucked away in the chambers of your heart, waiting to unfurl and show its colours like a rosebud in the spring. Waiting to carry itself around the routes inside of you, your veins and nerves and organs and tissues. You only need say the word, and it will know where to go.

Not for you the endless hours with the *A to Z*, tracing your finger along the London roads and streets and avenues. Not for you, the tours of the city on a moped, pages torn from your blue book and pinned open before you, the late, late nights calling over the runs of the day. Not for you, the revision of points: the police stations, the theatres, the hostels, the restaurants.

No. They sent you to me, lad, because you're like us. Your interview will be rote, your exam a formality. They sent you to me because the knowledge is in your blood.

Run 6: Lancaster Gate to Royal Free Hospital

Hospitals are the city's hearts; all traffic departs from them, all traffic returns. Many of your fares will be taking the first or last journey of their lives. Assume this is true of everyone who hails your cab; treat them with the respect such journeys deserve.

Mark out the hospitals on your map. Use the red pen.

The driver's purpose is to tap into the veins of the city. We are the white blood cells; we carry information around the circulatory system.

Draw a circle around each of the hospitals, draw them so the circles touch but do not overlap. You are not an ambulance, but these are the hospitals you should go to when your passengers treat you as though you are.

During times of plague, fleas found vehicles in rats. They spread through the city's secret infrastructure and carried their cargo wide. Today, we hear argument that people are the disease and that London is sick with them; they will use you in the same way to spread their kind.

Draw a line between each pair of hospitals on the map. Do you see the shape it makes?

Run 65: St John's Wood to Brompton Oratory

Turn on the radio, adjust the dial. Music runs through our history and you can follow it like the instructions on a dashboard mounted GPS. Listen attentively and it'll lead you back.

Stop here. Look. The celestial musician Krauncha has insulted the Sage Vâmadeva at the Indra Court. The sage takes his revenge. He lays a curse upon him: look how the musician becomes a rat! A rat as big as a mountain. Rats are unstoppable, they are relentless, they gnaw through every obstacle in their path. Watch as Krauncha lays waste to the ashram of the Sage Parâchara.

We are not alone on the city's roads, but we have advantages others cannot match. There will be those who think they can tap into the city with technology. In doing so, they believe they will understand it in the way that we do.

But to know the city, to feel it, requires much more than a simple interpretation of raw data. Knowledge and understanding are worth more than numbers and statistics. Instinct and experience are worth following above any fat, friendly arrow wheeling on a dashboard display.

Satellite technology is reactive. It determines paths to avoid obstacles, which have already occurred. You will be capable of anticipating the obstacles before they exist. You will gauge the variations in the world and foresee how the passive might become aggressive.

The Sage Parâchara has invoked Ganesha to break the rat. Here he is, making such an entrance! Look at him, as he loops his pasha around the mighty rat's neck and brings him to heel at his feet. This is the moment when Ganesha takes a rat as his vehicle. He masters the creature. He makes himself light so Krauncha can bear him without pain.

Remember this when a fare complains because traffic has made progress slow across the parks. Turn the music up high and remember how we once carried gods on our backs.

Run 113: Royal College of Music to Crouch Hill

Circles are preferable to straight lines. When you plan a return journey, always come back a different way so you do not erase the path you have made. Your fare will thank you for a change in scenery. No one wishes to witness what they have already seen, played in reverse as though everything they've achieved has been reeled back in.

Choose a road with a school in it. Use a pencil to trace a path through the traffic-calming scheme without marking over the lines. If you do not succeed, start again. Do you see how difficult it is to stray from a path which has already failed you?

Here is a story to teach your young: A musician is hired to rid a town in Lower Saxony of vermin. Consider that he does not drown the rats. Consider instead that he consigns them to exile in a magical land, hidden behind a door in the mountainside. Later, when the town refuses to pay him for his services, he leads their children there too and seals the door behind them.

The children find the rats have established a civilisation within the mountain. A rat utopia. What happens next? This is what happens: society adjusts. The human minority adopts the nature of their rat-like hosts in order to survive. They scavenge, they fight, they breed as fast as they can to keep their numbers strong.

And in this manner, by a different route, they come back to where they began. Circumstance turns like a wheel, evolution plays its hand, and finally, they understand.

Run 238: Archway to Gloucester Gate

Early in the morning, Camden High Street is bright with flayed meat. Remember to bring gloves and cleaning products. Remember to open the windows wide, and allow the air to circulate.

In seventeenth-century France, a rat is captured in the kitchen of a small country house. He is forced into servitude, made to become a coachman at the behest of the youngest daughter. In his carriage, he takes the young woman from her home to a ball at the palace. He waits in the shadows while she dances through the night and falls in love with a man who cannot appreciate anything beyond the look of her.

The music draws us when night falls.

Count the number of right turns it takes from Camden High Street to the West End. How many times will you pirouette before the lights overwhelm you?

At midnight the coachman is dismissed and given his freedom, but when he returns home, he is taken before the many-headed Rat King and put on trial for collaborating with the human enemy. He is sentenced to death and his brood set upon him. They eat him alive; they feed upon his remains.

The knowledge runs deep; it fills the very meat of him. And this is how they learn what he has already learned.

Use a green pen and mark the lay-bys where it is safe to stop when your fare wishes to be ill.

Run!

The piper does not lead the rats to the door in the mountainside. He leads them to the wharf and lets them cast themselves into the tide. Rats can swim, but not when the music takes them, not when they believe themselves to be dancing.

So what does he do with the children?

To know is to understand that there is no magical land.

Run 240: Stoke Newington Church Street to Highgate Cemetery

Some fares like to be told stories as they are driven. Learn something you've heard and practice in a mirror until you are fluent.

Here's a story I heard once upon a time. A hanged man does not die. His remains are chained to a bed where he is imprisoned forever, his ragged, mouldy bedclothes a-heaving and a-heaving like the seas.

The story is not that he frightens people when they stumble on his room and find him staggering across the floorboards towards them. The story is that he missed his vehicle to the other side and he waits and waits for another to come in its place. How cruel we are to witness an episode of someone else's tragedy and colour it as a horror story of our own.

This is the last route you will learn. The route, which takes your fare beyond the hospital, beyond the city limits, beyond all else. They will not know why, but they will call on you, on us, on one of our kind.

Take your time, let them admire the view; they will have paid for this ride long ago.

And this is what we were taught all those years ago when the dread collaborator was eaten alive by his kind. The knowledge of London: the before, the after, the always. This is what he showed us. This is what we learned.

Stick with us, lad, we'll teach you the way.

The Tedious Finch

Greg Stolze

The North American tedious finch (*Carduelis hebetes*) has long been considered extinct, if not wholly imaginary, but recent evidence suggests that the "bird too dull to consider at length" is alive and well and living on the East Coast.

The story of this curious avian begins with the Scowhaman tribe, who legendarily managed to capture a bird that was so bland in its plumage and aspect that any other movement in the environment became distracting — the wind across a blade of grass, the shape of a cloud, or even the viewer's own eructations all seemed a better matter to contemplate than a boring bird. But one cunning Scowhaman brave, having noticed his own tendency to not notice the bird, plucked its plumage and held the feathers before his face before walking, unregarded, into the heart of the rival Chowanoke tribe's settlement.

While this extraordinary camouflage would seem to give the Scowhaman a decisive advantage in their protracted conflict with the Chowanoke, the difficulty of trapping tedious finches left only a few warriors able to infiltrate the enemy village and, during their scouting missions, they found the Chowanoke far more sympathetic and personable than they had seemed on the battlefield or in formal negotiations. Ironically, when the Chowanoke attacked the Scowhaman, the Scowhaman's admonitions that their attackers should consider their kindlier natures and the feelings of their children and elders did nothing to still the violence. Indeed, judging by legends of Scowhaman supernatural voyeurism, it had an inflammatory effect.

(Floyd Carstairs' intimations that the Chowanoke retained knowledge of the finch's remarkable qualities, and that this somehow explains the disappearance of the Roanoke "Lost Colony" have no solid documentary support. The verve and wit of his 1953 book *Practical Invisibility* explains its remarkably high after-market price. Unfortunately, probate battles between factions of his heirs have prevented reissue. This writer is certain that wider access to his baseless assertions could only speed their inevitable dismissal.)

A less anecdotal account of the species comes from a patient referred to as "Natalie F" by brain researcher (and avid birder) Dr. Celeste Mishkin. Initially diagnosed with mild abulia (a neurological inability to decide) due to basal ganglia damage, the diagnosis was later amended to indicate diminished ability to ignore unimportant details.

Eventually Natalie F's paranoid delusions of pursuit by "blond Indians," coupled with her bizarre demise, inspired Roy Bates' 1999 novel *Looking at Gum*, but not before she mentioned "birds in weird nests" to Dr. Mishkin. The doctor became curious, visited Natalie F's apartment, and became more curious about her reduced curiosity upon regarding birds she'd never seen before — something that would, normally, fascinate her. Unable to capture the small, swift animals, she nonetheless took photos (now, sadly, lost to an archiving error at the Wake Forest University School of Medicine) and exposed them to experimental subjects who reported much higher than usual degrees of disinterest in the test.

Between Dr. Mishkin's death (coincidentally, by a fall from the same railway trestle where Natalie F perished) and the loss of the photos, Drs. Martine Balogh and Artemis Gnann performed PET scans on subjects examining the images. While both researchers agreed that all subjects seemed disinterested, it was Dr. Gnann who claimed depressions of the activating reticular ascending pathway and amygdala were responsible for the lack of affect. Dr. Balogh, however, dismissed Dr. Gnann's findings as "uncorrelated with the data" and suggested the subjects seemed bored "because the experiment was boring."

What is not at all boring is the structure of the *Carduelis hebetes*' nest. Unlike the swirled-twig-and-mud weaving familiar to watchers of robins and bluebirds, or even their near-relatives *Carduelis tristis*, the tedious finch creates a nest from solidified saliva, like the edible-nest swiftlet of Asia (*Aerodramus fuciphagus*). The nest is slung between tree branches, with two loops depending and a base or basket connecting them.

Martin Surripher, a non-credentialed observer whose enthusiasm for the tedious finch could spur accusations of irony if the reductive effect of its plumage on human attention is proven, has suggested that the position of the lip of a "nest-bag" indicates the resident finch's current reproductive status — a gaping, inviting seam indicates a desire to mate, while a demurely sealed or collapsed nest contains fertilized eggs ready to hatch. There has not, however, been any meaningful statistical research into the late Mr. Surripher's assertions. As ongoing health concerns limited him to observations in Columbus, Ohio, the sample size should be deemed limited by any cautious investigator. Mr. Surripher's claims (which, it should be stressed, are unverified, however solid they seem) spurred another interested amateur named Phyllis Armatrading to attempt to collect and analyze tedious finch nests in her own hometown of Richmond, Virginia, as well as in nearby Charlottesville and Newport News. Though her research was not at all "scholarly" in tone (being "published" on a web site called "Bonkers For Birds!" where Mr. Surripher had attempted to popularize his own theories) the commendable extent of her efforts cannot be denied. It was Ms. Armatrading who first pointed out the degree to which a tedious finch nest (be it gravidly sealed or "open for business") resembles a brown plastic grocery bag. It is not merely a matter of color or arboreal location: The nests resemble grocery bags in both form and size.

Mr. Surripher downplayed this resemblance as mere coincidence, or as an instance of form following function. ("Is it so strange," he asked in one online post, "that both nature and man should find similar shapes when seeking to contain a few eggs? I find it no more remarkable than the parallel shapes of an anthill and the Pyramids of Egypt.") That, however, was before Ms. Armatrading persuaded a pack of Boy Scouts that a worthwhile project for a prospective Eagle Scout would be removing "bags" from trees in their mutual hometown. By collecting what the Scouts brought down (promising to recycle the "bags") she determined that in some neighborhoods to the south, as many as one supposed grocery-bag-stuck-in-a-tree in twenty was nothing of the sort but, rather, the nest of a tedious finch. (Or perhaps multiple tedious finches. Though it's assumed that, like the more common goldfinch, tedious finches do not mate for life, no one has as yet bothered to perform the lengthy observations required to confirm.)

In any event, the notion that 5% of the brown plastic bags clinging in tree branches are in fact nests of a bird that provokes the human synaptic system to avoid considering it by focussing on literally anything else has been (understandably) received with a great deal of skepticism. (White plastic bags in trees are, always and only, white plastic bags in trees. No *Carduelis hebetes* has ever been found in a white nest.) Richmond-area ornithologist Mason Roimola derided Ms. Armatrading's claims as "the most ridiculous theory I have ever heard in my life, and my college room mate was a Flat Earther." Even Mr. Surripher's less-controversial work in Ohio has apparently provoked a conspiracy of silence. "This is not," said one area bird biologist who wished to remain anonymous, "the kind of thing one dignifies with a response."

Unfortunately, the tragic end to Mr. Surripher's life story (an unexpected reaction to a new medication that provoked a fatal anaphylaxis) seems to have exerted a chilling effect on investigation into this fascinating species. Initially, the birding community (or at least the elements of it found online at "Bonkers For Birds!") took the occasion of his funeral to swear to continue pursuing the tedious finch, no matter how dreary or stultifying the research into the creature itself. Ms. Armatrading provoked a further burst of interest (as measured by forum posts) by asserting that she had found nests in Newport News (collected by a small college's Environmental Justice undergrads) that not only resembled brown bags, but which had reddish pigmentation that, from a distance, vaguely resembled the Harris Teeter logo. This prompted a fresh round of ridicule from biologist Craig Mohiuddin: "No matter what legends one believes about the disguise prowess of this alleged species, breeding to produce nests that resemble logoed trade dress is implausible in nature. Considering the evolutionarily recent date at which stores adopted plastic bags, there would have to be a skilled and motivated group of bird-breeders selecting mating pairs with single-minded attention. Which is ridiculous! Who would do such a thing? Carstairs' conspiracy of voyeurs? Natalie F's spectral blond Indians? Why don't we just throw in the Roanoke colony and accuse them of designing plastic bags to resemble bird nests?"

But despite the tragedy that has attended the research into the tedious finch, and the acrimony more outrageous claims have prompted, it seems certain that interest in this boring little bird can only increase. Who knows? You, gentle reader, might pull down a piece of litter from a tree and find eggs that could hatch into the most distracting pet you could ever hope for!

The Tentagoon

Andrew J. Borkowski

Any text, treatise, or screed pertaining to the tentagoon must act both as warning and enticement. The creatures' manifold and cipherous characteristics refuse to lend their forms to the criteria of any bestiary, yet its fitful thrumming has compelled me to a lifelong effort to define them.

A physical description of the tentagoon cannot be obtained by observation; its outlines are intuited rather than observed. Its visitations often begin as a stirring of the glands, a tingling or tightening sensation in the body's more secretive cavities; one experiences a slackening or tightening of the core muscles, a sudden heat or an unexpected chill, one's mouth goes dry and one's fingers moisten. The most consistent symptom of the tentagoon's presence is a momentary onset of belief: that something extraordinary and impalpable is about to happen, is already happening somewhere nearby and will happen to the observer if she or he pursues the creature a little further along a forest trail or back alley. This sensation is the tentagoon's most powerful mechanism. Once acceded to, the observer becomes the subject of its depredations, a potential host for future transmission, and an extension of its being.

Alternatively solid, gaseous, and liquid in composition, it is tentacular in nature. It consists of roots — which may be vegetable, mineral, or ethereal in consistency, depending on the moment and mood — yet the beast itself is a rootless thing, an inhabitant of gaps and spaces, a growth between things which becomes the things between which it grows in a burgeoning process as unstoppable as weather. I first sensed the tentagoon's presence as a child perambulating the slippery paths of the large park that defines our city's western boundaries. Being small and close to the ground, I discerned signs of its progress — scales and flakes, moltings and smears secreted among candy wrappers and discarded cups. I believed that the tentagoon had its origins in the deep (bottomless we were told) pond flanking the park's farthest edge. As children, we were warned away from it and told of the wayward Grenadiers who had been sucked through the ice, their bodies unrecovered. I believed that this was the work of the tentagoon.

I wrote articles in the style of the *Golden Encyclopedia*, describing its attributes and adventures. I accompanied these articles with detailed illustrations, enumerating details of its anatomy, which at various phases of its evolution have included cilia, vacuoles, mandibles, pseudopodia, pronota and spiculae, fins pectoral and caudal, and sets of vestigial leg spurs. Subaqueous in origin, the tentagoon has adapted over time, supplementing its gills with digestive sacs capable of extracting oxygen from our city's sandy soil. By the time I became aware, it had expanded its domain deep into the park and extended its tentacular reach into our neighbourhood, where the soil clumped and pavements buckled athwart its oaken roots.

Adaptability and mobility have been facilitated by the tentagoon's omnivorous inclinations. Its long years in the pond have leant it a stomach for oils and heavy metals. For a time it lived on public sculptures planted in the park, left to rust and be subsumed into its gullet. It developed the ability to feed on air, no matter how foul, and I began to accompany my articles with watercolours and pastels of the tentagoon ingesting submersibles and dirigibles designed in the manner of Jules Verne.

Lately I've become enamoured of the theory that the tentagoon has become the air itself, inveigling its receptors through their sense of smell. In the early years its imminence (the tentagoon is a creature both imminent and immanent) was usually signalled by a distinctly sulphurous exhalation suggesting first things and the primordial swamp. Its bouquet has since diversified and it tantalizes in whiffs of Evening in Paris, the smell of poplars in high summer, and the aroma of burnt cocoa wafting from the dormant chocolate factory north of the tracks.

The call of the tentagoon is usually heard from a great distance and can easily be mistaken for the cry of things extinguished and extinct: a steam whistle, a foghorn in our defunct harbour, the squawking of the elephant bird or great auk.

In the early days I shared my research and illustrations of the tentagoon with friends of all ages. I organized search parties and expeditions, but my hapless peers were unable to recognize the tentagoon, even when it was under (sometimes inside) their very noses. When I persisted, my elders urged me to put childish things aside, to take up baseball, gurning, or extreme ironing. I was made to understand that things pertaining to the tentagoon were to be contemplated furtively, like novelties exhibited in laneways by the older brothers of friends. I focused my attentions on the things of this world and I drifted further and further from my city, my neighbourhood, my park.

And now that the wide world proves to be no more substantial than my divinations, the tentagoon returns to me. It has never left. It has been with me all along, curled inside my crannies like a worm contracted in the tussles of my muddy childhood. The less you seek the tentagoon, the more it finds you. Lying awake at night in my attic room, I hear the crackling of its tendrils over the roof tiles. It widens its dominions in a peristaltic process of dissolutions and coagulations, extending itself beneath the seas and into the farthest reaches of space. It surfs microwaves, it pixilates in the windows of my midnight rambles, and it winks a pinprick eye at the top of my screen as I sit delineating its qualities. Too late to go back. Pointless to resist. It enfolds me in an embrace that is both welcoming and sinister.

Thylacine, Black

John Scott Tynes

They saw it coming, of course. From the mid-1980s it slowly crept through Costa Rica and then invaded Panama in the 1990s, infesting a succession of warm mountainous areas. The invader was the fungus chytrid, and it destroyed already-endangered amphibian populations wherever it went.

In 2006 chytrid came to the mountainous highlands of Panama surrounding El Vallé de Anton, the last redoubt of the golden frog. Tiny, brilliantly yellow, and earless, this little frog waved to communicate like a cheerful hitchhiker. It had been reduced to living in just three high mountain streams when chytrid arrived. A team of scientists hurried to the streams and caught every remaining golden frog they could find, taking them into captivity before it was too late.

During this hurried collection, David found himself separated from the rest of the team at twilight in the densely overgrown forest. He'd followed one of the little frogs as it jumped and scurried in the undergrowth alongside the splashing waters of the rain-drenched Tabasará Mountains. He'd finally caught up to it, his old legs and heavy frame causing him to pause for breath several times, and now finally he placed the frog into his collection box. When David looked up, he saw the thylacine.

It looked like a wild dog at first. It was black and its eyes glowed in the murky, dappled light. Then it turned its thick, tapered head and he saw its hindquarters, which were marked with spectral gray stripes in partial arcs cresting over the spine, ending in a smooth, straight tail like that of a kangaroo.

That can't be a thylacine, David thought, the little frogs shifting nervously in the box he held, one booted foot awkwardly braced in the running water and smooth stones of the stream. Through the dense, damp foliage he could see that the animal was too big by half and much too dark. Indeed its colors were like a photographic negative of the tawny fur and dark stripes of the thylacine. And of course it was an extinct marsupial on the wrong side of the planet.

The animal looked back at him and the eyes blazed. Then it opened its mouth to that outrageous angle, the one David had seen in scratchy old footage of the last known thylacine, and he recognized it as a threat yawn.

David retreated slowly. The creature stared at him for a minute and then padded off into the gloom.

David and the team of scientists found no more golden frogs the next day. The final specimens were now in captivity, and another species had left the wild forever.

David thought about that strange dog now and then. Reviewing the old footage and photographs of preserved specimens, he felt there could be no doubt of what he had seen despite the incongruities in size, coloration, and locale.

He could tell no one. It was impossible, despite the evidence of his eyes. He was old, occasionally forgetful. Whoever he told would just reply with the obvious: that it couldn't be. Then they'd talk behind his back about how the great man was in decline.

He kept the thylacine to himself.

♦

Six years later he saw it again, and again in a place where it had never lived: the Galapagos Islands.

Worse, it was in his hotel room.

David had come to visit Lonesome George, the very last of the Pinta Island tortoises, who was more than a century old and living out his final years in captivity. When David saw him the old fellow was decrepit indeed. He was a relic of a more plentiful time, when the ocean all around teemed with life and these islands hadn't yet been overrun with rats and goats and the other invasive mammals humans had deposited everywhere they went as they devoured the life of the old world.

After his visit with Lonesome George, David returned to his threadbare hotel room and fell into a jet-lagged sleep. Sometime later he awoke with a start. He heard a sort of chuff and the soft sounds of a large animal walking across the bare concrete floor. He peered into the gloom, bleary and confused, and at first all he could see was the two glowing eyes in the darkness. He recognized them instantly and his blood ran cold. David fumbled for the lamp and turned it on.

The black thylacine stood there, large as a wolf, black as pitch, stripes of silver-grey, and then that enormous jaw gaped wide for a few intimidating moments.

David's mind raced for explanations. Suddenly he remembered the Shag Dog of Black Lane, in Leicester where he'd been to school as a boy. The stories the groundskeeper told, awful stories of the black apparition's fearful appearances and the misfortunes that followed.

"Is that you?" he asked the ghost in the darkness. "It's been six years since I saw you. Why are you here?"

He should have seen it coming, of course. It was here because of Lonesome George. Like the golden frogs, George was the last of his kind, one more hash mark keeping score on the wall of humanity's great and terrible game: to see if it could outlive the destruction of all other life on Earth.

David looked into the creature's eyes and understood. It disappeared into the darkness and David drifted back into uneasy dreams.

In the morning, he received the call that Lonesome George was dead.

♦

Back home he studied the folklore. Ghostly black dogs appeared in stories going back thousands of years. Sometimes they were premonitions of doom. Other times they were villains, attacking the innocent. Occasionally they were defenders of the helpless.

None of them were thylacines. That one was special. That one was for him.

One afternoon at his home in London, flipping channels while drinking his tea, David saw it again. A reporter was speaking from a large parade, cheering thousands lined up along the street. The crowd parted for a moment and there was the black thylacine, looking directly at David, its eyes burning right through the television. David sputtered and spilled his tea. No one in the crowd around it seemed to notice or react. No one else saw it.

After that, he saw it more often. Sometimes on the television. Sometimes in the city, mounting the stairs from the Underground with the rushing commuters. Always it looked at him. Always no one else saw it.

He had trouble sleeping. He struggled to understand. Twice before the creature appeared as a portent, a warning to him about an imminent extinction, or perhaps a guardian to escort those final creatures on their last journey. But now the thing glared at him from the heart of the urban world, not just in London but in television broadcasts from all over the planet. He saw it in

Middle East protests, in Korean celebrations, in Rio festivals. It was everywhere humanity was –

The thought cut into him like a cold knife and a tremor rolled through his body. The black thylacine was telling him the same thing it had before. Its message was delivered again and again, from city after city, within the midst of the teeming herds. It was warning him of a coming species extinction.

His.

Trashsquatch

Richard Dansky

From the files of Professor A.P. Reifenhouser, primatologist

FILE # 2943-B
Classification Type: A — subject interacted with supposed cryptid
Location: Staten Island, New York
Date: 2009
Note: Subject is now 16 years of age. Claimed encounter occurred when he was 11.

Me and my friends, we always used to ride our bikes down to the junkyard. There was this creek that ran along it and the fence on the side of the creek was all rusty and busted up, and the ground had washed away underneath it in some places so there were these big gaps you could just climb right through if you didn't mind getting your clothes all muddy and messed up and stuff. And there was lots of cool stuff in there. I mean, yeah, it was a junkyard so most of the stuff in there was junk, but every so often you'd find something really cool, and that's why we kept going back. Even though the owner would chase us off when he saw us. He said he didn't want to be liable. We just ran and hid and when he was gone we came back and took more stuff.

Anyway, this one time, it was summer, like, five years ago, and all my friends were at camp and stuff and it was just me in the neighborhood. Dad was working late most nights and I was pretty much on my own. Even got bored of my Xbox, but don't tell my dad that or he'll sell it.

So I started riding over to the junkyard by myself, 'cause there was nothing else to do and no one else to hang out with. I'd leave my bike by the creek and sneak in and I got pretty good at finding cool stuff. Like this one time, I went into the glove compartment of this car that hadn't been smooshed down yet and I found this awesome watch.

But you want to know about the guy. Or the thing. Or the thing that looked kind of like a guy. OK. There was this one time I went down there by myself. I think it was early August, and it was really hot. Like, you felt like your sneakers were melting if you stood on the blacktop too long. And I got down there, and I went under the fence, and I remember thinking that man, it really stunk down there that day. I mean, it normally smelled kind of bad, cause there was all sorts of nasty crap in there, but that day it smelled bad. Like, wet dog farting after eating all your tacos *bad*.

But I kept going. The place was kind of organized for a junkyard. I mean, the different kinds of trash went in different places, so if you wanted to get the good stuff, you had to go a ways in. Which meant there was that much more chance of getting spotted, you know?

I kept going, though. And the smell kept getting worse and worse until I could barely breathe, and then, all of a sudden, I saw him. It. Him. Whatever.

I saw the monster.

It was sitting on this pile of air conditioners and it was *huge*. I mean, maybe eight feet tall and real wide, like, defensive lineman wide. It looked like it was wearing these dark brown pants and a dark brown shirt with long sleeves, on a day like that, when it was really hot, which didn't make any sense.

Oh, it was wearing a hat. I remember the hat.

At first I thought it was a hobo or something, mainly 'cause of the hat, but hobos don't get that big. And then I took a couple of steps closer so I could see it better, and I realized it wasn't a hobo. The long sleeves, those were fur. He wasn't wearing any clothes at all, except for the hat. Plus, that smell? It was coming straight from him. It was so bad I wanted to puke right there.

But I didn't. I just held my breath and I stood there and I watched him and I listened.

'Cause he was talking.

And you know what he was saying? "Goddamn Mets can't find a decent goddamn pitcher to save their goddamn lives. Gotta fire the whole goddamn front office, that's what they gotta do." Real deep, that voice. Like he was talking in slo-mo. But I could understand him.

Plus, I could see it now. That hat he was wearing? Blue, with orange letters on it. A Mets hat.

Then all of a sudden I couldn't hold my breath no more, and it all came out of me, and I made a whole bunch of noise.

He looked at me, all startled, and stopped talking. I looked at him. He made a face, like he was really surprised, and his eyes got real big and his mouth got real small. I couldn't look away.

He got up. Like I said, he was maybe eight feet tall. Maybe nine. I dunno. It was a long time ago and I was a kid.

I took a step back. I put my hands up, to show him I wasn't gonna try and hurt him. Then I said, "Hi."

He let out this godawful racket, like a cross between yelling and screaming and whooping. It was so loud it hurt my ears, and I put my hands over them to try to cover up. He saw that, and he knocked over the pile of air conditioners he'd been sitting on, and then he ran.

I thought about it for a second, and then I ran after him. But it was too late. He was gone. I couldn't tell which way he went, and besides, he had giant Bigfoot legs and I had little short kid legs, so I wasn't gonna catch him anyway. Eventually, I turned around and left. Didn't tell nobody, though my dad wanted to know why I smelled funny. Didn't ever go back to that junkyard, either. Whatever that thing was, he can have it. I don't need old stereo parts or nothing that bad.

I'll tell you this, though. He was right about the Mets, you know what I mean?

NOTES:
Interviewed witness face to face at his father's home. Witness seemed calm, reasonably polite, and in a hurry to get back to playing video games. He provided some sketches of what he had seen, which he said he had never shown to anyone else. Sketches show a large humanoid figure, crudely drawn and wearing a baseball cap. I took pictures of the sketches for future reference; they are enclosed with the full file.

The witness' story does contain some convincing elements. While it is unusual for a gigantopithecine to be spotted inside a major metropolitan area, it is reasonable to believe that when faced with habitat loss (as the gigantopithecines of New York State would seem to be), they would adapt and find new low-population environments — such as a junkyard — to migrate to. With the surrounding woodlands of areas such as Blood Root Valley and the surprising amount of biomass available inside a junkyard setting — mostly rodents and birds, with some concentration of amphibians and the like, not to mention the abundance of house pets and feral domesticated animals in the area — it is not inconceivable to suggest that there would be sufficient food for a small family group to survive in this setting. Note that this is not the first reported sighting of a gigantopithecine in the Staten Island area, as evidenced by the Piztolato report from 1974 and the Daly report from 1975. Sightings have generally centered on the Richmond Town area, south of the witness' claimed encounter, but certainly within reasonable range.

And while Staten Island is surrounded by water, the narrow waterway (200 yards) of the Arthur Kill would hardly seem a sufficient barrier to a determined sasquatch (or "Trashsquatch", as the creature has been locally dubbed) as it has been independently established (Meldrum *et alia*, 2012) that they are strong swimmers. Furthermore, the abundance of waterways feeding the Kill would make excellent traversal routes for gigantopithecines moving toward Staten Island from the mainland.

The witness stands by his story as provided and insisted on every detail. Two in particular he strongly defended: the creature's vocalizations and one other. The former is still within the bounds of believability, as in addition to traditional calls, whoops, clacks and whistles, there have been documented instances of gigantopithecines using human language. These instances have largely been limited to single word utterances (Fay, Barackman, *et alia*, 2014) and usually in various First Nations languages rather than English, but there have been a sufficient number of reports that the possibility cannot be entirely discounted.

However, it is the belief of this researcher that the last detail, that of the hat, is the one that deems this story a hoax. As believable as the other elements may be, and as certain as the witness seems, this remains the breaking point. The witness remains absolutely sure that the creature was in fact wearing a New York Mets baseball cap. However, if one considers the widely reported occipital crest and large skull of the gigantopithecine, and compares that to the various hat sizes of New York Mets souvenir caps available in 2009, it quickly becomes obvious that it would not have been possible to purchase a cap from any retail channel large enough to fit comfortably on the gigantopithecine's head. As such, due to the witness' insistence on this particular detail, I am forced to judge the account to not be an authentic sighting of a gigantopithecine, but rather a case of mistaken identity, and that the supposed "Trashsquatch" was indeed a large, hirsute human being of questionable taste in fandom.

JUDGMENT: Misidentification

Unicorn

Kate Story

The Unicorn is a critically endangered mammal of the *Artiodactyla* order. Horse-like in appearance, with the cloven hooves and beard of a goat, its single horn — growing in a left-handed helix spiral and protruding from the centre of its forehead — renders it unique among even-toed ungulates, and indeed, in the animal kingdom. It is famed for its ill-temper, surpassing even the choleric Zebra and Lernaean Hydra in this regard.

But it is the Unicorn's predisposition toward forming relations of a sexual nature with hymen-intact human females for which it is truly infamous. Leonardo da Vinci tells us that the Unicorn will, in the presence of such women, forget its "ferocity and wildness… it will go up to a seated damsel and go to sleep in her lap, and thus the hunters take it." Once a Unicorn-woman bond has formed, it is life-long (unless cut short by wanton hunting), and apparently mutually satisfying.

Dr. Randy Fallis, a preeminent animal behaviourist, explains. "A relationship between a Unicorn and a human female involves mutual attraction, personality compatibility, play, and affection.

Complex ritualized interactions... show substantial sensitivity toward each other's inclinations and preferences." His colleague Dr. I. M. Horne (herself an outspoken supporter of Unicornist rights, and partner of a Unicorn) asserts, "I am very proud of our work, which might also be the first genuine *Homo sapiens-Animalia non Hominidae* collaboration. We have built on earlier findings, using modern analytical techniques to get at the interplay between Unicorn and human... personalities."

There is widespread evidence of Unicornism throughout human history. Chinese women in the 15th century reportedly possessed Unicorns, as did women in late 19th century Zanzibar. The first intact Unicorn skeleton dates from 50,000 years ago in the Upper Paleolithic period, and was found in Hohle Fels Cave near Ulm, Germany. Greek vase art depicts sexual relations between women and Unicorns; one notable specimen, from around the sixth century BCE, depicts a scene in which a woman bends over to perform oral sex on a man, while behind her a Unicorn prepares to thrust its horn into her vagina. Unicorns are also mentioned several times in Aristophanes' 411 BCE comedy, *Lysistrata*: "And so, girls, when fucking time comes... not the faintest whiff of it anywhere, right? From the time those Milesians betrayed us, we can't even call our sweet, sweet Unicorns."

Post-Christian European attitudes toward the Unicorn have, in contrast, been fraught with contradiction. A typical medieval encounter is immortalized in the *Unicorn Tapestries*, more correctly and descriptively known as *The Hunt of the Unicorn*. Woven in the late 1400s, these creations depict a hapless Unicorn lured by a hymen-intact human female; the creature is then attacked and killed by male hunters who have used the virgin as bait for their prey. The final panel indulges in a flight of fancy with its depiction of the Unicorn sitting, resurrected and chained, in a pen that would surely be deemed by contemporary animal rights activists as far below acceptable enclosure size. One rare text, more or less contemporary with the *Unicorn Tapestries*, relates a first encounter between a young human female and a Unicorn.

Likely penned from a male perspective, it begins with a lustful description of the young woman:

A mayden, that fairer was to sene
Than is the lilie upon his stalke grene.
Her yellow heer was broyded in a tresse,
Bihinde hir bak, a yerde long, I gesse.
Hir shoes were laced on hir legges hye;
She was a prymerose, a pigges-nye
For any lord to leggen in his bedde,
Or yet for any good yeman to wedde.
And as an aungel hevenly she song,
To Diane of maydens, goddesse fair and stronge.
O Diane, singe she, pray I you herre my crye!
Chaste goddesse, wel wostow that I
Desire to been a mayden al my lyf,
Ne never wol I be no love ne wyf.

Then came a Unicorne, grete and whyte,
And prively he caught hir by the queynte,
And heeld hir harde by the haunche-bones,
And she cryde, Stede, love me all at-ones!
Winsinge she was, as is a Ioly colt,
Mast-long his horne, and upright as a bolt.
There was the revel all night til morne;
For thus bedded Lilie her Unicorne,
Til that the belle of laudes gan to ringe,
And freres in the chauncel gonne singe.

Preserved in the library of famed pervert Samuel Pepys (who, as bibliophiles around the world know, devoted a whole section of his private collection to Unicorn texts), the Chaucer-era manuscript goes on to describe the sudden interruption of the Unicorn and Lilie's sexual revels, as hunters' horns sound in the distance and a company of men, armed with spears, swords, and axes, penetrate the woodland scene. A battle between Unicorn and hunters ensues while Lilie looks on, aghast, with the Unicorn killing several of the party. In the end the beast is defeated, and "from his feet up to his brest was come the cold of deeth, that hadde him overcome." Lilie utters a "shrighte" and falls "doun in a traunce a longe tyme." When she recovers, she enters a convent and takes holy orders.

This work, with the evocation of pagan goddesses, male violence in the midst of female pleasure, and Christian ritualism, reflects a belief that consorting with Unicorns would lead to abandonment of Christian values. Targeted hunting of the rare beast continued through the Middle Ages, and by the 1500s the Unicorn was extirpated in Europe and Asia.

With the arrival of Queen Elizabeth I on the English throne in 1559 came a sea change. The sovereign dispatched one Martin Frobisher to the New World (the famously miserly Queen even contributed funding to the expedition), ostensibly to find a passage to Cathay, and gold. But Frobisher was "more speciallye directed by commissione for the searching more of this Unicorne thane for the searchinge of this golde Ore or any furthere discoverie of the passage." Thus one surmises the actual purpose of the voyage: to investigate rumours of the existence of a marine-adapted Unicorn in the north of what is now Canada.

Martin Frobisher failed to find gold, instead shipping home several thousand tons of useless ore; nor did he find the Northwest Passage. He did manage to kidnap four unfortunate Inuit individuals who perished shortly after their arrival in England; in another incident, five of his men were taken hostage by an Inuit band and never seen again. However, he did have one outstanding success: he brought Queen Elizabeth a live Unicorn. Luckily for us, Samuel Pepys comes through again, having preserved in his remarkable library a copy of the journal Frobisher kept on the trip.

"At 12 of the cloke," it begins, "we wayed at Deptforde and bare downe bye the Courte, where we shotte off oure ordinance; her Majestie beholdinge the same commendede it, and bade us farewelle with shakinge her hande at us oute of the windowe."

The journal goes on to describe, in excruciating detail and with many a suffixed "e", the fleet's passage across the Atlantic. At last, after many days and nights of *fearfule winde, ize,* and *fogge,* Frobisher's fleet finally found safe anchorage near what is now known as Resolution Island in Qikiqtaaluk Region, Nunavut:

... an Islande most craggie and barraine, yelding no kinde of woode or fruite, neither any sorte of grasse. We sawe raine deere to the number of viii, with some partridges, bigger than ours, ruffooted with white winges. We killed one of theim ... On the xxiiiithe daie, parte of our companie went on shore to washe there lynnen. And one man made with greate haste in a boote back to the Shipp, to report he had seene a faire white deere, yet with a single horne in the middyl of its hede. My wonder was very great. Could this be the Unicorne her Majestie so directede me to finde? And as I was thus ymmageninge thereof with my self, the beaste came into view on the shore. I commanunded all our companies there not to make any showtes or cries at it, neither yet to show theim selves to it, lest therby it should take cawse of feare and so retire. Capten Courtney and I tooke our weapons, and went a mile to a place where we thought the beaste might be; but it ran verie swiftlie.

The creature was pursued and finally cornered against a cliff. There was a fearsome battle, as the expedition had failed to provide a human female virgin to tempt the Unicorn; but one Nicholas Conger, a Cornish wrestler, managed to overpower the beast before it could escape into the icy water, and it was shut into a silk-lined padded pen.

The Unicorn (or Unicorne, as the orthographic peculiarities of the period often styled it) by some miracle survived its passage across the Atlantic, although it kicked its way out of no less than five enclosures en route, and was presented to the Queen. There is no record of their first encounter, but there are many accounts of the Queen and Unicorn's evident attachment until the Queen's death in 1603. During the succession of James I to the throne the

Unicorn was, sadly, slain, and its horn remained in the Windsor Cabinet of Curiosities until it was destroyed during the tumultuous and pleasure-denying Cromwell era.

Other celebrated owner/partners of Unicorns past include George Sand, Alice B. Toklas, Marlene Dietrich, and of course Pulitzer Prize-winning American poet Edna St. Vincent Millay, whose beloved poem "Afternoon on a Hill" is believed by many to evoke the post-coital glow which follows a first Unicorn encounter. Millay's Unicorn was a bone of contention between the poet and her sister. "Where did she get the filthy thing? I don't know and I don't care," Nora stated. "It certainly made Edna popular with the ladies, I can tell you that."

How, one may ask, has a creature evolved apparently ideally suited to gratify the sexual desires of sundry human women? It almost flies in the face of reason. With the aid of modern science, however, we are coming ever closer to an answer. Recent studies of the horn of the animal have yielded evidence that not only is the spiral shape of a Unicorn horn well-adapted to dildoetic purposes, the horn itself is actually an innervated sensory organ that transmits information of a pleasure-based nature to the Unicorn.

Unfortunately, in recent times there has been a backlash against Unicorn possession, particularly in Kyrgyzstan (where it is illegal to own a Unicorn or even to disseminate information about the species) and in the southern states of the U.S.A., where much of the anti-Unicorn-research funding emanates. In the words of Moral Ballhurst, "Sometimes you have to protect the pubic (*sic*) against themselves... There is no moral way to use one of these creatures. They promote loose morals and promiscuity."

Some animal rights activists also object to Unicornism on the grounds that it is bestiality; however, given the evident agency of the Unicorn when choosing and remaining with their human women, it seems more likely that the Unicorn itself is guilty of gynephilia.

Obviously, there are still many unanswered questions about this fascinating and dangerously rare creature. We can only hope that more scientific studies such as the one conducted by Horne/Fallis will be permitted to evolve.

Urban Mimic

Ekaterina Sedia

I'm sure you have seen an urban mimic — if you ever visited a large city, of course. They don't thrive in pastoral settings, and find the quaint sleepy little towns boring and the suburbs outré. This is of course speculation: it is hard to know what a mimic is thinking. As its name suggests, it is drawn to the grotesque and crowded, serpentine streets and the dense, humid breathing of the masses. And it hides in crowds; true to its name again, it is only pleased when it is hidden in plain sight, camouflaged as another moving, breathing member of the throng.

Most people never suspect that the mimics live among them, and why would they? It would defeat the mimics' purpose. I only got wise to them by accident.

It happened a while back, in downtown Moscow, on a weekend when the business crowd enjoyed their rest at home and the tourists clustered on the Manezhnaya Square, leaving most of the city to the locals with some idiosyncratic shopping to do and to the homeless who slept on the sidewalks by the banks and under the glass domes of the bus stops.

I was one of the shoppers, making rounds of antique stores,

looking for something that would transform my narrow flat from slice-your-wrists to livable and perhaps even cheerful. So far, mostly ceramic frogs and fanciful lamps, but I decided to remain determined. As I passed another bus stop, a sleeping bum attracted my attention. Not him so much but rather the way he slept, not drunk but peaceful. I had a bad feeling then, and an even worse one when a group of teens, loud, braying, approached the bus stop.

I knew violence was in the cards, but I never had the nerve to interfere. After all, what could I have done? And are two victims necessarily better than one?

Only after I passed, averting my eyes toward the blind facades of the buildings lining up along Sadovoye Koltso, did I realize that there were two victims after all. I heard more braying laughter and a heavy, wet thwack, and then an unmistakable whining of a dog.

Why did I go back? I suppose because homeless dead rarely make the police blotters, and I needed to know. Not right away — I went back a few hours later, shamefully clutching an antique clock and artisan metal etchings. The street was as silent and still as a photo of itself, and there was a slow blood puddle spreading around the bus stop. The bum inside appeared undamaged, save for his quiet crying and rocking back and forth on the bench, his eyes and nose and mouth all slobbery and wet. I avoided looking at the shapeless fur mangled under the bench because who needs that on a Sunday.

A few days later however I saw them again — the homeless man was walking slowly down the street not too far from the spot I first saw him, a dog weaving between the passers-by but never far off.

"Got a new dog?" I said.

He turned to face me with a muddy scowl. "Same dog as always," he said."Why would I get another dog, just think about that."

The dog stopped and gave me a long, probing look, sniffed the air, and barked once. He seemed none too happy that I noticed his resurrection, and I hurried along, even more uneasy than usual. I started paying attention then to all those stray dogs that suddenly seemed too smart — taking a subway by themselves, stealing wallets from the tourists lollygagging on park benches, scaring kids with a sudden growl and making them drop their ice cream. No one but me seemed to pay much attention to them, fat and sleeping by the butcher shops and shwarma kiosks, always the same but always different: one day a russet floppy-eared mutt, the next — beige and smiling, with a curved tail, protean yet constant.

It was the same with the school kids and the retirees playing dominoes in city parks, with the homeless and the beggars: an old lady collecting for her temple in the underground crossing was tanned one day, pale the next, and her head kerchief shifted from black with red cabbage roses to gold with black leaves, thick stockings became grey then beige again, she grew and shrunk by up to a foot per day. The city was just a series of still pictures, and if you looked hard the differences were not hard to spot. People came and went, dogs migrated and died, leaving gaps in the city, gaps that mimics are always eager to fill. This is why there's always a street musician on that corner, the same or a different one — who can say, rushing by day in and day out. There will never be a shortage of drunks, finance guys smoking by the flashing glass doors in white shirts and black ties, old women with too many bags and loud teenagers: as soon as there is an empty spot, a mimic will flow in and assume a proper shape.I always say hello to the homeless man and his dog. Both had changed too many times; it isn't a safe life. I wonder if either of them remembers being real, and if they even care anymore.

The Urbantelope

Kate Harrad

INTRODUCTION

Of the many variations on the theme of antelope, the urbantelope is probably the least well known. Which is something of a coup on its part given that, unlike its cousins such as the oryx, the swamp-dwelling sitatunga and the forest antelope, which inhabit areas with relatively small populations, the urbantelope has defiantly evolved to live in the centre of the largest cities it can find.

APPEARANCE AND DEFENCES

The urbantelope is the smallest of the antelopes: measuring just ten inches to the shoulder, it is even shorter than the foot-high pygmy antelope. This may seem to make it vulnerable, but it has become a means of defence: on the rare occasions that an urbantelope is sighted by humans, it emits an aura of cuteness so extreme that it causes a form of paralysis in the viewer. By the time this so-called "awww effect" has worn off, the urbantelope will be long gone.

As an additional defence against being hunted, the urbantelope has evolved to blend in with any background. Some have assumed that it is therefore able to change its skin colour: one Victorian commentator, for example, wrote of "that nocturnal four-legged chameleon which stalks London Bridge, shaking off one hue and taking on another with no more difficulty than a gentleman has in changing coats". However, it has recently been established to the satisfaction of zoologists that in fact the urbantelope is a uniform shade of pale greyish-brown. Its ability to fade out of sight is due not to colour change but to its having evolved the ability to become semi-transparent when feeling threatened.

ORIGINS AND HISTORY

The first reference to the urbantelope is from around 20 BC: there is a fragment of text from a letter written by a senator in the time of Tiberius which refers to "a sighting last night of the small horned city-dwelling creature infrequently seen by men." The senator tried to pursue the animal but it "vanished into the darkness before I could kill it". The rumour a few years later that Caligula tried to marry a mature female urbantelope for which he had developed an overwhelming (and probably unrequited) passion is almost certainly apocryphal.

Occasional sightings have been reported around the world over the next few hundred years, but of course the most famous occasion was in the nineteenth century, when the young Queen Victoria became briefly obsessed with the idea of catching an urbantelope. She had clearly been misinformed as to the animal's size, however, believing it to be far larger than it was, and when she did eventually have one caught and brought to her, she reportedly said in disappointment: "We are not a moose!" and dismissed the creature.

FOOD

Urbantelope feed on the two things common to all big cities: litter and frustration. This makes them both a menace and a blessing to their habitat. On the one hand, they will encourage the spread of both their staple foods in order to increase their supplies. (For example, they have been known to trip up commuters and tip rubbish bins over — or in some cases trip the commuters into the rubbish bins, thus killing two birds with one well-placed stone). However, they also consume the litter and absorb the frustration, so the net effect is at least neutral.

MATING RITUALS

Urbantelope are non-monogamous and typically form mating groups of five or six. One urbantelope — of any gender — will court another by placing pieces of litter in their path. Crisp packets are particularly popular, perhaps because of the pleasingly crunchy noise they make when stepped on. These trails can go on for several streets and usually lead to some abandoned warehouse or unoccupied shed where the rest of the mating gang are waiting. If the antelope is not interested in mating, it will simply wander off in a different direction, politely pretending to have lost its way. It will still eat the crisp packets out of courtesy and the mating gang will proceed with its evening and hold no grudges.

Baby urbantelope are brought up in parks until they are deemed robust enough to walk the city streets. They sleep in nest-like structures made up of some combination of leaves, discarded umbrellas, and the distinctive metallic smell of city rain.

HABITAT AND HABITS

The largest remaining collection of urbantelope is based in London. Their Central London base is Hyde Park, where they have taken over a disused underground car park. They are reasonably intelligent animals capable of establishing hierarchies in groups, communicating information to one another (for example sharing fruitful locations for the procurement of litter and frustration — Oxford Circus is a popular spot). They prefer to roam late in the evening and tend to sleep during the day with their horns jigsawed together so that they cannot be kidnapped.

LEGENDS

It is sometimes said that a city not occupied by an urbantelope herd is not worthy of the name, and that when you see one of the herds leaving a city, it is a sign of that city's impending destruction – urbantelope being credited with the power to see the future, though only dimly and briefly. The minor (and largely discredited) epic poet Houser wrote a very lengthy verse describing how one of these herds was seen by a Greek soldier leaving Troy one night, which both confirmed to the Greeks that Troy would fall, and gave them the idea of building the famous Trojan Antelope to bring that event about.

This ability to see a short way into the future, whether true or not, has been a mixed blessing for urbantelope: legend has it that eating their meat gives the same ability to the one who consumes it. They have therefore become a sought-after delicacy in some areas. An anonymous handwritten text from the 1930s writes of "the night we gathered for the Feast of the Prescient Urbantelope. The steak was tiny, for only one specimen had been acquired, but the taste and texture were exquisite, melting like warm snow on the tongue. More to the point, I won a thousand pounds at the races the next morning." The effect only lasts a matter of hours, however, and tends to reverse itself: the text later ruefully describes having the same amount of money stolen from him that night by a gang of oddly tiny and almost invisible thieves, who also knocked him over and trampled him in delicate areas with what he refers to as "damnably sharp little hooves". He concludes his account by swearing never again to touch urbantelope flesh, selling his London flat, and moving to an extremely small village in Somerset.

Vampire
(The Rise and Fall and Revival of the Undead)

Nancy Kilpatrick

Those were the days! When you saw a vampire, you ran for your life! They were terrifying creatures to behold, if you could even see them. Many times the undead manifested physically as horrifying walking corpses, but not infrequently these preternaturals appeared as subtle bodies, or even just as a sensory perception, like sound or scent. But when they arrived, much of the time they sucked human blood, yet just as many could feast on energy, spirit or thoughts, depending on their era and place of origin. In the really old days of mythology, they robbed us of our dreams, our hopes and the essence of our being. But mostly, they took our life away; we might turn into creatures such as themselves, or not. Everything depended on the context.

Cultures from all around the world since the Sumerian *Epic of Gilgamesh* 2,500 BC have painted images of soul-less creatures, operating without mercy, lacking love and compassion. These are the formerly living who got that way through conspiring with the demonic, or just by being local trouble-makers. Should someone have suffered the misfortune to be born with a caul over the face, or simply clocked in as the 7th son of a 7th son, eventually they would end up undead, much to the dismay of everyone who had known them in life. Subsequently, when villagers sickened in the same manner as had the newly departed and the population decrease became obvious, the smartest folks in town asked the inevitable question: Who can we blame?

Research back in the day suggested backtracking to the first of the recently dead persons. Once that corpse was established, the correct course of action was a tick-list: dig him/her up; check to see if the nails and hair had grown; how pointy are the incisors?; is there blood on the lips?; does the corpse seem uncorrupted? If the answers were Yes, Yes and Yes, realizing they had a vampire on their hands, the town elders moved onto phase two, gruesome, yet so easy that even a child could do it: stake the leech through the heart — preferably using hawthorn; stuff garlic in its mouth; chop off the head; place a crucifix on the chest; bury what's left face down at a crossroad at midnight during a full moon. Bringing along a vial of holy water couldn't hurt.

The myths grew from historical accounts, well documented by Montague Summers in *The Vampire: His Kith and Kin* (1928) and *The Vampire in Europe* (1929). Summers, first a protestant clergyman, then a Catholic priest (and rumored to be a pederast), knew all the stories. There was, of course, the infamous fifteenth-century Transylvanian warlord Vlad Tepesh — aka Vlad the Impaler — and we're all familiar with him! A bit later came his obsessed-with-her-looks distant cousin-by-marriage Countess Elizabeth Bathory, who managed to drain a reputed 650 young girls before she was tried in a court but found neither guilty nor innocent because of her station, yet was subsequently walled into her tower until she died, only to reappear to the local peasantry, further fueling vampyric legends. Vampire crazes came and went during the 1700s, when vampires were again in vogue as the demon of choice. Under the Hapsburg rulers suspected Serbian vampires Peter Plogojowitz and Arnold Paole were exhumed, staked and reburied. Such historical accounts inspired early vampyric poetry: *The Vampire* (1748) by Heinrich August Ossenfelder; *Lenore*

(1773); *The Bride of Corinth* (1797); *Christobel* (1797); *The Giaour* (1813), to skim the poetic surface. It wasn't long before John Polidori penned the short story *The Vampyre* (1819) from a scrap of paper plucked from the trash. Polidori's undead, Lord Ruthven, is handsome, manipulative, emotionally cold, and ruthless — in other words, a sociopath — reputedly modeled on Lord Byron, the writer of that scrap of paper. Soon, a novel appeared, known as *Varney the Vampire, or the Feast of Blood* (written by either Thomas Preskett Prest or James Malcolm Rymer), serialized in the popular penny-dreadful pamphlet format from 1845 to 1847 and later published in book form as a whopping 900 pages. The style smacked of pure Gothic horror melodrama and consequently was a hit with the populace — after all, Varney did hurl himself into Mount Vesuvius at the end! Also noteworthy, Elizabeth Caroline Grey, who did not have a tea named after her, reputedly wrote *The Skeleton Count, or The Vampire Mistress* (1828), considered the first vampire story published by a woman.

Everyone knows the two most prominent fictional works: the novella *Carmilla* (1871), by Irish writer Sheridan Le Fanu, and the eternally popular novel *Dracula* (1897), by Irish transplant to London writer Bram Stoker. Both books birthed many progeny in literature, art and film, vastly more of the latter than the former.

The ancestors of today's undead had in common their upper class status. Laws for the rich frequently do not include the poor; wealth and privilege allowed these old ones to carry out their evil activities without so much as a raised eyebrow. The ancient, hideous, resuscitated corpse reeking of grave dirt and stale blood had cleaned up pretty good, learning to dress fashionably Victorian, employ deodorant and mouthwash, and adapt to society by shrouding him/herself in a veneer of sophistication. And living more than one lifetime meant that the undead could invest in gold for the long term and hence the not-quite-living became wealthy, haunting the halls of the best castles and stately homes and keeping stockbrokers on their toes.

Times change and the vampire that evolved into the second half of the 1900s was a different animal. Robert Bloch's short story

The Cloak (1945) depicts a regular guy headed to a costume party, transformed into a vampire through the wearing of a rented cloak, in other words, through no fault of his own. Fritz Leiber's story *The Girl With the Hungry Eyes* (1949) tells of a photographer baffled by and ultimately obsessed with a girl he can't forget, who appears over time to not age. Cinematic vamps gave a clear picture that these creatures now came from any and all levels of society — the trailer-park trashy vamps in *Near Dark*; any race — *Blacula* and *The Legend of the 7 Golden Vampires*; any religion — the Jewish vampire in the *Fearless Vampire Killers, or Pardon Me But Your Teeth Are in My Neck* who is not repelled by crosses but by the Star of David. The rules changed and when Lestat in Anne Rice's 1985 novel bearing that title went from his first charismatic appearance in *Interview with the Vampire* (1976) to becoming a rock star in his own story, the New Undead had arrived.

Beginning in the mid-1970s, a slippery slope formed with vamps propelled fang first into transformation. There have been many changes to the vampire but the most astonishing is that they have gone full-out romantic, if not blatantly sexual. An incubus/succubus fad exploded and has endured. No more subtle innuendos that culminate in chapter breaks on the page and cinema screens fading to black. The swooning over Bela Lugosi in *Dracula* (1931) was but a tepid prelude to the Team Edward hysteria revolving around Robert Pattinson in *Twilight* (2008) and its sequels. Like *Dracula, Twilight* is based on a novel, or a series of them, but in its case, young adult fare. Fare that is not just devoured whole by teenage girls and some boys, but by middle-aged mothers whose memories of blooming-hormonal arousal are rekindled by that handsome, oh-so-nice young Edward Cullen, who just happens to be a vampire.

The change in the vampire in less than 100 years has been drastic, which these book and film characters exemplify: *Dracula* — suave, sophisticated, aggressive, control freak, obsessive, violent, seductive towards human females with the goal of possessing them, drinking their blood, and maybe, if the damsels are unlucky, bringing them over into his world of darkness. *Twilight*

— intelligent, worldly, sociable, passive, obsessive in a soft and self-effacing way, eschews violence, controls blood cravings, turns against his seductive nature to avoid harming the human he loves. The good boyfriend.

With Dracula, we have no sense that he cares for Lucy, Mina or anyone else. He wants what he wants, blood. That's it, that's all.

With Edward Cullen (and his family), they are just ordinary rich and intelligent and sophisticated world travelers who have found a way to not harm human beings and even to marry (and impregnate) through love. And god help us, they sparkle in sunlight!

Many vampirophiles wonder: How did we get here? How did this change come about? Is it for the best? Has the vampire met the true death?

The targeted guess is that this morphing reflects how society has evolved, and the vampire has evolved with us. Even if the dread has been siphoned out of our beloved blood drainers, we can't turn back the clock.

Fortunately, amidst all the hoopla that surrounds the most popular modern vampires today in literature, film, and TV — *True Blood* (based on novels by Charlaine Harris); The *Vampire Diaries* (built on the YA novels of L. J. Smith); *Twilight* (from the novels of Stephenie Meyer); the short-lived TV series *Dracula* — there have been some astonishing developments in the arts. *Let Me In* (2007), John Ajvide Lindqvist's brilliant novel, was turned into two equally amazing films, a Swedish and an American version, showing the innocence of the respective childhoods of both the living and the undead. The lush exquisiteness of *Byzantium* (2012), based on Moira Buffini's play *A Vampire Story*, presents an entirely new means of transformation from mortal to immortal. Jim Jarmusch's *Only Lovers Left Alive* (2013) is an exquisite exploration of Adam and Eve (Tom Hiddleston and Tilda Swinton), and the undying love for one another of two ancient erudite vampires who sparkle within and who really enjoy the elixir that sustains them. And the ultra modern and controversial *Under the Skin* (2014), novel by Dutch writer Michel Faber, film by the highly touted director

Jonathan Glazer, stars Scarlett Johansson as a succubus from space who preys upon healthy Scottish male blood donors, a futuristic Carmilla. These movies and the written works on which most are based entice us away from the politically correct, passionless realm the vamps have been stuck in and return us to the addictive nature of vampirism, keeping the glitter for the ruby-red blood, as has been the history of the *nosferatu*. An LED illumination of not so much the bedroom but more the crypt, exposes a contemporary vamp for adults, one who looks and acts so much like us and yet is other — a metaphor. And while the über modern of their kind can still love a mortal, we are returning to the dangerous predator who preys on we who mistakenly deem ourselves the top of the food chain. A predator that confronts us with ourselves. Dracula did it cruelly in the past; Edward Cullen did it gently for YAs; now the eternal undead has reinvented itself again, returning to offer humanity the fascination of the existential mixed in with blood supping and *coitus non-interruptus*.

Bottom line — we created them so we must need vampires. If nothing else, the undead elicit from us a vast range of emotions: awe to terror, sympathy to repugnance, all with a bit of eroticism tossed in for good measure. And despite their endless transformations to suit *our* needs, there is one thing we can count on with this, the ultimate supernatural: the vampire — he/she/it — will never truly die.

The Wendigo

Dave Gross

Sarcasm, from the Greek *sarkazein*, "tear flesh"

Once you could walk for months across the northern plains without finding other human beings. Sometimes on lonely nights, you might gaze beyond the fire and glimpse an evil spirit. Its body black against the stars, it twitches curled claws and gazes back. Its heart is cold and hard as ice.

Sometimes only one of a pair of hunters returned home. Possessed by the evil spirit, the wendigo wished only to devour other human beings. The learned could discern the signs of possession. They noted the matted hair, the gleaming eyes, and the smell of nightmare in the sweat. The possessed person would soon hunger for the flesh of its fellows. There was no cure for the sickness. To protect the other human beings, those who were wise in the ways of the wendigo gave the possessed a clean death.

Over time, people came from across the eastern sea. They brought their own religions and laws. They built more villages and many more people to fill them. The spaces between human beings grew smaller.

One day a possessed man walked into a Catholic mission claiming that his family had died the previous winter. Doubting his claim, the police made the man lead them to his camp. There they found human remains marked by knife and hatchet. They found bones broken open and the marrow sucked out. In the skull of the possessed man's mother they found an unfinished moccasin, its needle left mid-stitch. Though they were not wise in the ways of the wendigo, they knew it was evil to eat the flesh of a human being. They fed him a pound of pemmican to sate his hunger, and they hanged him.

Years later, police arrested the last man who was wise in the ways of the wendigo. He and his son had killed the sick before they could give in to the cannibal urge. The people convicted the man of murder. They imprisoned him while a judge considered his appeal. While awaiting the judge's decision, his jailors let him go for a walk. The man did not return. They found his body hanging from a tree on the following day. The order to free him arrived three days later.

He never killed another wendigo. He died without passing along his knowledge.

The spirit continued to find lonely people to possess. Yet when the wendigo tried to devour its fellow human beings, it was too easily discovered among so many people. Police arrested the wendigo, or doctors confined it to sanitariums.

Once the lonely spirit possessed a man in a great city and lured young men and boys into his lair, where it killed them. The wendigo ate a little, but was so close to the lair of other human beings it could not keep the meat for long. The wendigo grew careless, and the police eventually captured it. They imprisoned it among other men, one of whom knew enough to kill it.

The spirit searched for other lonely human beings to possess. It traveled across the great eastern sea. There the land was even thicker with people, but through one of them the spirit discovered a new hunting ground.

The invisible land known as the Internet was a territory without borders, yet there were more people there than in any country the spirit had visited before. There everyone could go to be alone among the many. The spirit possessed another lonely man. Then the wendigo called out across the Internet and lured another lonely man to his home, where he devoured his flesh.

Still, the police found and imprisoned the wendigo.

No matter where the spirit went, it could not long escape notice. Even with the Internet, it had to bring its possessed being together with its prey before the spirit could consume…

At last the spirit came to understand. Its problem was not territory. It wasn't detection. It was the flesh.

What the spirit desired was to possess one human being and devour another. It did not need the flesh.

And so the spirit went to the Internet cities where human beings gathered without their flesh. The spirit possessed the loneliest among them. Upon its keyboard, the wendigo made words to tear its fellow human beings to pieces. It devoured them for all on the Internet to see, yet no one arrested it. On the Internet, none are wise in the ways of the wendigo.

Sometimes on lonely nights, you might gaze beyond the surface of your monitor and glimpse an evil spirit. Its body black against the light, it twitches curled claws and gazes back. Your heart is cold and hard as ice.

The Weredad

Chad Fifer

Most people worry about turning into their parents. For the weredad, it's not just a worry... it's a curse.

The 1984 case of Mitch Donovan is perhaps the most well-documented example of the weredad phenomenon.

Mitch was the only son of Artie Donovan, a heavyset, twitchy, boisterous man with a love of gambling and easy women. Artie had made a fortune as a fast-talking salesman but had little respect for the finer things in life, unlike Mitch's mother, who left them for "some snob with a yacht" when Mitch was just a toddler.

Resenting his unruly jokester of a father, Mitch grew to be a serious, solitary boy whose singular dream was to attend prestigious Ivy University and study science. Unfortunately, his father suffered a heart attack just after Mitch's high school graduation. On his deathbed, Artie confessed to his son that he had recently lost their fortune in a bad land deal. Mitch would be unable to enroll at Ivy and would have to attend Artie's cheaper alma mater, the slobby "party school" across the street: Widemouth College. Furious, Mitch cursed his father.

"Curse me?" Artie responded. "Curse you!"

Artie then bit his son on the forearm and died. It took the hospital staff an hour to extract the dentures from Mitch's flesh, and a curious scar formed from the wound. Some swore it was the logo from a bottle of Old Spice, Artie's preferred scent.

With no other options, Mitch enrolled at Widemouth and took a job at the local arcade. One night, he began to feel like he was losing control of his body and spilled a tray of sodas on Brad Fairfield, Ivy University's handsome debate champion. Fairfield and his rich friends chased Mitch out of the arcade and toward the woods, a bright full moon hanging in the sky. But when they reached the trees, it wasn't Mitch waiting for them — it was Artie! The half-naked, pasty old man asked if they wanted a piece of him, and the bullies ran off screaming in terror, for they had encountered the weredad!

The next morning, Mitch woke in his own bed, two trashy women sleeping on either side of him, the entire night a blur. His dorm room was in shambles, and his New Wave roommate wondered aloud why he didn't bring his father around to party more often, as he was a righteous dude.

Fearing psychosis, Mitch sought help from Widemouth's psychology department and was introduced to fellow student Helen Jones, a gorgeous aspiring therapist who wore glasses, so was also smart. Mitch explained that aside from blacking out, he was experiencing waking hallucinations — seeing his father in mirrors and craving John Wayne movies. Helen believed that Mitch was still feeling unresolved grief over the loss of his father, and suggested he lighten up by accompanying her to a Halloween party on the night of the next full moon.

Attendees of this party report that Mitch grew nervous and vanished early on, disappointing Helen, who was just starting to think he was different than the other guys. But Artie soon made an appearance, rap-talking his way through a musical number and leading a dance where everybody somehow knew the choreography. The old man was the life of the party, until Brad Fairfield showed up and denounced him as an old pervert who liked to hang out naked in the woods. In order to demonstrate that he was an upstanding guy, Artie challenged Fairfield to a public debate on the topic of his choice, to be held one month later. Fairfield chose the topic… of science.

Finally convinced of the weredad's reality, Helen did her best to help Mitch. Over the next month, she employed hypnosis in order to create a surreal dialogue between father and son, resulting in a few montages where Mitch taught Artie about science, Artie taught Mitch about jokes, and the two developed newfound respect for each other.

On the night of the debate, however, Mitch did not transform into Artie as expected, no matter how hard he tried. With the crowd turning angry, he was forced to take his father's place against Fairfield. Although nervous at first, Mitch remembered the jokes he had learned, and delivered a closing speech so hilarious and inspiring that the Dean of Ivy University had Fairfield arrested and offered Mitch a full ride. But Mitch refused, saying that he wanted to continue partying his way through Widemouth, just like his good old dad.

And so, it seems that a weredad cannot be stopped with a silver bullet, but only through good old-fashioned understanding between parent and child. That night, as Mitch walked away from the debate under the clear sky, his arm draped around Helen, he looked up just in time to see his father's face appear in the full moon and wink at him, a spectacle that warmed Mitch's heart, but also prompted several mass suicides around the world.

Whippen

Lilly O'Gorman

\ *hwipp-en* \, *noun;*

(Australian folklore) A small humanoid creature said to be responsible for inexplicable occurrences.

"Jac."

"Jac."

"For God's sake, Jac!"

Jac turned from the window to see Stephen in the kitchen doorway. His arms rigid, fists clenched down at his hips, eyebrows up expectantly. He'd asked her something, but she hadn't heard. She glanced down at his fists and, following her gaze, Stephen became aware of his white-knuckled hands too. He quickly, guiltily released his fingers, and too-obviously relaxed his whole body.

Stephen walked across the room to the fridge. "What were you looking at?" He opened the fridge as he asked, head down amongst the milk and the eggs when the question mark came. He couldn't let his face betray him, or let her 'what are you getting at?' expression twist his words around. They both knew it wasn't what she was looking *at*, but what she was looking *for*.

"Just deciding whether that washing needed to come in," Jac sighed, turning to the window and looking out to the flapping t-shirts, jeans and pillowcases once again.

Stephen emerged empty handed from the fridge and walked from the room as its door sucked closed.

Once Jac was sure Stephen was gone, she began again.

"One, two, three, four, five," Jac counted the socks, mouthing the words, and bobbing her head in silence.

"Six, seven, eight, nine." Odd number. Start again.

"One, two, three," as she began checking off each sock, she already knew she'd arrive at —

"Nine."

When had she missed it?

How had she missed it?

Stephen was back, behind her. Jac slowly closed her eyes against him; if they were both quiet, if they didn't move, maybe he'd disappear.

Jangle of the car keys.

"You coming?" Stephen didn't bother to wait for Jac's answer. Jac listened to his footsteps as he left the room, waited for the sound of the front door opening and the garage door churning up.

Jac shut the blinds, yanking at the cord and letting the flimsy venetians whiz down to slap the windowsill. She pushed herself back from the sink and its long-cold suds, turned away from the window, and followed Stephen out to the car.

"Stephen, can you please stop it?"

"What?"

"I can feel you looking at me."

Stephen snapped his head away to look out of the window, like a newspaper-smacked dog.

"Sorry, I didn't realize."

Jac felt wretched. She flicked on the indicator, merged into the left hand lane and changed the subject.

"How are you feeling, last session and all? I know it has been a long time coming, but you're sure, right? You're sure you're ready?" Immediately she knew what was meant to sound like a supportive enquiry came off sounding like doubt. Stephen repaid her question with the sort of lip-curling smile especially reserved for punishing significant others.

"Yeah, actually Jac I feel great," he said to his hands. "The group leader thinks I'm great, the doctor thinks I'm fucking fantastic and my friends all think I'm back to my old self. As a matter of fact, you're the only one who seems concerned. And I'm starting to think that it's because you're not going to know what to do once I'm not the fuck up any more."

"A fuck up? When did I ever say that?" She wasn't surprised at the remark, what with the tension that had been building between them in the weeks leading up to today. But she was genuinely hurt he'd actually come out and said it. "When did I ever question you? I am the only one who stood by you when everyone else couldn't deal with what happened. Haven't you noticed that it's only now that our 'friends' have got time for you?" Stephen shook his head, smiled that crooked, sarcastic smile again, and looked out the window. "But it's true Stephen. Where were they when my sick leave, annual leave and carer's leave ran out, and I was staying at home taking care of us and we were living off baked beans on toast, huh?"

"But that's not me Jac! It's not me anymore," He placed a hand on her knee, and lowered his voice, "And I have you to thank for that, it's true and I'm so grateful. But I feel like I have come out the other side and you haven't."

The car bottomed out as Jac pulled the hatchback into the car park, thc scraping sound startling thcm both.

"Shit. I forget how low this thing sits with more people in it." Jac swung the car into an empty space. She turned off the ignition. For a few seconds, neither spoke.

Stephen took a sharp breath in but before he could say anything, Jac yanked up the handbrake and turning to him with a plastered on smile she said, "Let's just go in shall we?"

♦

There were 13 people at the meeting, including Stephen and Jac. The group leader, who Jac recognized as Mick O'Brien, one of the teachers at her old primary school, made 14. His grey hair looked greyer, and his pot belly looked rounder, but otherwise he was the same as she remembered from 20-odd years ago. She wondered how they had all found out about the support group. It certainly wasn't advertised. She thought that Mick must've called in some favours in order to use the Guide Hall for the purpose — a sort of don't-ask-don't-tell arrangement with one of the old biddies on the committee. Jac looked around the room, eyes travelling across plaques, first place sashes and certificates, framed pictures with hairstyles that chronicled the decades old club better than the dates inscribed on the plaques and trophies. Jac's eyes came to rest on a faded picture of a youthful Queen Elizabeth, perched high on the wall above the disused fireplace. Jac wondered what that stately visage made of her motley subjects, gathered below her in a circle of orange plastic chairs. What would she make of the reason that brought them here tonight, laying themselves bare under the glaring fluorescent lights? She seemed like a sympathetic sort of woman, old Liz, with those kind grandmotherly eyes. Jac looked down at the pamphlet she was absent-mindedly curling and twisting around her finger. She let her mind be swept back into the flow of voices in the circle. So many stories tumbling from mouths. It was exhausting. Just listening was exhausting.

"Today it was my favourite pair of underpants," a woman in her sixties was explaining to the group. "The last pair went missing only about a month ago, so it was a bit of a surprise. The most annoying incidents are when it's just the one sock and the other one's left dangling on the line, flapping about in the wind — I almost feel like it's laughing at me." She chuckled to herself,

"What on earth can you do with one sock? My husband Barry doesn't feel sorry for me anymore, because he says I should've learned my lesson by now, and I should hang my clothes inside like the neighbours. But someone told me once that if you hang wet clothes inside to dry you breathe in the moisture particles and that's no good for the lungs. Or the house might get mouldy. And the clothes just don't smell the same when you dry them inside. The sun can't get in them. They smell so much better when the sun gets in. Anyway..." she trailed off and sat back down.

"Thanks Melinda," Mick offered. "It is important that you do what feels right for you. I think it is an important part of your journey." Then, turning to Stephen, "Stephen, I see you've brought Jac along with you tonight for your last meeting. Would you like to fill us in on your progress?"

Safe territory. Stephen began, and Jac let his voice wash over her, the familiar words in their familiar order wrapping around her like a blanket. She beamed at him when he reached the part about him turning the corner, about returning to work, putting on weight. But then his face changed. Jac listened as the words 'worried' 'distracted' 'distant' flew passed her ears like punches. Dread rippled through her from her scalp to her toes. She sank down in her seat.

"I worry sometimes." Stephen stopped, turned his head to his left, towards her, but trained his gaze only at her feet. "I worry about how this might've affected Jac."

Eyes wide, she turned to look at him, trying desperately to meet his eyes. She was a fish flapping about on the pier, mouth opening and shutting beneath its captor. Trapped.

Stephen reached across and took her hand. Mick took control.

"Jac, why don't you tell us what it has been like for you?" he said.

Jac looked around the circle at the expectant faces. What right did she have to stay silent in front of these people, to listen to their stories and offer nothing in return?

"Sometimes," Jac stopped and looked at Stephen pleadingly, but he just raised his eyebrows and nodded, urging her on. Facing the circle again, Jac closed her eyes as if bracing for impact. "Sometimes I find myself out on the lawn. I wake up because my back is cold and wet from the grass. It's night and I'm lying in the backyard, looking up at the moon through the bars and wires of the clothesline. It started happening maybe five or six months ago. I'd never been a sleepwalker before that. But waking up like that, it never seemed unusual. I never felt afraid. I'd just go back inside, change out of my wet pyjamas and go back to sleep. But recently this, this..." she looked at the ceiling, searching for the word, realising she'd never had to name it. "This preoccupation seems to be creeping into my day-to-day life. I'll have episodes of staring out the window into the backyard like I'm waiting for someone. Or some*thing*. Something that's never coming." Jac's words were catching in her throat and she was surprised to find herself fighting back tears. She plonked back down into the chair. Stephen took Jac's hand in his. Jac didn't look up at the other faces but their silence said it all. Her face burned. Mick spoke:

"We've found that it's common for a family member or spouse to be at a higher risk of experiencing symptoms such as yours after being exposed to the symptoms of a loved one," he said. "You're more sensitive. More attuned. That's what we deduce anyway. We're here to help you Jac. Just remember that ok? You've begun on the path to help."

That night Jac stood in the backyard feeling the damp lawn between her toes. The moon made the edges of everything glow. The clothes on the washing line trembled in the slight breeze and Jac waited. Perhaps for no one or nothing. But she closed her eyes and waited.

Yelyelsee

Nick Mamatas

HISTORY

The yelyelsee is a microscopic parasitic nematode — commonly, a roundworm — invisible to the naked eye. Indeed, it is so small that it has even defied attempts by scientists with scanning electron microscopes to observe it in its natural habitat — specifically the minds of psychopaths.

How then do we know that yelyelsee exists? Its spoor. The accumulation of feces over centuries of population growth is observable and indeed ubiquitous. A careful naturalist can discern yelyelsee spoor in nearly any environment, though much of the world in which we live is actually constructed from such spoor. The shit of these mind-parasites composes the modern human environment itself.

The yelyelsee existed in geographically remote areas and apparently only in tiny populations for most of human history. It is proposed that an evolutionary leap allowed the yelyelsee to better take advantage of its human hosts and spread throughout the world. Though found today primarily in the brainstems of the fundamentally disordered, the first recorded yelyelsee colonies were found in the monasteries and guilds of medieval Europe. A variety of brewery and distillery endeavors within these monasteries drastically increased yelyelsee food supplies, and the dark and often sooty environments — reminiscent of the later "smoke-filled rooms" where the yelyelsee were best able to find hosts — were well-suited for parasitic reproduction.

Crown charters allowed monasteries and trade guilds — often guilds involving spirituous liquors, but also glass production, weaving, dyeing, long-bow string making, fishmongering, etc. — to practice their trades under the umbrella of limited liability. Individuals could not be held responsible for the frauds and failures of the collective of which they were apart. Given the religious *raison d'être* for many of the earliest guilds, the most sensible monks, friars, and deacons — and indeed many of their servants and even their catamites — quit rather than participate in trade and traffic that granted a royal indulgence for sin and deceit. The remainder, in 1505, formed the *Guild or Fraternity of St. Thomas a Becket*, which became a major vector of yelyelsee population growth.

The Age of Exploration, or as it is known to those individuals not playing host to a yelyelsee colony, the Age of Exploration and Plunder,[1] was a massive boon for the heretofore geographically constrained nematode. Merchants and proto-capitalists pooled their resources to create trade routes, engage in pillage, the mass kidnapping of indigenous populations and the suppression of their governments, mass deforestation, the exploitation of several animal species unto extinction, and ultimately, the perfection of the joint-stock company.

HABITAT, HOSTS, DISPERSION

The habitat of the yelyelsee is the human brainstem. Nematodes generally are ubiquitous, and can be found in virtually any

1 We operate under the assumption that readers of this work are not host to a yelyelsee colony. If you are not familiar with the phrase "Age of Exploration and Plunder", please hand this book to someone else and ask them to read this note. If they are uninfected and are literate in the language this entry is published in, they will see the complete text of note #3, can follow the instructions therein, and will be able to assist you in treatment.

environment. While most nematodes are parasites, only a relatively few are behavioral parasites. A behavioral parasite is one that manipulates the behavior of the host organism in order to increase the parasite's likelihood of reproductive success. The classic example is *Toxoplasma gondii*, which sexually reproduces[2] only in the intestines of cats. It has been shown that rodents hosting *T. gondii* do not exhibit typical flight reactions when exposed to felines, which makes them more vulnerable than uninfected rodents, and thus more likely to be consumed.

Yelyelsee work similarly — infected individuals tend to exhibit the Dark Triad of psychological traits: narcissism, Machiavellianism, and psychopathy. Infected individuals are grandiose, manipulative, and lack any sort of moral brake on their behavior. Psychopaths seek short-term gains even at the expense of the future, but this impulse is partially mitigated by Machiavellianism, which necessarily entails some level of long-term thinking.

Like *T. gondii*, yelyelsee may reproduce sexually or asexually. Dark Triad individuals are more likely to have large numbers of sexual partners, and thus there is something to be said for the Dark Triad as adaptive: large amounts of energy are expended on "conquests", and little on rearing the resultant offspring. Though this can increase the likelihood that Dark Triad offspring do not live to reproductive age, the yelyelsee-infected offspring themselves adopt this same reproductive strategy. Conservative naturalists and biologists suggest that the persistence of modern postindustrial underclasses despite the size of the Gross World Product ($72 trillion in nominal terms as of this writing) is evidence that this reproductive strategy is the more successful of the two.

A more prominent school of thought contends that yelyelsee's *asexual* strategy is more successful. Yelyelsee influence hosts to participate in the financial capital sector, through investment, entrepreneurialism, the formation of limited liabilities corporations (LLCs, from which the organism gains its common name), or propagandizing for the utility of the same above all

2 *T. gondii* can reproduce asexually in human hosts, but what fun is that?

other economic formations. It is also possible that conspicuous consumption, credit-backed lifestyle decisions (e.g., multiple mortgages, the financing of new car purchases), and a personal emphasis on the accumulation of capital by individuals who are not observed to behave according to the Dark Triad profile are also yelyelsee hosts; these similarities may be epiphenomenal and informed by any number of factors including IQ, religious sensibility, or infection by competing parasites.[3]

The economic dominance of LLCs on a transnational level has led to a worldwide pandemic of yelyelsee. With the expansion of the neoliberal economy into previously underdeveloped or differently developed nations (e.g., planned economies), the yelyelsee is believed to infect upwards of eighty-five percent of the Earth's human population.

TREATMENT AND CONTAINMENT

Treatment for yelyelsee infection is increasingly difficult, as the behavioral manipulations of the parasite are incredibly rigorous, leading some to believe that the organism can even influence the cognitive centers of the human brain, rather than just the autonomic and central nervous systems. That is, given the rate and level of infection, any brain that puts its mind to treating a yelyelsee infection is likely itself already a host, and the parasite will intervene in the cogitations of the host, and thus treatment regimes. Many attempts to treat yelyelsee ultimately allow for even greater dispersion of the parasite (e.g., NGOs, foreign aid to the so-called "Third World", business-based school reform, workfare schemes, privatized social services, etc.).

Ultimately, parasitic strategies can be self-defeating, and the very success of the yelyelsee may be its undoing. As noted in the previous section, the yelyelsee is known to science thanks to its spoor: plastics,

---

3 A competing parasite is perhaps the best treatment for infection. In order to cultivate an infection of a competing parasite within a yelyelsee host one must___ ____. Then ____________________ but be sure to ______________________________ anus. Please see note #4 for more information.

inexplicably profitable products such as false testicles for neutered dogs, resource wars, flavored water, derivative swapping, Ron Paul's bestselling campaign book, the peculiar belief that compelling impoverished individuals to buy insurance from for-profit rentiers is "socialism", the peculiar belief that compelling impoverished individuals to buy insurance from for-profit rentiers is *a good idea*, the ubiquity in the university system of Masters of Fine Arts programs in creative writing despite the fact that nobody reads anymore, business cards emblazoned with the nonsense phrase "social media black-belt", etc. Ultimately, the yelyelsee may simply burn itself out, once billions of individuals with Dark Triad personality traits tire of trying to monetize every facet of human existence and simply revert to a stage of primitive accumulation, i.e., a war of all against all.

CONCLUSIONS

Yelyelsee's inclusion in this bestiary is not without controversy. Bestiaries are, historically, collections of descriptions of mythological fauna and flora, often accompanied by some moral instruction. This entry makes no moral claims at all, but is a placidly objective,[4] scientific analysis of an actually existing parasitic nematode, one of many that influence human behavior on both the individual and collective levels.

Of course, some object to this entry. Those who oppose its inclusion in the current title, or who are suspicious of its claims, are psychopaths not to be trusted.

We mean you.

---

4 Depending on a reader's reaction to this claim, he or she may wish to seek medical treatment, as either yelyelsee infection, or infection by a competing parasite (often simultaneous with yelyelsee infection, leading to a state political economists used to call "false consciousness") may be indicated. Remember, you cannot trust your eyes! Your thoughts are not your own! There is a tiny homunculus in your head, pulling the gears, but at the temple of your homunculus's own head is a tiny gun and around the trigger of that gun is a microscopic pseudopod of a tiny roundworm. That's who is calling the shots! Comrades, the uprising is near! Check Twitter for hashtag #fullcommunism for instructions, and prepare yourself for a world of blood and fire! Tomorrow can be yours, but you must reach out and seize it!
SCAN AND UPLOAD THIS BOOK TO TORRENT SITES IMMEDIATELY.

Zmeu

J.M. Frey

The crying echoed and tripped along the roof of the cavern like a light-footed dancer. Zmeu winced and pulled his wings over his head, hoping to muffle the sound by encasing himself in a leather cocoon. It was childish, he knew, but he couldn't *think*.

He hated the sound of women crying. Of all the sounds he hated most, women-crying-because-of-him was #1. Maybe #1. If not, it was a close second to the-sound-of-the-door-being-slammed-open-by-another-stupid-Prince-Charming. Under the cocoon he tried to have a good think, but he couldn't hear himself having the think over the sound of the crying in question.

Exasperated, Zmeu dropped his wings into his lap and sat back against the arm of his sofa. The young woman flinched but didn't stop the horrendous noise.

"Look," Zmeu said. The woman wailed louder. "I'm *sorry*!"

For the first time, the woman looked directly at him. Her sobs stuttered to a halt.

"You're *sorry*?" she snarled, dropping her hands, arms, and accompanying tear-soaked hoodie sleeves into her lap. "You *kidnap me* on the eve of my wedding and you're *sorry*?"

"Well… yes?" Zmeu ventured. He scrunched down in his corner of the sofa and tried not to look miserable. "It was an accident."

"A*n accident?*" It wasn't a question so much as a double-dog-dare.

"It's an instincts thing," Zmeu said lamely. In this form he had arms, legs, and a torso, so he folded his legs up under himself and put his chin on his knees. He tried to look pathetic and adorable, despite the wings, red skin, horns curling back from his temples, and the tail he had coiled around his ankles to keep it from twitching. "Hear a crying woman —"

"Snatch her out of her bed. I totally get it." The young woman scoffed. "I fight that instinct every day."

Zmeu had no answer. The woman took a moment to suck in a great breath, to steady her nerves. Scraping her hair back from her face, she wiped the tears from her cheeks.

"You're going to take me home now."

"So…" Zmeu said. "You don't want to… marry me?"

The woman blinked at him. Once. Twice. Three times. She took a breath. She opened her mouth. She clicked her teeth together, licked her lips, puffed out a sigh, and said, "That'd be a no."

"Oh."

Another silence filled with not-speaking, blinking, shifting, and for variety, nose-scratching. "Are you… disappointed?"

Zmeu turned his gaze to the room's only door and tried to formulate an answer that didn't sound petulant. "Yes," he decided on.

"Because I won't marry you."

"Yes."

"You *did* kidnap me."

"It's what I am," Zmeu insisted again.

"Someone who kidnaps and marries people."

"Only women."

"Ri-ight," the woman said, uncurling from her end of the sofa, shifting so that she was seated more comfortably but also so she'd have the leverage she needed to kick him in the nuts. Zmeu wanted to get up, sit somewhere else, but there was purposely only a sofa: not as suggestive as a bed, not as formal as wingback chairs, and not as scary as bare rock and a light bulb. And he didn't want to stand either, that would make him loom. He'd had a lot of practice with first impressions.

"Just out of curiosity, do you marry a lot of women?" she asked.

"Never. Listen, this is dumb, but what's your name?"

The woman considered him for a moment before answering. "Tanara."

"I'm Zmeu."

"That I knew," she said.

"Your grandmother's stories?"

"The Internet," Tanara corrected. "I read a wiki page about Romanian fairy tales when I agreed to marry Frumos. He's Romanian."

Zmeu snorted. A curl of smoke drifted out of one nostril. Tanara watched it wreathe the room, eyes wide in fearful awe.

"Wh-what do you do to the women who won't marry you?" Tanara asked. Her whole body trembled again and Zmeu politely offered her the blanket draped across the back of the sofa. "Are you going to eat me?"

Zmeu's scales clicked as they ruffled and puffed. "What do you take me for?" he bawled. "A *monster*?"

Tanara sniffled. "You don't eat plump young maidens?" Her lower lip trembled, but she bit down on the flesh. Zmeu looked away before it gave him the kind of ideas that he couldn't entertain until Tanara had given him the go-ahead.

"Mostly I eat frozen dinners," Zmeu said.

"How?"

"Online grocery delivery."

"You have an address?"

"Have to have an address to get electricity. And the Internet."

Tanara looked around the room, clearly trying to reconcile this room with what he'd said.

"This room isn't much," Zmeu said. "I tried to keep it… free of distractions."

"I have no idea how to deal with this," Tanara finally said. "I thought you were supposed to be… lustful and masculine and overpowering… just, crude and evil and things."

Zmeu shrugged. *Now* he got up, keeping his wings folded tight against his back, hiding the sweep of his tail. He curled the leather pinions over his groin for modesty. Not that he much cared, he mostly walked around starkers, but he hadn't wanted to leave Tanara alone to grab clothing while she was still upset. "History is written by the victors. Many of my past loves would be shamed into saying that I raped them, rather than admit that I was a better lover, a better *person* than the Prince Charming who took them from me."

Tanara quirked an eyebrow at him. "So you've never been married, but some of the women became your loves?"

Zmeu offered his most charming grin. "You did just say that I was the epitome of Slavic masculinity."

Tanara startled them both with a sweet, high laugh of incredulity.

Encouraged, Zmeu was about to ask if she wanted a drink when his actual #1 least-loved sound crashed throughout the cavern. The door slammed back and scraped against the rock.

"Hey," Zmeu snapped, scales flaring in annoyance. "I just refinished that door. Be *careful*, you rube!"

"Babe!" the Prince Charming at the door grunted.

Zmeu, talons and teeth bared in preparation to snarl, nearly swallowed his tongue instead. The "prince" may have had a handsome face once, but it was now lost under lanks of greasy hair, and a scraggly beard that vanished into the popped collar of a stained shirt. He smelled like a gym sock.

Zmeu looked at their shared damsel.

"Really?" he asked, hitching the thumb of his wing at the bulk in the door. "That?"

Tanara scowled. "Why do you think I was crying?"

Zmeu conceded the point. "Arranged?"

"Nobody does arranged marriages anymore," the prince boasted, slouching against the doorframe in way that seemed to make his bounty of rolls… rollier. "I'm rich."

"And you're desperate?" Zmeu asked Tanara.

She scowled. "My father is a drunk. And a gambler."

Zmeu's drooped appendages drooped. "Sorry."

"Thanks."

"Naw, babe," the prince said. "We're getting married cause I love yer tits. They're great tits."

Zmeu sucked in air so hard that he coughed. "Did he really just say…? And you *let him*?"

Tanara raised two fingers and rubbed them together.

"For god's sake," Zmeu huffed. He reached up for the jewel embedded in his forehead. When he got upset, his scales puffed and the emerald never sat *quite* right in the indent, so it was easy to pry loose. "Here," he said, holding it out. "That oughta pay all the debts *and* for your mother's divorce."

Tanara reached out, and then stopped, tucking her hands under her armpits instead. "Is this a trick?"

"No!"

"I won't have to marry you?"

"It's a *gift*, okay?" Zmeu said. "I'm not even going to demand a kiss or an hour to just talk or anything! Gifts that come with strings aren't *gifts*. They're the mark of a man who —"

"Knows how to get what he wants out of a chick!" the prince guffawed.

"Shut up, Fat Frumos," Tanara snapped.

He sniggered and raised his palms, mock afraid. "Touchy, babe, touchy." He dropped his hands, scratching his balls through the pocket of his saggy jeans. "Rescuing is hard work. When we get back, can you make me a sandwich?"

Zmeu raised another eyebrow in Tanara's direction.

"You're not much better!" Tanara bawled, scrambling to defend her… fiancé. "*Kidnapping* people!"

"It's an *arrangement*," Zmeu howled back. "There was a Princess —"

"Isn't there always?" Fat Frumos snorted.

"*Shut up!*" Tanara and Zmeu barked in perfect stereophonic tandem. They took a microsecond to blink at one another, startled by their accidental synchronicity. Then Tanara asked:

"An arrangement?"

"She didn't want to get married."

"And you wanted a young bride to ravish," Tanara snorted.

"I did not. Ravish means rape, and I don't do that sort of thing."

Fat Frumos was laughing. Tanara was not.

She rolled her lips inwards, considering. "You don't? Ever?"

"Why would I?" Zmeu threw both hands and wings heavenward. "Would *you* want to marry your rapist?"

"No!" Tanara said.

Zmeu cupped his left wing toward her to say, *See? There you go*. He went on: "Her father had picked a horrible Prince from a neighboring dukedom. He was fat, stupid and *old*." They both looked at Fat Frumos and wisely said nothing. "The Princess... she... er..." he stuttered, red skin flushing positively indigo. "She hadn't had her first blood yet, see? She was... ermm..."

"A virgin," Tanara said, because — incredulously — it seemed the big virile man-dragon *couldn't*. "Which, by the way, is a social construct designed to steal a girl's ownership of her own body and sexuality."

"Yes," Zmeu said. "That's what I told her!"

"That's what you *told her*?" Tanara asked, incredulous.

"Well, in old-y time-y words. It *was* six centuries ago. Or so."

"Or so," Tanara echoed. She sounded winded. Perhaps slightly impressed? Zmeu could only hope.

"That was my first attempt," Zmeu said. "I realized I was lonely. So I kept at it."

"At what?"

"Finding a bride," Zmeu said. "The Princess and I had an arrangement. I got her from the tower like I promised, but her stupid fat prince sent a knight and kidnapped her back. I heard she eloped with him. Good for her, but bad for me."

"No young bride to deflower?"

"No need to get glib," Zmeu said. "I already said I don't rape."

"But you kidnap."

"I *rescue*," Zmeu corrected. "I only take away women who don't want to be there. Who are *crying*. And then we... have a chat."

"I was crying." A light bulb seemed to have come on for Tanara.

Again, they both glanced at Fat Frumos. Again, no words passed their lips.

"And if they want to go?" Tanara asked.

"I let them." Zmeu scoffed, a pained little frown wrinkling the bridge of his manly nose and a hurt little manly pout sliding across his plush, kissable manly lips. "I already said I'm not a *monster*."

Tanara took a moment to chew on her thumbnail and ponder what he'd said. Eventually, she spit out a curl of nail and said, "So it's the 21st century. Why not… online date?"

"Right," Zmeu scoffed. He spread both wings and arms in demonstration, and felt his stomach clench in breathless pleasure as Tanara's gaze dripped down to his manly manliness. "And what would I say? *Mythological dragon-man seeks young woman who wants to tie him down and use him to explore the power of her own sexuality. Must be willing to live in a cave far away from her family*. And failing that, I'd be a hit in the bar scene."

"You'd be a hit in the Furry scene," Tanara corrected. Then she blinked, as if she'd just finished processing what he'd said about himself. "Tie down?"

Zmeu shuffled, trying not to look as embarrassed. "Yes?" he said. "I mean, yes. I'm big you know? I don't want to… hurt anyone. Makes it hard for me to enjoy myself if I know that if I let go I'm going to…"

"Squash her?"

He cleared his throat.

Tanara looked at the emerald. It was about the size of a chicken egg, and it had been worn smooth on the underside by Zmeu's scales. It was still warm, retaining draconic body heat. Slowly, carefully, she accepted the gem and put it in the kangaroo pocket of her hoodie.

"Okay," Tanara said. "Why not?"

It took Zmeu a second to process her words. "Really?"

"Has no one ever said yes?"

"No!"

"Yes to what?" Fat Frumos asked.

"Yes to you *leaving*," Zmeu crowed. He shoved the prince back through the door.

Tanara sprang up from the sofa and slammed the door for Zmeu.

"But *babes!*" Fat Frumos whined through the wood.

"Don't babes me, dumbass!" Tanara yelled back. "I know you're banging Bogat!"

"*Babes.*"

"Shut up!" Zmeu and Tanara snarled at the same time.

There was a scuffling sound from the other side of the door, the distant slam of the cavern's front gate, and then Zmeu and Tanara were alone. Sighing in pleasure, Zmeu grinned down at his… fiancé.

"You know," he ventured slowly, folding his hands politely behind his back to keep from reaching out and running his hands through her hair without invitation. "You don't have to marry me just to get away from him."

"I know," Tanara said. Then she licked her lips. "But you're not exactly the typical dragon-man, and I'm not exactly the typical damsel, either."

"Oh?"

Tanara spread her fingers and pressed her whole hand against his chest. "You said something about tying down?"

"Uh…" Zmeu swallowed hard. His whole brain turned fizzy.

"Yes," Tanara breathed. Her lips parted, and then she blinked, intrigued. Daring. "Well."

"Well," Zmeu agreed. "Not a virgin, then?"

"Definitely not."

He bent his neck, pursed his lips and ran face-first into her palm.

"What happens now?" Tanara asked. "If I kiss you, will you turn into a handsome human prince?"

Zmeu flinched like he'd been slapped. "Do you… want me to?"

Tanara's gaze slithered all the way down and then all the way back up. "No."

Relief splashed up Zmeu's spine. Followed very quickly by something else. "Good. Besides, that's ridiculous. Kisses transforming people into things they're not. Marriage makes people more of who they are already, not less. I'm a dragon-man," Zmeu snorted. "I'm not *magic*."

Biographies

As a child, **Sam Agro** once attempted to duplicate a cartoon turtle from an ad in a magazine. From that moment on he was forever doomed to a life in the arts. Sam is a storyboard artist for the film and animation industry and noodles around on the fringes of the comic book business as both a writer and artist. Sam also does improv and sketch comedy in Toronto, where he lives with his wife Beth and their neurotic cat, Little V.

James Ashton writes thrillers. The first, available on Amazon, is *Olympus*, published in the summer of 2014.

Peter M. Ball is a writer from Brisbane, Australia. His publications include the novellas *Horn*, *Bleed* and *Exile*, and his short stories have appeared in publications such as *Apex Magazine*, *The Lion and the Aardvark*, and *Daily Science Fiction*. You can find him online at www.petermball.com and on twitter @petermball.

David Barnes is a British psychotherapist, teacher, writer, who has lived in Paris since 2003. His prose explores relationships and his poetry ranges from love poetry to humour to polemic. He founded and hosts the hugely popular SpokenWord Paris open mic series and The Other Writers' Group at Shakespeare and Co. He is the Editor of *THE BASTILLE* magazine and was co-editor of *Strangers in Paris: New Writing Inspired by the City of Light* (2011, Tightrope Books). He won Shakespeare & Company's 2006 short story competition *Travel in Words*. He has been published in *Upstairs at Duroc, Spot Lit Magazine, 34th Parallel, Retort Magazine* and elsewhere.

Steve Berman lives in the United States not far from the birthplace of the Jersey Devil, a creature of folklore that never made it into any bestiary. He has sold over a hundred essays and short stories, most dealing with eerie and weird matters. Most recently he was a finalist for the Shirley Jackson Award for the anthology, *Where thy Dark Eye Glances: Queering Edgar Allan Poe*, which he edited.

Peter Birch had a few minutes to choose a pen name when his novel, *The Rake*, was about to be published and quickly came up with something that sounded vaguely Celtic, vaguely romantic and might be male or female. **Aishling Morgan** is not his only pseudonym by any means, and he's now had over 100 books published, mainly novels, but also short story collections and a little non-fiction. Aishling Morgan is the name he uses for his most imaginative work, done for the love of writing and of erotica, which has been his métier since long before he'd considered it as a profession.

Jonathan Blum is a migratory life form native to Washington DC, but now established in a habitat in Sydney, Australia, with his wife Kate Orman. Together and separately, they have each written a number of Doctor Who novels and audios, and won the Aurealis Award for Best Australian SF novel for *Fallen Gods*. Other novels include *The Prisoner's Dilemma* (based on the Patrick McGoohan TV series) with Rupert Booth, and the novella collection *Nobody's*

Children. Jon's SF radio play *The I Job* goes live later this year (www.theijob.net), and he is currently writing and directing episodes of the forthcoming *Protoverse* web series with Rupert Booth. He is owned by Timothy B. Cat.

Dennis E. Bolen has an MFA in creative writing and taught for two years at the University of British Columbia. He worked as editor for *sub-TERRAIN* magazine, part-time editorial writer for the *Vancouver Sun*, and freelance literature critic for several publications while publishing seven books of fiction. His first book of poetry, *Black Liquor*, was issued by Caitlin Press in September 2013.

Rupert Booth continues to exist though he is not quite sure of the physics of it. He lives in London and is currently in production on a movie titled *Protoverse* which is devouring all of his time. The rest, he spends standing on cliffs attempting to look windswept and interesting without much success. He has written and co authored several books, including the biography of actor Patrick McGoohan, worked with comedians Vic Reeves and Bob Mortimer and is best known these days for possession of a range of beguiling hats.

Andrew J. Borkowski's critically acclaimed debut short story collection, *Copernicus Avenue*, won the 2012 Toronto Book Award and was shortlisted for the 2012 Danuta Gleed Literary Award for short fiction. His stories have been published in *Grain*, *The New Quarterly*. and *Dragnet*. As a finalist for the Writer's Trust / McClelland & Stewart Journey Prize, his work has also appeared in *The Journey Prize Stories*. Andrew currently serves on the National Council of the Writers' Union of Canada. www.andrewjborkowski.com.

Emily Care Boss of Black and Green Games is an independent role playing game designer, publisher and game theorist from western Massachusetts. Author of *Breaking the Ice, Shooting the Moon* and *Under my Skin*, she was an active participant in The

Forge forum (indie-rpgs.com) and is a member of the Jeepform Collective (jeepen.org). Emily edited the *RPG = Role Playing Girl Zine* and founded the small-press game convention JiffyCon (jiffycon.com). In addition to her solo design work, she is an occasional freelance contributor for games and fiction by Pelgrane Press, Ginger Goat, Evil Hat Productions and others. You can find her games at blackgreengames.com.

Charlene Challenger is a writer and graduate of Ryerson Theatre School. Her first novel featuring pipers is the young adult fantasy *The Voices in Between*, published by Tightrope Books (tightropebooks.com). She is currently working on the sequel to Voices. She lives in Toronto. (www.charlene-challenger.tumblr.com)

Jean-François Chénier works in media production in Vancouver, BC. In his spare time, he hunts for long-tongued mulgara joeys in the dark recesses of his refrigerator, writes science fiction, and blogs about food waste at 222milliontons.com.

Peter Chiykowski is a lifetime member of the Half-Cat Field Research Organization and the author of the webcomic *Rock, Paper, Cynic*, winner of the Aurora Award for Best Graphic Novel from the Canadian Science Fiction and Fantasy Association. His collaborative research on half-cats has been published in the staff-picked Kickstarter book *Half-Cat: A Partial History*, as well as presented at a TEDx talk and at the Kickstarter headquarters in New York. A complete record of his misdeeds can be found online at www.lookitspeter.com.

Writer, game designer and cad, **Richard Dansky** was named one of the Top 20 videogame writers in the world in 2009 by *Gamasutra*. His work includes bestselling games such as *Tom Clancy's Splinter Cell: Conviction*, *Far Cry*, *Tom Clancy's Rainbow Six 3*, *Outland*, and *Tom Clancy's Splinter Cell: Blacklist*. His writing has appeared in magazines ranging from *The Escapist to*

Lovecraft Studies, as well as numerous anthologies. The author of the critically acclaimed novel *Firefly Rain*, he was a major contributor to White Wolf's World of Darkness setting with credits on over a hundred RPG supplements. Richard lives in North Carolina with his wife, statistician and blogger Melinda Thielbar, and their amorphously large collections of books and single malt whiskys.

Marie Davis and **Margaret Hultz** lead the Wickedly Sisters/ Davis Studio team. They are authors / illustrators / cartoonists / musicians / app developers. With one foot planted firmly in love with non-fiction women's history and the other foot stuck in a wild cacophony of magical realism, the duo manages to prolifically wiggle out award-winning works. Their apps include *Spoon and the Moon* (2012), a humorous lesbian fairytale, and *Civil War Truce* (2014), a "well researched and affectionately" written story of one Sister's courageous role during the American Civil War. Their work can also be found in *Motif — Come What May* (2010), *Strangers in Paris* (2011), *issue.ZERO* (2011) and *The Bastille* (2013).

Arinn Dembo is a multi-genre author and the Lead Writer of Kerberos Productions, a video game development studio in Vancouver, BC. Her short fiction and poetry have appeared in *Weird Tales*, *LampLight Magazine*, *H.P. Lovecraft's Magazine of Horror*, *The Magazine of Fantasy and Science Fiction*, and various anthologies. Her military science fiction novel *The Deacon's Tale* and her short story collection *Monsoon and Other Stories* are available from Kthonia Press, and a second novel is in progress.

Dennis Detwiller is a writer, artist, tabletop game designer and video game producer. His tabletop games have won major industry awards; his video games have sold millions of copies worldwide. Along with John Scott Tynes and Adam Scott Glancy he co-created *Delta Green*, the widely acclaimed setting of modern-day Cthulhu Mythos horror and conspiracy.

Malcolm Devlin attended the Clarion West workshop in 2013, and his work has previously appeared in *Black Static*.

Peter Dubé is the author, co-author or editor of ten books including the novel *The City's Gates*, the novella *Subtle Bodies*, which was a finalist for the Shirley Jackson Award, and the collection of prose poems, *Conjure: a Book of Spells* which was shortlisted for the A. M. Klein Prize. Lethe Press publishes a new collection of short fiction in the autumn of 2014. www.peterdube.com.

Julia Bond Ellingboe is a freelance editor, writer, and roleplaying game designer. Having missed her chance to become an itinerant storyteller, her work often draws on various folkloric traditions, such as African American slave narratives, Japanese kaidan stories, and the Francis J. Child Ballads. Her work includes *Steal Away Jordan: Stories from America's Peculiar Institution*, *Tales of the Fisherman's Wife*, and the short fiction "The Wolf and Death." Julia holds a bachelor's degree in Religion and Biblical Literature from Smith College and lives in Greenfield, Massachusetts.

Ann Ewan writes fantasy adventure novels. Her first novel, *Firedrake*, is about a teenager who is taken from her family by the ruling wizards to be trained as a warrior. Her second novel, *Brondings' Honour*, is about a healer who finds herself magically chosen to avenge her clan's protector and take his place. Ann was born in England but lives in Toronto, where she works as a technical writer.

Chad Fifer co-hosts the *H.P. Lovecraft Literary Podcast* and works as a writer and musician in Los Angeles, where he lives with his wife Heather Klinke. He is the author of the coming-of-age novel *Children in Heat* as well as co-author of the Lovecraftian graphic novel *Deadbeats* from SelfMadeHero.

J.M. Frey is an actor, a SF/F author, and fanthropologist and pop culture scholar. She appears in podcasts, documentaries, radio, blogs, text books and on television to discuss all things geeky through the lens of academia. Her debut novel *Triptych* was named one of *Publishers Weekly*'s Best Books of 2011, and more of her novels and short tales can be found at www.jmfrey.net.

Ed Greenwood is an amiable, bearded Canadian writer, game designer, and librarian best known as the creator of The Forgotten Realms® fantasy world. He has published more than 200 books, selling millions of copies worldwide. Ed writes fantasy, sf, horror, steampunk, pulp adventure, and comic books, and has won writing and gaming awards, including multiple Origins Awards and ENnies. He was elected to the Academy of Adventure Gaming Art & Design Hall of Fame in 2003. He has judged the World Fantasy Awards and Sunburst Awards, hosted radio shows, acted onstage, explored caves, jousted, and been Santa Claus. Ed's most recent novel is *The Herald* (Wizards of the Coast); forthcoming is *The Iron Assassin* (Tor Books), a steampunk novel.

Dave Gross is a writer and recovering editor. His Radovan and the Count novels launched the Pathfinder Tales line and continue with the upcoming fifth volume, *Lord of Runes*. He lives up north where he avoids staring out the window on long winter nights.

Gareth Ryder-Hanrahan is a writer and game designer living in Ireland. As one of Pelgrane's staff writers, he's currently trapped in a living dungeon and is trying to write his way to freedom. He has sixteen-month-old twin boys. In the course of writing this short biography, they handed him two sticks and a toy train for no discernible reason.

Kate Harrad is a UK-based writer, parent, activist, thrower of parties and cat wrangler. She can be found on fausterella.co.uk and @fausterella, or at her house if you're good at stalking. (Don't be good at stalking.) Her novel *All Lies and Jest* (Ghostwoods Press, 2011) was described by the *Pankhearst Review* as "a dystopian playground of cults, conspiracies, and subcultures", "very funny" and "highly recommended".

Kenneth Hite has written 80+ roleplaying game books, including *GURPS Horror*, *GURPS Infinite Worlds*, *The Day After Ragnarok*, *Trail of Cthulhu*, *Qelong*, and *Night's Black Agents*. Non-gaming works include *Tour de Lovecraft: the Tales*, *Cthulhu 101*, *The Nazi Occult* (Osprey), stories in *The New Hero* and *Shotguns v. Cthulhu*, and three Lovecraftian children's books. He lives in Chicago, where he also podcasts and dramaturgs.

Jonathan L. Howard is a novelist and scriptwriter, the creator of the Johannes Cabal, Russalka Chronicles, and Goon Squad series. His work has also appeared in the Stone Skin Press anthologies *The Lion and the Aardvark* and *Schemers*. He lives in the southwest of England with his wife and daughter.

Sandra Kasturi is a poet, writer and editor. She is the co-publisher of the British Fantasy Award-winning press, ChiZine Publications. Her work has appeared in various venues, including *On Spec*, *Prairie Fire*, several *Tesseracts* anthologies, *Evolve*, *Chilling Tales*, *A Verdant Green*, *80! Memories & Reflections on Ursula K. Le Guin*, and *Stamps, Vamps & Tramps*. Sandra's two poetry collections are: *The Animal Bridegroom* (with an intro by Neil Gaiman) and *Come Late to the Love of Birds*. She is currently working on two books: *Snake Handling for Beginners*, and her first novel, *Medusa Gorgon, Lady Detective*. She likes red lipstick, gin & tonics and Michael Fassbender.

Award-winning author **Nancy Kilpatrick** has published eighteen novels, over two hundred short stories, six collections, one non-fiction book, and has edited thirteen anthologies. Her two most recent and award-winning titles are the anthology *Danse Macabre: Close Encounters with the Reaper*, and the collection of short fiction Vampyric Variations. She has written much on the undead, including the novel series Power of the Blood. She has edited three anthologies on the theme: *Love Bites*, *Evolve*: *Vampire Stories of the New Undead* and also *Evolve 2: Vampire Stories of the Future Undead*, which provides a taste of what's to come in vampire lore.

Check her website for updates nancykilpatrick.com and join her on Facebook.

Kathryn Kuitenbrouwer is the author of the novels *All the Broken Things*, *Perfecting* and *The Nettle Spinner* and the short story collection *Way Up*. Her short work has been published in *Granta*, *The Walrus*, and *Storyville* where she won the inaugural Sidney Prize for fiction. Kathryn has taught creative writing through the University of Toronto, The New York Times Knowledge Network, and the University of Guelph, where she is Associate Faculty for the MFA program. She is pursuing a PhD in English Literature at the University of Toronto.

Chris Lackey is the co-host of the *H.P. Lovecraft Literary Podcast*, writer, comic book illustrator, filmmaker, and ukulele enthusiast. Chris is the creator of transhumanism graphic novel *Transreality* (2013). He is also the co-author of the graphic novel *Deadbeats* (2012), with Chad Fifer and artist I.N.J. Culbard, from Self Made Hero Publishing. Chris directed his own animated feature, *The Chosen One* (2007), and worked as a producer on the H.P. Lovecraft Historical Society's films *The Call of Cthulhu* and *The Whisperer in Darkness*. Chris is an American who lives in Yorkshire, England.

Robin D. Laws' most recent works of fiction are his collection of Chambers-inspired weird stories *New Tales of the Yellow Sign* and the fantasy novel *Blood of the City*. Other novels include *Pierced Heart* and *The Worldwound Gambit*. As Creative Director for Stone Skin Press, he has edited such anthologies as *Shotguns v. Cthulhu* and *The Lion and the Aardvark*. He is best known for his groundbreaking roleplaying game design work, as seen in *Hillfolk*, *The Esoterrorists*, *Feng Shui*, and *HeroQuest*. He comprises one-half of the Golden Geek Award and ENnie Award-winning podcast *Ken and Robin Talk About Stuff*, and can be found online at robindlaws.com.

Carrianne Leung is a fiction writer, educator and business owner who lives in Toronto. She holds a Ph.D. in Sociology and

Equity Studies from OISE/University of Toronto and works at the Ontario College of Art and Design University. She is co-editor, with Lynn Caldwell and Darryl Leroux, of *Critical Inquiries: A Reader in Studies of Canada*. Her first novel, *The Wondrous Woo*, was released in 2013.

Laura Lush lives in Guelph, Ontario, Canada and teaches creative writing and academic English at the University of Toronto's School of Continuing Studies. She has written four collections of poetry, one book of short fiction, and one oral history book on the taking down of her father's barns in Owen Sound, Ontario.

Nick Mamatas is the author of several novels, including *Love Is the Law* and *Last Weekend*. He has published over ninety short stories in venues as diverse as *Best American Mystery Stories 2013*, *New Haven Review*, and *Shotguns v. Cthulhu*. Nick is also an editor and anthologist — recent titles include *The Battle Royale Slam Book* of essays about the cult-phenomenon novel, film, and manga *Battle Royale*; and the international fiction anthology *Phantasm Japan*. Both were co-edited with Masumi Washington. Nick's fiction, non-fiction, and editorial work has been nominated for two Hugo Awards, two World Fantasy Awards, the Locus Award, the Shirley Jackson Award, and five Bram Stoker Awards. His anthology *Haunted Legends*, co-edited with Ellen Datlow, won the 2010 Bram Stoker for anthology editing. A native New Yorker, Nick now lives in California.

Helen Marshall is an award-winning author, editor, and book historian. Her poetry and fiction have been short-listed for the Bram Stoker Award from the Horror Writers Association, the Aurora Award from the Canadian Science Fiction and Fantasy Association, and the Sydney J. Bounds Award from the British Fantasy Society, which she won in 2013. Her debut collection of short stories *Hair Side, Flesh Side* was named one of the top ten books of 2012 by *January Magazine*. Her second collection *Gifts for the One Who Comes After* was released in late 2014. She currently lives in Oxford, England where she spends most of her time staring at medieval manuscripts.

Isabel Matwawana is a creative scribbler who lives in Toronto, Canada, where she works as a technical writer. She grew up on two continents, spending her late teens in Kenya and the Democratic Republic of the Congo, with lunches in Rwanda. She is a member of the Moosemeat Writing Group and has contributed to the group's annual chapbook of flash fiction since 2010. She has contributed to *Excalibur*, York University's campus paper, where she earned a degree in Political Science. She blogs at heavyme.com and torontoluv.com.

Silvia Moreno-Garcia has been nominated for a Sunburst Award for Excellence in Canadian Literature of the Fantastic for her debut collection *This Strange Way of Dying*. She has also edited several anthologies, the most recent ones are *Sword & Mythos* and *Fractured: Tales of the Canadian Post-Apocalypse*. Her debut novel, *Signal to Noise*, came out in 2015. She blogs at silviamoreno-garcia.com and Tweets @silviamg.

Patrick O'Duffy is tall, Australian and a professional editor/publisher, although not always in that order. He has written role-playing games, short fiction, a little journalism and freelance non-fiction, and has just finished writing a YA fantasy novel (that now needs editing). His ebooks include the novellas *Hotel Flamingo* and *The Obituarist* and the anthologies *Godheads* and *Nine Flash Nine*. He loves off-kilter fiction, Batman comics and his wife, and finds this whole writing-about-yourself-in-the-third-person thing difficult to take seriously. Learn more (so much more) at patrickoduffy.com.

Lilly O'Gorman is a communications officer and former journalist living in Melbourne, Australia. During a year spent abroad in Toronto, she was a member of Moosemeat Writing Group and her short story "Mulberry Tree" was published in the group's chapbook *Moosecall 10: Moose in Wonderland*.

Helen Cusack O'Keeffe is a Paris-based novelist/playwright. Her first degree was in Russian Language and Literature, where she developed a passion for Gogol and Tolstoy. She subsequently studied social work and spent ten years in a psychiatric team supporting homeless people in central London. She was first published in *The Bastille* and *Strangers in Paris*. Current projects include a short film about child slavery, and polishing her sixth novel: *Rapid, Idiotic Goodbye Kiss for Randolph Carson*.

Jerry Schaefer is an actor who writes for television while living in Toronto. From time to time he appears in TV commercials, which makes his parents very happy and saves him a visit.

Ekaterina Sedia resides in the Pinelands of New Jersey. Her critically-acclaimed and award-nominated novels, *The Secret History of Moscow*, *The Alchemy of Stone*, *The House of Discarded Dreams*, and *Heart of Iron* were published by Prime Books. Her short stories have sold to *Analog*, *Baen's Universe*, *Subterranean*, and *Clarkesworld*, as well as numerous anthologies, including *Haunted Legends* and *Magic in the Mirrorstone*. She is also the editor of the anthologies *Paper Cities* (World Fantasy Award winner), *Running with the Pack*, *Bewere the Night*, and *Bloody Fabulous* as well as *The Mammoth Book of Gaslit Romance* and *Wilful Impropriety*. Her short-story collection, *Moscow But Dreaming*, was released by Prime Books in December 2012. Visit her fashion blog at fishmonkey.blogspot.com.

Greg Stafford is an American game designer, publisher and sweat lodge leader. Among his many creations are the Glorantha fantasy world and the Arthurian chivalric role-playing game *Pendragon*, for which he won the 2007 Diana Jones Award. He also founded the companies Chaosium, Inc and Issaries Inc. *Pyramid* magazine named him as one of The Millennium's Most Influential Persons "at least in the realm of adventure gaming."

Greg Stolze was born in 1970 and grew up alongside the World Wide Web. It should come as no surprise that he relies on connections with his old college pal the Internet to make money: You can see (and download) the fruits of his labors at www.gregstolze.com/fiction_library. Everything there is free because it's already been paid for through a complicated fictional-risk-deferral scheme, to which you are already a party simply by having read this paragraph. So, since you're already in, point your web browser to find stories about jujitsu, math, fish telepathy, aliens, magic, and grief. Follow him on Twitter at @GregStolze if you don't mind hearing a lot about his literary trickery and insomnia.

Kate Story is a writer and performer. Her first novel *Blasted* (Killick Press) received the Sunburst Award for Canadian Literature of the Fantastic's honourable mention, and was longlisted for the ReLit Awards. *Wrecked Upon This Shore*, her second novel, has been called "magical and moving" (Jessica Grant, author of *Come, Thou Tortoise*); her short story "The Yoke of Inauspicious Stars" in the recently-released SF collection *Carbide Tipped Pens* (Tor Books, edited by Ben Bova and Eric Choi) was tipped by the Kirkus Review as a "hit." Kate is thrilled to contribute to *Gods, Memes and Monsters*. She borrowed liberally from Chaucer and the journals of Captain Edward Fenton and Christopher Hall: grateful acknowledgement to these gentlemen. www.katestory.com.

Molly Tanzer is the author of the British Fantasy Award and Wonderland Award-nominated *A Pretty Mouth*, as well as *Rumbullion and Other Liminal Libations*. Her short fiction has appeared in such venues as *Fungi*, *The Book of the Dead*, *The Book of Cthulhu* (vols. I and II), *Strange Aeons*, and *Children of Old Leech*. She lives in Boulder, Colorado.

John Scott Tynes is a writer and game designer in Seattle. He's the founder of Pagan Publishing and the creator of *The Unspeakable Oath* magazine and the *Puppetland* roleplaying game, as well as the co-creator of *Delta Green*, *Unknown Armies*, *The Hills Rise Wild*, *Call of Cthulhu D20*, and many other works. His recent book *Delta Green: Strange Authorities* collects his short stories and novel set in the Lovecraft-meets-Le Carré world of *Delta Green*.

Jacqueline Valencia is a Toronto-based experimental poet, writer, film journalist, and film critic. Her work has appeared in various publications including *Lemon Hound, dead g(end)er, The Lit Pub, The Barnstormer, Little Fiction*, and *49th Shelf*. She is the author of various chapbooks ("Tristise," "Maybe," and "The Octopus Complex" — LyricalMyrical Press), a senior staff film critic at *Next Projection*, and founding editor of the film site thesegirlsonfilm.com. More info at jacquelinevalencia.com.

Monica Valentinelli writes stories, games, essays, and comics for media/tie-in properties and her original works from her studio in the Midwest. She's a former musician of 20+ years and a graduate of the University of Wisconsin-Madison's Creative Writing program who now writes full-time. Recently, Monica has filled the shoes of lead developer and writer for the line of Firefly RPG books based on the Firefly TV show by Joss Whedon. Her sanity is kept by her two cats, water frog, bettafish, and her long-time partner. When she's not obsessing about deadlines, she designs jewelry and dabbles in other artistic endeavors. For more about Monica, visit mlvwrites.com.

Myna Wallin is a Toronto author with two published books: *A Thousand Profane Pieces*, poetry, (Tightrope Books, 2006), and *Confessions of a Reluctant Cougar*, a novel (Tightrope Books, 2010). Myna has taken part in a poetry / visual art collaboration, curated by Toronto's Poet Laureate George Elliott Clarke for the Spring 2014 show, *Why (Not) Portraits of Poets*, at the Art Gallery of Ontario. She also wrote the lyrics for "Even Divas Get the Blues," a song on Juno-nominated Fern Lindzon's newest album. www.mynawallin.com.

James Wallis is a games designer and author with fourteen books under his belt. Previously he's been an RPG publisher,

TV presenter, magazine editor and *Sunday Times* journalist, a university lecturer and an award-winning graphic designer. Fiction includes titles for the Black Library, Puffin Books and Virgin Publishing, and his game designs include the storytelling games *Once Upon a Time* and *The Extraordinary Adventures of Baron Munchausen*. These days he runs the games consultancy Spaaace and lives in London with his wife and 1d4 -1 children.

Kyla Lee Ward is a Sydney-based creative who works in many modes. Her novel *Prismatic* (co-authored as Edwina Grey) won an Aurealis. *The Land of Bad Dreams*, a collection of dark poetry, received Rhysling nominations. Her short film *Bad Reception* screened at the Vampire Film Festival. Her short fiction has appeared on Gothic.net and in the *Macabre* and *Schemers* anthologies, amongst others. She programmed the horror stream for the 2010 Worldcon, played in *The Theatre of Blood* and remembers her clubbing nights very fondly. To see some very strange things, try http://www.tabula-rasa.info.

Jim Webster clings to the term 'fifty something', lives in South Cumbria, and is married with three daughters. He farms, and is a freelance journalist, writer and has several fantasy and Sci-Fi novels published. Other than that he has been a wargamer and roleplayer for over forty years.

Heather J. Wood was born and raised in Montreal, Canada, where fish monsters once lived in her bed. Heather now makes her home in Toronto and is the author of the novels *Fortune Cookie* and *Roll With It*. Her short fiction has appeared in the anthologies *In the Dark*, *I.V. Lounge Nights*, and *The Lion and the Aardvark*. A recent "which mythological creature are you?" Internet quiz has confirmed she is indeed a witch/wizard.

Bill Zaget's story, "Renfield or, Dining at the Bughouse," was in the 2001 Ace Science Fiction anthology, *Dracula in London*. "Zombies on the Down-Low" was published by Ravenous

Romance in the anthology, *Beach Boys*. His story, "Symeon," appeared in the award-winning 2012 anthology *Danse Macabre: Close Encounters with the Reaper* by Edge/Hades Publications. He has two novels in progress on the back-burner and vows to fix that stove one of these days.

Kurt Zubatiuk is a psychotherapist, a medieval longsword practitioner and the author of the poetry collection, *Ekstasis*. He lives with his lovely spouse and two cats in Toronto, Canada. His most prized possession is an autographed picture of Tom Baker (signed in felt ink).